DEEP AND DEADLY

Inspector Torquil McKinnon Mystery Book Seven

Keith Moray

SAPERE
BOOKS

DEEP AND DEADLY

Published by Sapere Books.

24 Trafalgar Road, Ilkley, LS29 8HH,
United Kingdom

saperebooks.com

ISBN: 978-1-80055-867-0

Keith Moray is represented by Isabel Atherton at Creative
Authors.

In memory of my Uncle Joe, and happy days fishing on the River Findhorn

It is estimated that over 1,900 seals were shot in Scotland between 2011 and 2020 in order to protect fisheries. The Scottish government banned seal shooting by the fishing industry on June 17, 2020.

PROLOGUE

The old writing box had a musty odour and was unremarkable to look at. It was the record of a family. Not a family that anyone was proud of, or one that anyone particularly remembered, but a family nonetheless. Yet the scribe who had kept such meticulous records had enough feeling to record each death and store it away, rather like a spider kept tasty morsels wrapped up at various points in its web.

That was an apt description of the scribe known as Mungo. A spider sitting in plain view, yet strangely invisible. Ever watching, gathering secrets, spinning tales full of venom and then delighting in watching victims squirm as he sent out his poison-pen letters.

Now, Mungo was dead, but there remained the writing box and its contents.

The bloody box. Mungo's legacy.

His lawyer had no idea what it contained, nor had he shown any interest. To him it was merely a legacy from a deceased client. Its appearance was so unremarkable that its contents may never have been seen again, had not the legatee's curiosity been roused by the dying ramblings of the poisonous scribe.

The box was not imposing enough to be called an antique, more the sort of thing that could be picked up in a bric-a-brac shop or a flea market. Just an old walnut wood writing box. A hammer and screwdriver would have opened it, but the whole cloak-and-dagger ritual of getting the old barrel key that opened it had provided amusement after a fashion. It had been sealed away in the lawyer's safe with instructions that it was to be sent one week before the box itself was delivered. When it was finally unlocked and all of the meticulously arranged paraphernalia inside it was carefully examined, it was as if Pandora's box had been opened.

The life of the spider at the heart of that great web was revealed, with all the dirty secrets it had hoarded and used to make its victims suffer.

Everything in the writing box had its own little niche, and each component had been carefully maintained. The tools and instruments of a virtuoso.

A little drawer contained the gloves. White gloves such as a magician or a conductor would wear. Gloves that stopped the wearer from being contaminated by filth, and, equally importantly, they left no trace.

There were the little neatly labelled postcard-sized file-cards containing all the dirt Mungo had gathered on his community. And then like a pearl in an oyster there was the diary. The whole seedy story was in there, but it was more than a diary: it was a manual detailing how to exact revenge. It was as if it had been meant to fall into the hands of one who would have the courage and the wit to use it. Mungo's heir.

Reading the diary and studying the little card entries brought clarity. It exposed those guilty of the greatest sins against the family. Had the writing box not been opened, they would undoubtedly have taken those sins to their graves. But it had been read now, and it had produced the powerful emotions it had been intended to.

A plan started to germinate with the sifting through all the dirt. A fresh web would need to be spun, but Mungo's box would be used again, and there would be a final reckoning.

No, wait. Words mattered. A final execution was an altogether better description.

CHAPTER ONE

It was 3 a.m. Arran MacCondrum had been out at sea all night. Even when the boat was being buffeted and the rain was lashing down it was his usual escape from all of his cares and stresses. Lately there had been far too many of them and on this night the boat was no escape at all. He was alone in the small wheelhouse of the *Betty Burke*, the old boat his father had christened decades before and which had done their salmon farm such good service.

Why hasn't the bugger texted? he thought tersely as he looked at his mobile for the tenth time in as many minutes. *I've done as he wanted and made myself available all night.*

As he thought it, he felt another pang of fear.

Bastard! He has me over a barrel and is enjoying getting me scared witless. But not here. Not now. Here I'm master of myself.

Being scared was not a normal part of his psyche and he was loath to admit it to himself. It was another point he mentally added to the score he was going to settle. In one way or another the sea had given him his living and he never feared it. Like his father and grandfather before him he had been a fisherman, and when his father and his uncle had started the salmon farm back in the early nineties he had joined them with alacrity. And now they were both gone and it was all his. Or most of it, at any rate. At least he'd made sure of that.

As such, he was an employer, a provider of both food and wealth to the local economy. It should have made him happy, content even, but other folk obviously thought otherwise.

When he was in a dark mood, he didn't mind being out in the *Betty Burke* during squalls like this one as he wandered far from West Uist. With the clouds concealing the moon and stars, there was darkness all around apart from the lights inside his wheelhouse and on the boat and the pinpoint of light from the automatic beacon on the clifftops of West Uist. The boat was one of the three places that gave him succour. The salmon farm itself and the hatchery were the others. But only if he was by himself. He did not crave human contact at those times.

It would be light soon enough and the staff would be getting up to head out to one or the other of the farm's sites. Half a dozen to the farm to do all the checks on the fish, the water and the conditions and get ready to do the feeds. Two or three of the most qualified fish technicians would head to the hatchery to tend to the developing eggs, alevins, fry, parr and smolts.

He reached into a pocket, pulled out the crumpled envelope and from it took out the letter that he had screwed up when he had first read it. Scanning it quickly he felt his temper rise again, just as it had a few hours before, when he was stone-cold sober. Scowling, he quickly crammed it back into the envelope and stowed it back in his pocket.

Who the hell does this Mungo think he is that he can write this shit to me?

He scratched his beard and looked expectantly at his phone again.

But how did the bastard get my number? Pen and paper and the Royal Mail were good enough for him until he made it clear he didn't just want to piss me off.

He scrolled to his messages and the last one he had received. He looked at the little illuminated screen.

DEAR FM, BE WHERE I TOLD YOU AT 3 AM AND EXPECT MY MESSAGE. I'LL TELL YOU WHERE TO

COME, WHERE THE REVELATION I PROMISED WILL BE MADE. YOU CAN DECIDE IF YOU WANT THE WORLD TO KNOW YOUR DIRTY SECRETS. COME ALONE OR YOU'LL BE LIKE A DODO.

FM! Farming Mannie! You bastard. Whoever you really are.

Arran stooped and reached into the old duffel bag on the cabin floor and pulled out the bottle of Glen Corlin malt whisky. It had been full when he left Kyleshiffin, but was now half empty. Uncorking it he took another large swig but spilled some into his full beard and moustache. He was wiping his mouth with the back of his hand when his phone beeped and the awaited message appeared.

DEAR FM, MEET ME AT YOUR EGG SHACK IN ONE HOUR. REMEMBER, COME ALONE AND DON'T BE LATE. ITS YOUR ONLY HOPE. DON'T DRINK TOO MUCH.

Arran glanced at his trusty old .308 rifle that he had brought with him and propped up in the corner and wondered if he would have the nerve to use it if he had the opportunity.

Then he pictured his father, Inver MacCondrum as he used to be. A strong man, a man's man with a full beard just like his own, with gnarled and calloused hands, and a sod-them-all personality.

Na làithean math, athair. The good days, eh, Father. We did everything by hand, touch and good old know-how. Now it's all about sensors, monitors and computers that do all the thinking. Worse, at the farm we have bloody cameras everywhere. Inside, outside and under the water, for goodness' sake.

The rain continued to pelt the wheelhouse screen and the wind howled.

And you wouldn't have hesitated, would you, Father? Them or us, you would have said. That's what you said about the bloody seals. You wouldn't have held with all these damned regulations and prissy organisations and people I have to deal with nowadays.

He snorted as he recalled how the old boy had taught him how to shoot and who had then been at his side encouraging him when he'd made his first kill.

They can all go to hell. I own this bloody business now and I'll deal with these thieving seals the way I want, never mind putting down namby-pamby sound deterrers or whatever you call them. Our family worked this farm for thirty years, me on my own for the past fifteen, and I'm damned if I'll be dictated to by the bloody powers that are threatening to ban us from protecting our own stock. He grunted. *And I'll be damned if I'll be spoken to by this bastard Mungo who thinks he's going to blackmail me.*

But another pang of fear gripped his heart and he took another swig of whisky. Then he turned the wheel and headed back to the coast and the hatchery. Glancing again at the .308 rifle, he wondered if he had the nerve. A killing might feel the right thing, but there would be consequences.

Dire consequences.

Arran tied up at the hatchery moorings and, armed with the rifle and his duffel bag containing his Glen Corlin, he let himself in and switched up the intensity on the dimmed lights as far as it was safe to do so for the developing fish. His footsteps echoed around the large hangar-size building, which his father and uncle had installed and which he had extended on the west coast of the island.

The bugger hasn't arrived yet. He must be expecting me to let him in. He clutched the .308 and snorted. *Well, he'll get a surprise all right.*

It usually gave him a sense of pride to think that here was where their freshwater team oversaw and nurtured the life cycle of the salmon all the way up to the young adults. He looked over the trough and box systems where they incubated and hatched the salmon eggs into tiny alevins with their yolk sacs. There was a continuous trickling sound that was pleasing to the ear, as the exact conditions of the water were maintained to incubate tens of thousands of eggs in each trough.

Then there were the large round fry tanks where the juvenile fish developed. Then the parr tanks with their feeder systems where they gradually grew into smolts, when they were changed from freshwater tanks into the acclimatising salt water, preparatory to being transported out to the salmon farm.

With a grunt of satisfaction that all was well, he walked on towards the technicians' station, the enclosed cabin with all its computers and gauges and the technology that monitored oxygen saturation levels, water pH, temperature and flow rates in all of the complex hydraulic systems, and the appropriate nutrient levels. As much as he despised it all, he had to acknowledge the science that had become so much a part of his business.

His anger flared again. *The cheek of the sod, calling me Farming Mannie and this hatchery an egg shack. Well, if he thinks he's going to blackmail me, he can think again.*

Opening the door of the technicians' station, he flicked on the light and then gasped at the sight of the female body slumped in the chair in front of the computer bank. She was stark naked and seemed to be asleep. He didn't recognise her because long black hair covered her face.

Then through his whisky-fuddled mind the fear suddenly engulfed him. What if she wasn't alive? A corpse in his hatchery station!

'What the hell is this?' he shouted at her. 'Wake up!'

He moved into the room and reached out to prod her, but the arm that suddenly snaked around his neck from behind him made him drop the duffel bag and the rifle. His hands went up to grasp the arm that was already compressing his windpipe, choking him. Then a hand clapped a large pad of some sort over his face and he was momentarily aware of a pungent, overpowering smell.

Then he knew no more.

CHAPTER TWO

Detective Inspector Torquil McKinnon had not slept well for a few nights. His wedding was not too far away now and there were so many changes that he was going to have to make in his life. Not the least was going to be leaving St Ninian's manse, which had been his home ever since his parents had drowned in a boating accident in the Minch when he'd been a youngster, and he'd come to live with his uncle.

Crusoe, the tri-coloured collie that he had rescued from the sea a couple of years before, was waiting patiently at the bottom of the front stairs as he came down.

'*Madainn mhath*,' he called out as he heard his Uncle Lachlan pottering about in his study.

'And a good morning to you, too, laddie,' came the reply, amid a rattling of drawers and a rustling of paper.

Grabbing the dog's lead from the umbrella stand and pulling on his leather bomber jacket, Torquil smiled wistfully at the corridor, which seemed so bare. For years it had been home to an assortment of motorbike parts that belonged to a classic Excelsior Talisman motorcycle that he and his uncle had been slowly 'rebuilding'. At long last, after many hundreds of hours tinkering they had completed the task. They had both considered it apt to do so with the wedding looming, as it would be symbolic of the changes that were coming.

It was raining hard on their walk and although Torquil always carried a lead when walking Crusoe, he rarely used it. Getting wet never seemed to bother Crusoe. He was always ready to fetch and return tennis balls when given the opportunity. It had surprised Lachlan to discover some time ago that the dog was remarkably well behaved on the golf course and that he would squat down on the golf tee and watch while he drove his ball down the fairway. The sound of the ball being struck never bothered him and the padre had deduced that at some stage someone had given him rudimentary training as a gun dog.

Torquil entered the small copse of rowan trees, partly to get some shelter from the rain and partly so he could get out his phone without it getting wet to send a text message to Lorna. Crusoe followed him, tail wagging furiously as he spun the ball in his mouth.

His thumb dashed dexterously back and forth across the keyboard on his phone: *Don't let Lumsden get under your skin, darling. Please remember to bring back some of those oat and apple dog pretzel treats from Dunrobbin's.*

Superintendent Lumsden had been Torquil's senior officer until the Hebridean Constabulary had been absorbed into Police Scotland, and Torquil had transferred to the detective force. There had been history between them and since Lorna was a sergeant in the uniformed branch, they both knew only too well that the superintendent did whatever he could to make life difficult for them. He refused to allow her to be stationed back on West Uist, giving the fact that Sergeant Morag Driscoll was already in post.

Twenty minutes later Crusoe was eating his breakfast from his bowl in the corner of the kitchen while Torquil washed his hands in the old enamel sink.

His uncle, the Reverend Lachlan had breakfast prepared for them. He poured porridge out for them both and waited until Torquil took his place before saying a brief grace.

There was an obvious resemblance between them. Both had the same slightly hawk-like features and shared many of the same mannerisms. Torquil had been the youngest ever inspector in the Hebridean Constabulary, but was now the detective inspector for West Uist and Barra. He was thirty, with raven black hair. By contrast, his uncle had a mane of wiry snow-white hair that rarely saw either comb or brush, but instead was roughly swept back when he ran his fingers through it. With the healthy, weather-beaten complexion of the outer islander, he looked far younger than his sixty-five years. As usual he was wearing his horn-rimmed spectacles and the dog collar that proclaimed his calling as a Church of Scotland minister.

Lachlan sprinkled salt on his porridge and passed the cellar to Torquil before reaching for the milk jug. 'The post came while you were out walking Crusoe,' he said, nodding at a neat pile of mail beside a large teapot. 'I have to say that the new postie always delivers nice and early, no matter the weather. I had a word with her this morning and she told me she just loves coming across on the early morning ferry and then aims to get back across on the eleven o'clock. She said that all the fresh air and scenery of being a rural postie on the outer islands fair beats pounding the streets of Glasgow where she used to live.'

Torquil nodded at the pattering rain against the window. 'Aye, well, I understand what she means. Why would you want to live anywhere else when you have good clean air like this?' He grinned as he raised a spoon of porridge to his mouth as he thought of his text exchange a short while before. 'Though maybe we could do with less rain and fewer squalls.'

Lachlan gave a short laugh. 'Aye, I could do with it brightening up later when I play a few holes. What about you, will you be going across on the ferry to Barra today?'

'No, I thought I'd take Crusoe and go out to the Piper's Cave and give the pipes a go first thing, but I'll need to get into the office and phone my DC later this morning. She's over there now, following up on some leads. She and Lorna should be back in a few days for their next diving lesson.'

Lachlan finished his porridge, pushed the bowl aside and dabbed his lips with his napkin. He took a slice of toast and hummed as he dithered over whether to take marmalade or honey. 'Is this the drugs again? The county lines you hear about?'

Torquil poured them both tea. 'Aye, it's getting everywhere. At one time, no one would have thought that organised crime from the big cities on the mainland would use kids and young folk to supply drugs on the islands, but it's happened. It's worse, though. We think there's cuckooing going on.'

Lachlan raised a quizzical eyebrow. 'Cuckooing? That's a new one on me. What is it?'

'It's when criminals groom a vulnerable person and then take over their house, often by using drugs or threatening violence. You'd be surprised how they work it.'

Lachlan shook his head. 'I'm never surprised by evil and the things wicked folk do to get other people to bend to their will.' He sighed. 'I've written many a sermon about it over the years.'

'It's a huge problem nationally, but the thing is that people from all walks of life use drugs. We both like a drink, don't we?'

'We do.'

'Well, alcohol is a drug and it's often the one that folk start on.'

Lachlan nodded. 'I've beat that drum many a time, laddie. As the great Roman playwright Plautus said, "Moderation in all things is the best of policies." Or as the old saying goes, "One's enough, two's too many, three's not half enough."

Personally, I'd argue about two being too many, as I'd call it par for the course, but three is certainly a bogie.'

Torquil shook his head and chuckled. 'You always bring it back to the hallowed game of golf, Uncle.'

'And I make no apology for doing so. The handicap system makes it a great leveller. Keep your score and try to better it each time, and you won't go far wrong. Doctor McLelland always talks about counting alcohol units and keeping the number down to safe limits. I agree with that and aim to be a fourteen handicapper in alcohol terms. Fourteen units per week is my allowance to myself.'

'Aye, but drugs are another problem. There are so many different ones, not just the weed that some of the fishermen used to smoke. I don't have a great problem with the occasional recreational user, but it is the dealers that get me and who we need to get off the streets and out of the system. I'd go so far as to say that there is a case for the legalisation of drugs in a controlled way.'

'Now, from a police officer that's controversial, Torquil.'

Torquil finished nibbling the last of a crust of toast and wiped his hands on his napkin. 'I've been thinking a lot about it and talking about it with Penny and Lorna. Penny has had more experience of drugs and county lines, having moved here from Leeds. You can imagine how big a problem organised crime groups are down there in England. She saw lots of it, dangerous and violent gangs, coercion of kids to act as mules. The problem is that the so-called war on drugs is based on the Misuse of Drugs Act, which is half a century old. But what does it achieve? Arrests boost statistics, fill prisons, but they do nothing to stop the availability of drugs. Big drug seizures look good in the press, but they are an illusion. An illusion that is used to make political capital, but it doesn't reduce the drug market. The big organised crime gangs just change the shape of the market. That's what's caused the problem with county lines.'

'So how would legalising drugs help?'

'First, I'm not sure that we should, but criminalising it just seems to make more addicts. If drugs like cannabis were legalised, it would be possible to control the amount of the active ingredients. Tetrahydrocannabinol or THC is one of over a hundred constituents of cannabis. We could reduce that, make it safer. If we went further and did the same with other drugs, reducing the price to the user, we could reduce addicts and reduce crimes that addicts commit to feed their habit. Then we'd have less overdoses and less deaths.'

'I can see that, but what about the other side of the coin? If you make it easier for someone to get something, won't more folk start experimenting? The lady in the wool shop, the butcher, the baker, the candlestick maker, and even, dare I say it, the church minister!'

'Aye, there are all sorts of counter-arguments. I just wonder whether we should be talking about it more, rather than just enacting draconic measures. Every addict needs help rather than more punishment.' Torquil sighed. 'But we are officers of the law, and we have to follow and carry out the law. That means cracking gangs, exposing county lines and helping kids and vulnerable folk who may be being exploited.'

'Like these cuckoo nests. Your hands are tied, I can see that.'

'Oh, we have some leeway with the users. It's the dealers that we need to sort out.' With a sigh of resignation, Torquil pushed aside his plate and started going through his mail. It was all commonplace, a mix of junk circulars and various statements and bills. He picked up the remaining item, a brown envelope with his name and address written in ink in amazingly precise capital letters. He slipped a thumb under the gummed-down flap and slit it open. Taking out a single, neatly folded piece of blue paper, he began to read.

'*Bròn math*!' he exclaimed a few moments later, sitting upright with indignation. 'It's another poison-pen letter from that nuisance, Mungo. He addresses me as "Dear Piggy Windbag Player".'

Lachlan had also been going through his letters and had just opened a small blue envelope with his butter knife. With a raised eyebrow he pulled out a sheet of blue paper, neatly folded in four. He opened it out and read it to himself, his face expressionless. He had seen too much of life to be shocked.

'Snap! Our Mungo has been busy again. It's funny the way he seems to have reared his ugly pen after lying low for a few years.' He clucked his tongue. 'Mind you, he certainly has a twisted way of using his words.'

Torquil carefully folded his letter again and pushed it back inside its envelope with the handle of his teaspoon. 'Whoever the scunner is, I don't care what he writes about me, but I'm peeved that he's written about Lorna. He's called her a "hoor". When I find him, I'll —'

Lachlan tutted. 'You'll let the law deal with him properly, of course, won't you, laddie? Still, he must be getting on in years. It must be well over thirty years that he's been at it. Certainly, before you were born. It's as if he gets a craving every few years and starts up again.'

'He's one poison-dealer that the police have never caught up with. As you say, he just seems to create havoc for a while and then he disappears again. I'm thinking you are right: it is a craving or a sort of addiction he has. He gets the need to upset as many folk as he can, and then once he's satiated he crawls back under his stone.'

'But he's never been unmasked, so you don't know where the stone that he bides under is. He could be any one of your neighbours.'

'Well, he's hardly a master criminal, just a wee nyaff with a mental problem. We've had to open the file again, not that there's much that we can charge him with.'

Lachlan nodded. 'Like you say about addicts, he needs help. I can't say that I care for being addressed as Minister Mannie and being called a fairy-tale peddling old alcoholic with my hand in the collection box, but that's what Mungo says I am.' He handed over his letter for Torquil to inspect. 'From what I can recall from ones I had in the past, he must be using the same stencil.'

'Aye, it's a good one, though. None of the letters are joined up and they are so precisely written.'

'You'll be wanting to take this letter to the station, I suppose?'

Torquil read the letter, written in the same manner as his own, and blew air through his lips. 'I suppose we need to find him before someone else does and throttles him.'

Lachlan smiled as he started clearing the breakfast things away. 'There's a task for you, then, Inspector McKinnon. But best to prevent folk getting throttled, I always think.'

CHAPTER THREE

The rain was lashing against the upstairs windows of the work room of the *West Uist Chronicle*, and a regular drip of rainwater from the leak in the ceiling produced an almost melodic plopping sound as it hit the strategically placed bucket in the middle of the room.

'Is it not time that we had that roof fixed, Calum?' asked Cora Melville with a yawn, standing up from her desk and stretching. 'It's been raining all night, if you hadn't noticed.'

Calum Steele, the local newspaper editor, stopped tapping at his keyboard and momentarily looked away from his computer. As usual he was working with his sleeves rolled up and wearing a vintage telegrapher's eyeshade that he had purchased on eBay. He smiled and pushed his wire-framed spectacles back onto the bridge of his nose from which they habitually fell. 'Oh, aye, maybe sometime, my wee darling,' he replied unconvincingly before returning his attention to his screen.

'But I've emptied it once already and it's four in the morning. If the rain doesn't stop after we leave, we'll come back to a wet floor.'

'The rain will stop, never fear. It's only a drop water, lassie. Anyway, we'll soon have this edition finished and ready for printing.'

'But the drip is irritating, Calum.'

'Och, I like it. It's a bit Zen, don't you think?' he replied without looking back. 'I thought you would too, what with your yoga and eating seeds and all that.'

Cora Melville was Calum's assistant and fiancée. Her great aunt, Bella Melville had been the local schoolteacher who had taught Calum and his friends, all of whom revered and remained slightly in awe of her. She had introduced them at a *ceilidh* one New Year when Cora was in her final year of her journalism degree at Abertay University.

Never able to refuse Miss Melville anything, in a state of intoxicated magnanimity Calum had promised to employ Cora at the *West Uist Chronicle*. Up until that time he had not only been the editor, but the sole reporter, photographer and printer. He had forgotten about it until one day some months afterwards Cora breezed in, started tidying up the office and reminded him of his promise to employ her. Much to his amazement, she proved to be an asset both journalistically and technically. Not only was she dragging him into the twenty-first century, but with her enthusiasm for reporting and her almost dewy-eyed reverence and respect for him and his work she completely turned his head. While he had once held a candle for Kirsty Macroon, the news anchor-woman of Scottish TV, now he only had eyes for Cora.

'Shall I give a roofer a ring later in the morning? Who do you normally use?'

'Och, you know I do most of the maintenance jobs round here myself, Cora. Besides, Padraig couldn't go up there in the rain.'

Cora went to the window and pulled the blind in the hope of letting in the first grey light of morning, but it was still dark. She glanced at her reflection in the window and leaned forward to look at her face. Cora was twenty-five years old, seven years younger than her boss and boyfriend. She had short crinkly blonde hair and a penchant for large hoop earrings. She blinked several times and then leaned closer to see if she had rings round her eyes after their all-night work session. Satisfied that she had none, she glanced at her nose and imagined what it would look like if she finally had a stud.

'So, are you going out on the roof yourself after the rain stops, Calum?' she asked doubtfully.

The editor continued typing. 'Maybe, although when the rain stops it won't be a problem. Not an urgent one, anyway. You know my principle, Cora. The newspaper copy always comes first, the wee touches on the *West Uist Chronicle* offices can come later.'

Cora sighed resignedly as she turned round to look at their place of work. The *West Uist Chronicle* offices was Calum's somewhat grandiloquent term for the two floors of the building off Harbour Street. The reception room and 'news desk' where either she or Calum interviewed people and took orders for photographs that had appeared in the paper was on the ground floor. It was one of two rooms, the other being a multi-purpose repository where he kept artefacts from old stories, and an old grocery delivery bicycle with a large basket on the front which he usually persuaded one or other of the lads to use when they delivered the special editions around the town. Cora had artistically decorated the advertising panel on the frame with the words 'The West Uist Chronicle Writes the Truth'.

The actual office where they worked was upstairs and housed two desks, one for each of them as the full staff of the newspaper. Calum worked at a cluttered oak desk illuminated by an old green glass telegrapher's lamp, where he wrote his articles and columns on what was now a vintage personal computer or, when he was feeling 'modern', on a spanking new laptop.

Sitting between the two computers was a dusty old Remington typewriter, which served no real purpose other than to help him feel the part of a writer. In his mind he felt that he had the same passion for investigative journalism as Woodward and Bernstein, and that he had been touched with the literary genius of writers like Ernest Hemingway and the incisive mind of Sir Arthur Conan Doyle. Although he had not yet actually tried his hand at fiction, he was sure that he had at least one novel inside him. His plan was to write on the Remington.

By contrast, Cora worked from a brand-new desk devoid of clutter, which was big enough for the three computer screens and the wireless keyboards and mouse that she operated like a piano virtuoso, designing the website, the blog and dealing with the social media side of the newspaper.

The walls were covered in pinboards with posters, memos and timetables of high and low tides, ferry times and jottings about radio and TV programmes to catch up on. Piles of past issues of the *Chronicle* and the special issues that came out at erratic times took up floor space between the filing cabinets, bookcases and other paraphernalia of the newspaper business.

Cora's eyes fell on the cracks on the ceiling, the aged wallpaper that had peeled off in places and the evidence of Calum's repair-work. Sellotape ancient and new was much in evidence, as were drawing pins, nails and masking tape. She smiled as she recollected how he had reacted when she had first remarked upon them.

'Aye, lassie, that's a subliminal lesson about journalism for you,' he had replied. 'Papering over the cracks, that's what people do. As journalists, we need to be able to spot the papering and peel it back to expose the cracks. These,' he said expansively, waving towards them, 'are constant psychological reminders to keep doing what we do and to maintain the fundamental principles of solid journalism.'

She loved his homespun philosophy and the little nuggets of wisdom about his vocation that he kept coming out with. Of course, she had soon become wise to him and realised that admitting errors or mistakes was not something that came naturally to him.

She recalled one time when she was reporting on a dispute between two local businessfolk, both of whom told her forcefully that she didn't know what she was talking about and they didn't want to discuss it further. Calum had drawn himself up to his full height of five foot six and told her in the sometimes-bullish manner that he adopted, 'Always give the impression that you know what you are talking about, lassie. Just wait for the other guy to fluster and give himself away. Let these words be emblazoned on your mind; it's my motto as a newspaperman and it has held me in good stead — *bi dàna agus seasmhach*. Be bold and persistent.'

Cora had repeated that in her mind. *Be bold and persistent!* She liked that because they were two attributes that she considered she had herself. She realised that they were two more reasons why she was so attracted to the West Uist newsman. They thought the same way.

With a final flurry of fingers on the keyboard, Calum clapped his hands and spun round in his seat.

'That's done. I've just put in another piece about the resurfacing of our local geriatric nuisance Mad Mungo. In the piece I did on him a fortnight ago, I think I was too kind and said he was likely psychologically damaged and that I strongly advised him to seek professional help. But since then we've had a lot of our readers complain about the poisonous stuff he's been sending out, so in this article I've ended by telling folk just to bin his rubbish. I've told him in the article that we're not going to give him any more attention.'

Cora giggled. 'I still can't get over the fact that this Mungo, whoever he is, is writing poison-pen letters and sending them through the post. Who would do that these days when we have social media? You can find all sorts of bile and venom by anonymous accounts on Twitter and Facebook.'

'Aye, but this is West Uist in the Outer Hebrides, Cora. Folk here still write letters and read newspapers. I'm pretty sure it's an old person; he has spells of activity then disappears for a couple of years before starting up again. That's why I called him our geriatric Mungo.'

'Isn't this second article a complete *volte-face*, then?'

He winked at her. 'Sometimes you have to backtrack on things you have written a week or more before, but if you do, always be assertive, Cora. That's the key. Now we're all done and dusted, ready to print.' His hands went to his bow-tie and tugged the ends as he proudly beamed at her.

'Okay, boss. I've updated the website and finished the latest digital issue, which is also ready to go online after you add any other editorial posts you want to go in.'

'Aye, we'll deal with it after we've printed the newspaper, Cora,' Calum replied with an emphatic nod of his head. 'The actual *West Uist Chronicle* that folk can hold and read by their fireside or sitting in their garden, or when they're bobbing along on the ferry, that's what real local journalism is about — always remember that.'

Cora knew that the local newspaper was Calum's *raison d'être*, having taken it over when it had been little more than a listing of wool and potato prices, times of the tides and occasional bits of gossip that masqueraded as local news. Working every hour he could, he had transformed it into a newspaper that sold not only in West Uist, but also in Barra, Benbecula and some of the smaller isles. But it was falling behind now that many younger folk had computers and smart phones. To combat that, Cora had set up a website, a digital edition and a blog so that *The West Uist Chronicle* was gradually building up a social media following. Although the paper depended on local advertising, she knew that eventually other advertisers would be attracted to their expanding online presence.

Cora was astute enough to realise that she had to be cautious about introducing changes, and the best way was to make Calum think the ideas for progression were his own. She beamed at him. 'So, after we get the morning edition printed and ready for delivery, can we discuss a couple of ideas I have for features I think we should do? They're all sea-based.'

Calum tapped his slight paunch. 'A good idea.'

'I have three ideas, actually,' Cora went on, adopting a bold and persistent manner. 'Firstly, you know that the girls and I have been having diving lessons with Ross McNab's "Wave and Dive" School ahead of Lorna's hen-do?'

'Of course, once a week. Mad, the lot of you. I'd rather stay on *terra firma* than go skulking about underwater with a tank on my back.'

'Well, we'd like to do it more frequently, but we're limited with Lorna's shifts. She is still kept busy on Lewis most of the week. But what you maybe haven't taken in is that our next dive will be our fourth open water one. That will give us our scuba certification. Then for the hen-do Ross is going to take us to dive down to the wreck of the *SS Lister* out beyond the Cruadalach Isles.'

Calum gaped for a moment. '*Gràdh math*! That's not a normal hen-do, is it? I mean, diving and drinking don't seem compatible. And having a man with you doesn't seem right.'

'We won't be drinking then, silly! And Ross will only be with us on the dive. He won't be at our celebratory dinner.'

Calum looked perturbed. 'It's not that safe out there, you know. I'm guessing Torquil won't be too happy about Lorna diving over a wreck. You ken that his parents drowned in the Minch when he was a wee lad. That's how come his Uncle Lachlan came to bring him up.'

Cora pursed her lips and nodded. 'Yes, Great Aunt Bella reminded me of that, too. And Lorna said that although Torquil isn't keen, he knows it's what she wants to do and it is her hen-do. Morag Driscoll is her matron of honour and she's a great organiser.'

Calum frowned and sucked air through his lips. 'Aye, well, there you have it. The bride-to-be and the matron-of-honour are both police sergeants, so it's bound to be well organised. More than can be said for Torquil's stag-do. If it was just up to me I'd have it all tied up already, but since he's having five of us as best men we're having a wee bit of bother agreeing. Camels and committees come to mind.'

Cora nodded sympathetically, although she was well aware that Calum himself was more than likely to be one of the main hindrances. She pressed on. 'The point is that Ross McNab's school could do with a bit of publicity, and so I thought we could do a feature on the way he's been teaching us, culminating in the big dive.'

'And when is this hen-do dive?' Calum asked, a tell-tale grin beginning to erupt. 'Or should that be a duckie-do dive?'

Cora could never resist her fiancé's jokes and puns. 'Oh, Calum, that's so bad its almost hilarious.'

Pleased as ever to impress his fiancée, Calum suddenly adopted his best editorial tone of seriousness. 'Well, I think it sounds like good copy, so is there a main thrust to it?'

'There is, actually. As part of it I'll run a parallel thread on the history of the wreck. I've already done some research. The tramp steamer *SS Lister* sank twenty-five metres off the Cruadalach Isles in 1922, carrying an assorted cargo of canned fish, sherry and jute. It would be a double feature then, as we see if we come up with anything new from the wreck. Ross says there are still tins and the odd bottles strewn on the seabed, all covered in barnacles and stuff.'

'I am liking it more and more. Good idea, so let's run with it, lassie.'

Cora picked up her notepad and made a tick against an entry. She sat on the corner of her desk and tapped her pad with her pen. 'I'd also like to do one on food and foraging. It's really popular these days, and since we have The Crow's Nest Café just up Harbour Street —'

Calum snapped his fingers. 'Of course, Henson Dingwall took it over nine months ago and has transformed it from a paper cup takeaway into one of those gastro-cafés.'

'I think you mean a bistro-café, darling.'

'Aye, I did. But maybe it could be gastro, too,' Calum said with a guffaw, 'especially as he does all that foraging for seaweed, mushrooms, samphire and whatever he can drag out of rock pools. Maybe we should do a feature and warn the good folk of West Uist about food poisoning.'

Cora shook her head and gave him a reprimanding look. 'We will not. As you just said, he's taking The Crow's Nest somewhere. He won awards on the mainland before he came here, and he may even get a Michelin Star someday.'

'The landlady at the Bonnie Prince Charlie just down the road from him isn't so keen. He's taken away a lot of her trade.'

'But you must admit the food we've had when we've eaten there has been delicious.'

Calum screwed up his nose. 'Aye, I suppose so, but I'm a traditionalist, as you well know. I prefer a good mutton pie or a burger and chips.'

'Well, the girls are having our celebratory dinner cooked by Henson. Morag has it all arranged.' Cora eyed him questioningly. 'So, is that a yes for a feature?'

'Aye, have your way. Now, what's the third?'

'How about The Salmon War?'

'What war?' he queried, shoving his spectacles back up his nose. 'Am I missing something?'

'The Salmon War. I thought it was high time that we brought it out into the open. Perhaps the *West Uist Chronicle* should make its position clear.'

Calum eyed her askance. 'You're losing me, Cora. It's not clear to me what position you think we should take, because I don't know what you're talking about.'

'Now you are being deliberately evasive. The MacCondrum Salmon Farm and the WUCE guardians.'

Calum harrumphed and cast his eyes at the ceiling. 'Oh, not this old chestnut again. You want us to side with the Wookies!'

Cora whooshed air through her lips. 'Calum! Just calling them that is bad enough. As you well know, they are the West Uist Coastal Ecology guardians.'

Calum jokingly covered his mouth. 'Och, there's me not being PC again. But the thing is, Arran MacCondrum has been running that salmon farm off the west coast for fifteen years or so, ever since his dad died. Old Inver MacCondrum and his brother Cormac had been in there right at the start of salmon farming with wooden square pens, hand feeding, the whole lot. He's run it ethically, as you will see if you look back through past features I've done on them.'

'I have done, darling. And I can see that you have always been very positive about the farm.'

'The farm has been good for the island's economy and it still provides employment to a number of folk.'

Cora nodded. 'But the West Uist Coastal Ecology guardians have done studies, just like other groups on other islands and on the mainland wherever there are salmon farms. They say they are poisoning the seabed, attracting sea lice and devastating the marine ecology.' She waited until she had his full attention before adding, 'And they are one of the independent salmon farms with a history of shooting seals.'

Calum shrugged his shoulders. 'I think the Wookies have got to you, darling. The thing is that seals hunt and eat fish. It's inevitable that they'll get into the pens which are full of food every now and then. That causes leaks of fish into the sea. It's legal to shoot so many seals every year, you know.'

'For now it is, but I'm guessing it won't be for long. There are groups petitioning Holyrood. Look, as you just said, seals breach the pens and the fact is that every leak is a potential disaster. That's one of the things the WUCE guardians have been agitating about. The sea lice they are infested with have infected wild Atlantic salmon.'

'Arran treats them for the sea lice, Cora. They use anti-thingy-me-bobs.'

'That may also be causing problems. It's poisonous to other creatures — crabs, lobsters and all the smaller crustaceans.'

Calum took off his eyeshade and tossed it onto the desk and removed his spectacles to rub his eyes. 'I don't know, Cora. It's a tricky one. The *West Uist Chronicle* doesn't want to be seen to be biased. Apart from that, I know that Arran hasn't been himself lately.'

Cora looked unconvinced. 'Do you mean he's one of your drinking pals, Calum?'

He looked aggrieved. 'I see him occasionally in the Bonnie Prince Charlie or in the Barrel Bar at the Commercial Hotel, and he's a good lad. I don't want to upset him. He has a temper, you know. I wouldn't want anyone to think that we at the *West Uist Chronicle* were being biased, or you know, politically correct.'

'You mean environmentally conscious, don't you? And anyway, since when did you worry about being biased? You've always told me to find the truth, publish and be damned.'

Calum picked up a pen and started to fiddle with it, realising that Cora was outmanoeuvring him by tossing his own maxims at him. He tapped his notepad with his pen and beamed at her. 'Look, why don't we think about this one and set the printer off? Then we could have an early breakfast.'

Cora stood up and pointed to the open door and the closed door on the other side of the landing. One of the things Cora had arranged after they'd become engaged was to get rid of the old camp bed that Calum had used in his bachelor days when he'd had late nights or too many bottles of Heather Ales or drams of whisky. She had replaced it with a very comfortable and serviceable king size bed.

Raising an eyebrow, she gave him a suggestive sidewards glance. She held out her hand. 'I have a better idea, darling. What about an aperitif before breakfast?'

She was quite confident not only of her persistence but also of her powers of persuasion.

CHAPTER FOUR

Sergeant Morag Driscoll had been up early to drop her boyfriend Sandy King, the Scottish Premiership and Scottish international footballer at Kyleshiffin harbour, so that he could get back to Dundee for his training.

They passed all the market folk who were already setting up their market stalls and wares alongside the harbour seawall and parked outside MacOnachie's Chandlery on Harbour Street. They got out of the police station's Ford Escort and sauntered over to the wall where he rested his hold-all. The rain had gradually eased off and turned into a fine drizzle before finally stopping. The sun seemed to be about to break through.

'It's maybe going to be a fine morning after all that rain last night, which just makes me more depressed to be leaving you, Morag,' Sandy said, reaching to put his arms round her. He was a tall, broad-shouldered young man in his late twenties with shoulder-length blond hair. Morag was slightly older — a thirty-something mother of three who had been widowed at the age of twenty-six when her husband had had a massive heart attack. From that day she had become a fitness addict and now had the trim figure of a distance runner.

Conscious of all the people milling around and descending the nearby steps to the harbour itself, where the Macbeth ferry *Laird o' the Isles* had docked, she took hold of his wrists and stopped him from encircling her waist in too intimate a hug. 'Sorry, darling, but I'm in uniform.' She winked at him and gave him a wistful smile. 'We've had a lovely weekend, what with my kids being on holiday with my sister and her family, but now we both have to come off cloud nine and get back to work.'

He gave a lopsided grin. 'Ah, yes, duty calls, but you get to stay in this fabulous place. It's like a picture-postcard, even in the rain.' He turned and inclined his head towards the old town clock, the multi-coloured shop-fronts of the crescent-shaped Harbour Street and then to the flotilla of yachts, cabin cruisers and fishing boats that bobbed up and down in the right side of the harbour. 'And I hate that I have to go back to the city and won't see you for a fortnight.'

Suddenly, Sandy and Morag became aware of a lot of noise with horns and people shouting.

Looking over the wall, they saw a cluster of people lined across the harbour road with placards, squeezing claxons and beating makeshift drums.

'Oh-oh, looks like you were right about duty,' Morag said.

'Won't Eggie MacOnachie know what's going on?' Sandy suggested, pointing to the chandlery where baskets containing fishing rods, crabbing nets and assorted fishing and recreational wares were already stacked on the pavement around the door.

'He might, but he'll be down there himself,' Morag replied. 'He's the harbour master and has to be down to check everything when the ferry comes in. Look, there he is, in the thick of it.'

Sandy followed her pointing finger to the small group of demonstrators who were clearly intent on blocking the passage of a lorry. Some of them were arguing with five or six other people dressed in waterproofs, some of whom also had life jackets on. In the middle were two men with clipboards. One was wearing a brown shop-coat and an official black cap, while the other was in a black uniform with a braided cap.

The driver of the lorry they were preventing from advancing along the harbour road started to beep his horn, which stimulated those behind to do the same. As a result, all the stall-holders and early passers-by on Harbour Street had crossed to look over the seawall to see what all the commotion was about.

'He's with Willie Armstrong, the Macbeth representative, and it looks like they've got some bother on their hands. Come on, Sandy, let's go down ready to get you on, although that might be delayed if the cargo and passengers can't get off.'

They went down the steps by the old Second World War mine that had been converted into a collection box for the Shipwrecked Fishermen and Mariner's Benevolent Fund and made their way through the crowd that was waiting to meet those coming off, or already waiting to embark.

'Ah, I thought so, it's the WUCE guardians,' Morag said as they threaded their way on.

'The Who?'

'WUCE. The West Uist Coastal Ecology guardians. They are activists against the use of dredgers, trawlers and the salmon farm. Since we haven't had any dredging or trawling for over a decade, their focus is almost exclusively on the salmon farm.'

As they approached the group of ten or so protesters, all of them local folk, they could read the placards they carried with an assortment of messages:

WUCE GUARDIANS UNITE
PROTECT THE SEABED
STOP THE POISONING
STOP SHOOTING AND SAVE THE SEALS
EAT PLANTS

'Ah, Sergeant Driscoll!' cried Tam MacOnachie, the septuagenarian harbour master and ship chandler. He took off his hat and ran a hand exasperatedly over his bald head, the reason for the soubriquet by which he was known, thanks to the mischievous wit of the Drummond twins. 'I was just about to call the station. We have a serious public disturbance here and it's about to cause mayhem.'

Willie Armstrong, the dapperly dressed Macbeth representative who was also the local butcher, was looking flustered and irate. 'Aye, we need some arrests here. These people are halting the ferry and blocking the cargo carriers and passengers from disembarking. We cannot let the cars off until these front lorries are allowed to leave.' He pulled back the sleeve of his jacket to look at his watch. 'And I'm on a tight schedule myself. I've still got the mealie puddings and sausages to make. This lot are bringing the island to a halt.'

The two men were in the middle of two groups. On one side were the placard-waving group, six women and four men strung across the harbour road. They were dressed in anoraks or raincoats with green high-vis vests with the letters WUCE emblazoned on the backs, and with matching green baseball caps also with the same wording on them. They were all chanting, 'Save our Coast!'

Facing them and gesticulating angrily were six people, five men and one woman all dressed in orange waterproofs, three with lifejackets.

Morag gritted her teeth and, leaving Sandy, strode into the middle to join Tam MacOnachie and Willie Armstrong, who were looking out of their depth.

'So, what is the problem here, Tam?' she asked.

'These Wookies are not allowing the lorry to pass,' a stocky man in waterproofs and a life jacket wearing a black beanie hat said, pre-empting the harbour master.

Morag saw the driver in the lorry cab shaking his head angrily as he honked his horn three times again. Taking a few steps sideways, she saw in large lettering on the side of the lorry *ABOVE PARR*. Underneath it were the words: *Suppliers of feed and treatments to the Salmon Farming Industry.*

A tall, good-looking woman with a greying auburn ponytail protruding from under her baseball hat stepped forward. She was in her mid-forties and clearly was the leader of the protesters. She introduced herself as Elspeth. 'We are not Wookies, we are WUCE guardians,' she said assertively, 'and we are taking a stand to protest about the contents of that lorry.'

'That's a container of feed for our farm and some chemicals we need up at the hatchery,' replied the man. 'Sergeant Driscoll, we need to get on with our work, and already we're late getting off to the salmon farm. We have to get the salmon fed and we need to maintain our supplies.'

'Did you not hear what he said?' Elspeth queried loudly. 'Chemicals they are pumping into the sea and into the fish.'

'Ach, just sodium thiosulphate and cleaning alkalis,' he returned. 'We keep things clean and safe. The MacCondrum Salmon Farm operates its farm and hatchery to the highest standards.'

Tam MacOnachie frowned and pointed over his head to a docking space on the other side of the harbour. 'Aye, well, talking of keeping things clean, we need to get this cleared up, Rab MacQuittie, my man. But your boss is already out there, I think — can you not see that the *Betty Burke* is out? He left the harbour last night.'

All of the salmon farm staff turned in the direction of the harbour and one, a young woman with purple-dyed hair, put her hands to her mouth.

'Oh no, he's not had another all-nighter has he?' She tugged on Rab's sleeve. 'We'd better get out and see that he's all right. He shouldn't be out at the farm on his own.'

'Well, you'd better just turn this lorry back,' said Elspeth. 'Because we're not moving.'

Morag addressed the WUCE leader, having decided it was time for her to intervene. 'You'll have to stand aside. You're causing an illegal obstruction.'

Elspeth raised her voice, lifting her head at the same time to address a wider audience on the harbour. 'My name is Elspeth McLauchlan of the West Uist Coastal Ecology guardians. And you should all know why we're here. We want to stop this criminality that is on-going and causing an ecological disaster.'

'Och, stop the woman from havering,' said Rab MacQuittie. 'The MacCondrum Salmon Farm has been in operation here for thirty years, ever since old Inver MacCondrum and his brother Cormac started it. There isn't anyone on the island that doesn't know Arran, his son. You know us, who work for him, too. We've done everything possible, used all the latest methods to farm the best, most wholesome salmon that goes on your dinner tables.'

All of the people waiting on the harbour had moved in around the protestors and the salmon farm staff to hear what was being said. All the while the chanting continued along with the beating of drums and the honking of claxons.

One of the WUCE guardians had produced a pile of leaflets from a rucksack and started distributing them to members of the crowd.

'Be careful of your language, Elspeth,' Morag warned. 'Don't make allegations against people that you can't back up.'

'Can't back up! You're kidding, aren't you?' Elspeth returned. 'We've got scientific studies, seabed videos, pictures of sea lice infestation. It's all on our website and on the leaflets my colleague is handing out. This scandalous salmon farm is polluting the seabed and we have abundant evidence that the sea lice are infecting the wild Atlantic salmon.'

All of the salmon staff reacted angrily, with rebuttals and further urging for them to move out of the way. The lorry driver climbed down from his cab and joined the salmon farm staff. He shook his head angrily and folded his arms in front of his broad chest. 'Come on. I've a busy day and need to make my deliveries.'

Murmurings from the audience that had been attracted were rising in intensity, adding to the overall noise from the protestors and counter-protestors. And then other people started crying out, voicing their opinions. Soon there was an angry hubbub blocking the harbour.

'We are totally ethical and follow all the latest science,' the young salmon farm woman chirped up loudly. 'I'm a qualified fish technician with a master's degree in marine biology, and I can honestly say —'

'You can say what, Marie Urquhart?' Elspeth asked contemptuously. 'That you're using that muck, the load of emamectin I'm sure you've got in the lorry. And the feed that is made from other fish, including salmon. You're turning these salmon in the farm into cannibals.'

This brought cries of support for the WUCE guardians.

'That's nonsense,' said Rab. 'Tell him, Marie.'

'Emamectin treatment is proven beyond doubt to kill sea lice. I can show you all the figures you want. I did my dissertation on —'

Elspeth put her hands on her hips. 'So, you've got a vested interest. Well, we have data, too. Benthic studies of the seabed and the harm that the salmon poo and the emamectin is doing to the crustaceans. The crabs, lobsters, shrimps, clams and cockles.'

The crowd became angrier and it seemed to be more active, as if people were being jostled. To Morag, it seemed as if the two sides in the argument had equal numbers of supporters.

'But we're doing more than that,' Marie tried to shout loud enough to be heard. 'We're doing a trial with wrasse fish in two pens. Already we've —'

But she was barely heard and slapped her sides in frustration.

Morag raised her arms and cried out for quiet, but it was ineffective. And then she saw Calum Steele and Cora Melville pushing their way through the crowd and her heart sank further.

'Excuse me! Press coming through,' she heard the local newshound cry out, as they approached. There were flashes of light as Cora took photographs and collected a leaflet along the way.

Elspeth and her fellow WUCE guardians looked delighted at their arrival and let them through.

Both Calum and Cora looked flushed, and the newspaper editor was grinning like the proverbial Cheshire cat. After a curt nod at Morag, Tam MacOnachie and Willie Armstrong, they separated, Calum heading for the salmon farm team while Cora joined the WUCE guardians, her phone at the ready to record an impromptu interview with Elspeth MacLauchlan.

Duty! Morag thought disconsolately as she saw Sandy looking sympathetically at her over the heads of the crowd.

CHAPTER FIVE

When the situation was eventually resolved and the WUCE guardians and the MacCondrum Salmon farm team had separated, and Tam MacOnachie and Willie Armstrong were able to do their jobs, the ferry traffic was allowed to roll off.

Morag rejoined Sandy at the side of the harbour wall while he and the crowd of other would-be passengers waited for the last of the traffic to come off before Willie Armstrong and the ferry crew finally allowed anyone to embark.

'A grand job there, Morag,' he said, squeezing her arm and avoiding any stronger show of affection.

'Never made easier when Calum and Cora show up. Cora is lovely, but whenever she gets under Calum's influence she turns all investigative journalist and you have to watch what you say. Still, the WUCE guardians will have been happy that they appeared. The more publicity they get, the more they'll like it.'

'I hadn't realised there was such strong feelings on West Uist. I know salmon farming is contentious these days, but it seems to be dividing the island if the little gathering this morning is anything to go by.'

The sound of assertive footsteps approaching made them both turn. A tall clean-shaven man in his mid to late forties smiled as he neared them. He had a deerstalker hat in his hand and had curly black hair with slightly longer than usual sideburns, high cheekbones and a healthy complexion. Dressed resplendently in a tweed jacket with plus-two trousers, a checked tattersall shirt with silk tie and highly polished brogue shoes, he looked every inch of what he was, the head gamekeeper of the Cruikshank estate. He greeted them with a wave of his deerstalker, before he put it on.

'Hello, Frazer,' greeted Morag. 'You've missed all the commotion, you lucky man.'

The gamekeeper inclined his head. 'I heard about it up on Harbour Street as I was parking my jeep. The Wookies again, so I'm guessing Elspeth MacLauchlan was giving the MacCondrum Farm folk a hard time. I was told they were trying to block the *ABOVE PARR* lorry?'

'They were, but thankfully they were persuaded to let them pass, otherwise there would have been a major riot.'

Frazer clicked his teeth. 'Well, it couldn't happen to a nicer chap than Arran MacCondrum, in my opinion.'

'Is that some antipathy between water and air you are showing?' Sandy asked with a grin.

'You mean between salmon farming and gamekeeping? Aye, well maybe a bit,' Frazer returned airily.

Morag put her hand on her boyfriend's shoulder. 'Sandy is waiting to get on board, and I have to say this wasn't the best way I could have thought of to keep him here a bit longer.' She pointed at the gamekeeper's shoes. 'I know you're always dapper, Frazer, but are you here meeting, greeting or leaving?'

Frazer nodded at them both and smiled. 'Meeting and greeting, Morag. I was a bit late getting started, which is why I missed the commotion you've had to deal with. I'm here to welcome a party that will be staying at the Cruikshank estate. One's that Irish actor Declan O'Neil.'

Sandy looked impressed. 'I remember him. He was in that boyband Quicksilver a few years ago. And then he turned to acting, didn't he?'

'That's the chap,' Frazer replied. 'He and his group are coming to get away from it all and to sample the island's delights.'

'Will you be taking him shooting, Frazer?' Morag asked, her professional interest piqued.

'A wee bit. They're using one of our cottages as a base, and they're hiring a couple of our vehicles. While they're here, they wanted to shoot deer. Unfortunately, as you know, the Scottish National Heritage only allow a cull of thirty deer this year and we have reached that already on the estate. So, I'll be taking them on a wild shoot for game birds, mainly woodcock and partridge at this time of year, and maybe some rabbit.'

'Or hares?' Sandy suggested. 'I'm partial to jugged hare.'

'Well, that you'll not get on West Uist. We never shoot hares,' Frazer stated.

Morag smiled at Sandy. 'Old island superstition. You never know if a hare is somebody's ancestor. You wouldn't want some incomer shooting your grannie, would you?'

Frazer winked at her. 'They'll only be shooting at all if they are competent with the guns, of course. I'll take them to the targets first, so don't you worry, Sergeant Driscoll.' He raised a hand to his mouth, as if to prevent anyone but them from overhearing and winked conspiratorially. 'Between us, I think it's his agent and a producer, so maybe they're going to be scouting the island,' he whispered.

Sandy gave a short laugh. 'I was just saying to Morag that it's a fabulous place, even when it rains. Just look at Harbour Street and as for the scenery, West Uist is Scotland in miniature.'

'Aye, well, I'm here to meet them and take them to the estate, so I've been given instructions from my esteemed absent landowner boss across the great Cyber-sea to give them a wee tour on the way to give them a feel of the island. I understand they are travelling in a convertible Mercedes. Maybe not the best of transport for the Outer Hebrides, but it's stopped raining now, so maybe they'll be fine and lucky the rest of their trip.' Again he raised a hand to cover his mouth as he grinned and whispered: 'Maybe I'll get a part alongside Declan O'Neil in a new television show *The Caretaker and the Gamekeeper*.'

But his attempt to prevent being overheard was unsuccessful, for a moment later Calum and Cora suddenly appeared again from the waiting crowd where they had been soliciting onlookers' opinions after having interviewed the main participants in the dispute.

'A fine job you did there, Sergeant Driscoll,' Calum said. 'Hiya Sandy, and Frazer. Did I just hear you say that the actor Declan O'Neil is coming to West Uist?'

Frazer smiled nervously. 'Aye, I did, but the thing is, he's come for a bit peace and to get away from —'

Cora Melville giggled. 'How fabulous. I'm so excited to be here to see Declan in the flesh. I was a proper teeny-bopper fan of Quicksilver when I was a wee girl and I loved all of them, but Declan most of all.'

Calum darted a covetous glance at her. Then with a cough to clear his throat, he was back in journalistic mode. 'So, what exactly is the attraction of West Uist for Declan O'Neil? Did I hear you say something about a new TV show?'

Frazer shrugged his shoulders. 'You have the hearing of a rabbit, Calum Steele.'

'And the nose of a newshound,' Morag added.

Calum grinned and prodded Frazer. 'Come on, Frazer, out with it.'

'It's not my place to say, Calum,' Frazer returned. Then he pointed to a cream-coloured Mercedes convertible that came slowly down the ramp. 'But speaking of the devil, I believe this must be them.' He held up and waved his deerstalker, immediately receiving thumbs-up signs and raised hands from the three men in the car. The driver parked up beside them and they all got out of the car.

The three men couldn't have seemed more different from each other. The driver, who looked to be in his mid-thirties, was a small, wiry, animated man with designer stubble and short hair. He was wearing chinos and a polo shirt under an incongruously garish waistcoat. The one who had been sitting in the front passenger seat was older, in his early forties, lanky with long hair tied in a ponytail and with a horseshoe moustache that reached his lower jaw. He looked an unlikely shooting party guest, for he had a slightly hippy appearance. He was wearing a T-shirt underneath a white cotton jacket, the sleeves of which were rolled up to the elbows, revealing multiple friendship bracelets on each wrist, knee-length walking shorts with multiple pockets and large rope sandals.

Yet it was the passenger who had been in the back that all eyes focused on. He was a handsome man of about fifty with thick black hair going grey at the temples, dressed in jeans, an open-necked shirt under a petrol-blue jacket and sporting designer sunglasses. Declan O'Neil looked every inch the celebrity. He smiled with the easy affability of a former boyband frontman turned soap star.

Frazer introduced first himself and then Morag and Sandy, before Cora and Calum.

The garish waistcoat-clad driver reciprocated. His accent was southern English and smacked of a public-school education. 'Great to be here, Frazer. I'm Alistair Pitcairn. After I organised things with your landowner Digby Cruikshank, we talked on the phone and we've exchanged emails. This is my good friend and client, Declan O'Neil, and this is my very old chum and associate, Steve Rollinson.'

'Great to meet you all,' said Declan in an unmistakeable melodic Irish brogue.

'It's a pleasure to welcome you, gentlemen,' Frazer interjected. 'I'm sure we'll have some entertainment on the moor tomorrow, and we've got a couple of extra vehicles as you asked. A Jeep and a Mini.'

'Talking of cars, I love your Mercedes,' Cora enthused. 'Though this is West Uist, we get sudden squalls, so you might need that roof up in a hurry.'

The hippyish passenger made a face and pretended he was about to throw up. 'We know about your squalls already, petal. It was a bumpy passage over here and not great for those of us prone to the good old mal-de-mer.'

Declan O'Neil patted him firmly on the shoulder. 'Good job there was a bar for you to get mal-de-mer medicine from, eh, my man!' He looked at Cora and raised his hand to his mouth as if about to throw back a shot from an invisible glass. When he rolled his eyes and pretended to go wobbly like a drunk, they all laughed.

Calum produced a notepad and pen with the dexterity of a magician. '*Sgonneil*! Or as we say in English, brilliant! I'm Calum Steele, the editor of the *West Uist Chronicle*. Declan,' he said, honing in straight away on the celebrity with all of his usual subtlety, 'what exactly brings you to our island?'

The actor winked at Cora and turned his head, indicating the ferry. 'This tub, the *Laird o' the Isles*, I think it was called, brought us here,' he grinned, revealing perfect, ivory white teeth. 'But seriously, my friends here brought me, thanks in no small measure to Frazer's team.'

'We're here to sample the delights of West Uist,' Alistair Pitcairn volunteered. 'We all need a holiday. Some hunting, fishing and golf — we're up for all that this island has to offer.'

'I'll drink to that. I guess we'll be having a few of those wee drams you have up here,' agreed Steve Rollinson, also in an English public-school accent, slurring his words slightly so that no-one was in any doubt that he had been drinking on the ferry over. A breeze wafted a faint hint of tobacco from him.

'Chin, chin,' said Declan immediately. 'Or what's that Scottish toast?'

'*Slainte* or *slainte mhath*,' Morag said with slight smile. 'It means "health" in most of the Gaelic languages. So, when we say it we mean "good health." The other person would then say *do dheagh shlainte*, meaning "your good health."'

Alistair turned to Morag. 'Thanks for the mini language lesson, Sergeant. And I guess as you are a police officer, we don't need to be reminded that we should all drink responsibly. But heck, do we have to learn all this Gaelic? On the drive up the west coast, we saw that all the road signs had both English and Gaelic names.'

'It is pretty controversial actually, Alistair,' Calum explained. 'It's a political football that's been kicked around for a few years. Ironically, that's especially on the mainland parts where Gaelic hasn't been much spoken for centuries.'

'Here on West Uist, you'll get by fine in English,' volunteered Frazer. 'But now, if you'd like to follow me, my Jeep is parked up on Harbour Street. Just drive up the ramp and turn left and you'll see it. I'll take you on a wee tour of the island before we go to the Cruikshank estate and get you settled in your cottage. Then when you are ready, later on we can go to the targets and do your shooting test.'

'I have to say, sir, you look the real McCoy,' said Alistair admiringly. 'Deerstalker and all.'

'A regular Sherlock Holmes,' chirped up Steve Rollinson, now actually swaying slightly on his feet, causing Declan O'Neil to steady him with an arm and chuckle.

'I think that a drive in the fresh air would be a real cool idea, Steve my man,' he said, addressing the gamekeeper with a short laugh. 'Then I guess he needs a bit of a lie down. Too many brandies and ginger to steady his seasickness,' he explained. 'Don't mind his sense of humour, such as it is.'

'We'll say goodbye then and hope you enjoy the island,' Morag said.

As the group turned to leave, Calum caught the actor's arm. 'Maybe we could have a proper interview with you later, for the readers of the *West Uist Chronicle*? It's not every day we get a celebrity on the island. I was a fan of your show and I liked the premise of a hitman in an old folk's home.' He made some erratic moves, which he thought resembled the martial arts skills that Declan O'Neil's character exhibited on the screen. 'Maybe I could give any new project you are planning a bit of local publicity?'

Alistair put a restraining hand on the newspaper editor's shoulder. 'Calum, isn't it? I tried to tell you, we're just here for a relaxing holiday and a bit of peace.'

But no sooner had he said that, than several other people who had been waiting recognised the former singer and actor.

'It's him!'

'Naw, it canna be.'

'Wow! It's that stunt mannie, the hitman himself.'

And like a flock of gulls people suddenly surrounded Declan, begging the actor for an autograph or a selfie.

Alistair strove to keep people at bay, but Declan went into showbiz mode, took off his sunglasses, flashed a smile and started signing tickets, newspapers and whatever folk had handy to thrust at him. He posed for selfies and even executed a few karate kicks and stood in action poses that impressively demonstrated his skill, strength and balance. Calum and Cora wasted no time and took numerous photos and video clips on their smart phones.

'He loves it all really,' Steve said softly to Morag and Sandy. 'This happens in every little fleabag place we go to. I think it sort of reminds him of past glory days.'

Morag and Sandy smiled dutifully then looked at one another, having both noticed the sarcastic barb. Neither replied to the reference to West Uist as a fleabag place.

At last, as the crowd started to disperse, Calum honed in on Declan again. 'So is that okay, Declan? About a proper interview, how about tomorrow, once you've settled in?' He produced a business card from inside his notebook and shoved it in the actor's hand.

'It's a deal, Calum. I'll give you a bell and maybe we can meet over a drink.'

Calum turned and pointed up to the Bonnie Prince Charlie Tavern in the middle of Harbour Street. 'That's the ticket. We have the best Heather Ale in the local hostelry, and they have an impressive range of whiskies.'

CHAPTER SIX

After riding out to The Piper's Cave and having a short practice on his pipes, Torquil opened up the throttle of the Norton 850 Roadster motorcycle and felt the air rush over his face as the speedometer steadily rose. He adjusted his Mark Nine goggles and glanced sideward as Crusoe, sitting in the Charnwood Meteor sidecar, hung his head over the side and barked as the air rushed past the small windscreen.

Down the Devil's Elbow series of hairpin bends they went, spraying water as they sped through some of the larger puddles. And then they took the headland road past Loch Hynish with its famous crannog and ancient ruin until they reached the edge of the machair that intervened between the heather and bracken slopes of the Corlins and the seaweed-strewn beach.

The road straightened and he saw Frazer McKenzie's familiar Jeep heading towards him on his way to the Cruikshank estate. He raised his hand to his Cromwell helmet as they passed each other and received a wave.

Travelling a couple of hundred yards behind was a flashy, open-topped, cream-coloured Mercedes E-class with a driver and two passengers. They were all clearly singing at the tops of their voices and music was booming out. As Torquil came towards them, the passenger in the front started pointing at him and gesticulating rudely as they all seemed to erupt into near-hysterical laughter.

'Impudent bunch!' Torquil grunted to himself, looking at them as he passed by. Glancing in his handlebar mirror, he saw the front passenger looking after them and seemingly shouting out derogatory remarks at both himself and his dog. 'Right! That's it,' he said, gritting his teeth. 'If you lot have been drinking…!'

He slowed down and did a U-turn in the road, then swiftly went through the gears as he accelerated to overtake them. He waved them down as he gradually slowed and pointed to the next lay-by.

'Hey! What's the idea with the road-hogging?' cried the one in the front, who he had seen gesticulating.

Torquil switched off his engine and dismounted. Removing his helmet and goggles and unwinding his tartan scarf, he deposited them all in the sidecar, unclipped Crusoe's restraining lead and walked back to the Mercedes.

'West Uist police,' he announced, producing his warrant card. 'Detective Inspector Torquil McKinnon. I believe you had something to say to me. Or rather, you did say something to me, or about me. Would you care to repeat it?'

The passenger in the front seat, a chap with a long ponytail and a Hulk Hogan moustache, would not have looked out of place had he been going to a music festival. He had a supercilious grin on his face. 'Repeat ourselves, Jimmy? Oh, I can't think why we should. We're just here on holiday, minding our own business. I always think that's a good policy, don't you?'

'My name is not Jimmy, sir. I just told you what it was, but to demonstrate the simple art of repetition, my name is Torquil McKinnon and I am a detective inspector with the West Uist and Barra branch of Police Scotland.'

The man grinned and clapped his hands. 'I'd never have known it, what with you not wearing a uniform. So, it's a bit like a guessing game. What a good idea.' He put on a puzzled expression, then: 'Er, what was the question again?'

The driver put a restraining hand on the passenger's arm. 'My name is Alistair Pitcairn, Inspector,' he said with an affable smile. 'Excuse my friend, Steve, he can't help being puerile. He meant no harm and was just rather taken by the sight of your motorbike with your dog in the sidecar.'

Steve slapped the door. 'You look just like those old cartoons of Dick Dastardly and Muttley!' He snorted with laughter. 'You know, the cartoon, Wacky Races. Or that other one, Wallace and Gromit.'

The man in the back reached forward and tapped his fellow passenger. 'Steve, you're being an idiot,' he said in Irish accent. 'Give Inspector McKinnon here a break and cut out the buffoonery.'

'Have you all been drinking?' Torquil asked.

Alistair waved his hand emphatically. 'I have absolutely not, Inspector. I never drink and drive. My friend here had a couple of drinks on the ferry over.'

I could breathalyse him, Torquil thought. *But he's obviously just trying to keep this fool quiet.* He turned and whistled to Crusoe, who hopped out of the sidecar and ran to him. 'This is Crusoe, my dog. As you can see, there is nothing funny about him.'

Without warning, Crusoe propped his paws against the door of the car and started sniffing and then began barking at Steve.

Taken by surprise, Steve cringed back in his seat. 'Get that mad dog under control.'

'What's wrong, boy?' Torquil asked. Crusoe continued barking and Torquil grew suspicious. 'Would you all mind stepping out of the car?' he asked assertively, leaving them in no doubt that they would be unable to refuse.

All three got out, the front passenger more reluctantly than the driver and the Irishman in the rear. Crusoe continued to bark at the one called Steve.

'I have reason to believe that my dog has detected a substance on your person, sir. Please turn out your pockets on the seat there.'

'Best do as he says, Steve,' Alistair urged.

The joker scowled at the dog as he acquiesced. 'Okay, just call him off.'

Torquil touched Crusoe's neck and he immediately sat, emitting a low growl.

The sound of a motor made Torquil turn to see Frazer McKenzie approaching in his Jeep. He coasted to a stop, got out and walked towards them.

'Is there a problem, Torquil?' he asked, touching his deerstalker cap as he came close. 'These three gentlemen are guests at the Cruikshank estate. I was just showing them round West Uist before I take them to their cottage.'

'Do you not know who we are?' Steve asked haughtily.

'I will in a moment, sir,' Torquil replied. Then to the gamekeeper: 'Just checking, Frazer,' he added casually as he pushed the various items around with a finger. 'Cigarettes, rolling tobacco and papers, lighter, wallet and what have we here?' He picked up a small polythene packet and sniffed it. 'Cannabis!' he exclaimed, looking Steve in the eye. 'You do know this is an offence? A serious matter indeed.'

Frazer shuffled awkwardly. 'Look, Torquil, could you —?'

Torquil silenced him with a frown, then turned back to face Steve. 'We take drugs very seriously in Scotland. I am obliged to confiscate this and I need to take your details.'

'Are you arresting him, Inspector?' Alistair asked nervously.

'If I thought that he was a dealer in drugs, you can rest assured that I would straight away and we would prosecute. If this is solely for his personal use, then I can use discretion. As an officer of Police Scotland, I can issue him with a Recorded

Police Warning. That means I won't be reporting it to the Procurator Fiscal, but it will be kept on our records for the next two years.'

Steve looked contrite. 'Then I apologise. Please go ahead, officer. Give me this warning.'

Torquil went back to the sidecar and whistled for Crusoe to get back in. He returned and did the necessary paperwork.

'Thanks, Torquil,' said Frazer quietly. 'That could have been trouble for me. That's Declan O'Neil in the back. He's a singer and an actor. They could be good for West Uist, I am thinking.'

'I thought I recognised him, but the law is the law, Frazer. The comedian in the front there will not be charged, but as I told him, he'll be on our records for two years.'

Once the Mercedes pulled away, Alistair and Declan remonstrated with Steve.

'You bloody fool, Steve,' said Declan. 'That must have been one of the stupidest things you've done in a long time. You could have screwed everything up for us.'

Steve shrugged. He reached under his T-shirt, unzipped a money belt and pulled out another polythene bag from where it had been secreted. He held it up and flicked it with his forefinger. This one contained white powder. 'At least that island flatfoot didn't find my stash of coke.'

This time, both Alistair and Declan laughed along with him.

'That'll go well with the whisky,' said Alistair.

Steve grinned. 'Don't say I don't look after you both.' Then suddenly, in a more serious tone: 'But one thing is sure: if I get a chance before we leave this island, I'm going to get even with that puffed-up bugger who gave me that telling off along with his stupid RPW, or whatever he called it. And maybe I'll just let his stupid dog have a real snort of this.'

'Don't be a fool, Steve. You'd kill it. That stuff is poisonous to dogs,' Declan warned.

'That's the idea, my good man. You know me, I'm a cat man, not a dog-lover.' He held up his wrists and shook his friendship bracelets. He pointed to the larger ones on each wrist. 'These belonged to Alcibiades and Pericles, my two best Persian cats, may they rest in peace.' His voice quaked slightly with emotion. 'I like to feel that they're with me all the time. Sort of looking after me.'

Alistair glanced sideways at him. 'Bit of a nutter, aren't you, Steve?'

But Steve did not look back at him. He was stroking cat collar and then running his hand over the closed fist, as if it had been transformed into his dead cat's head. 'The Egyptians worshipped cats, you know? Mummified them when they died. I should have done that with my beauties.'

Up ahead the Jeep turned a corner and was lost to view. Declan held his cheroot up above the shelter of the windscreen so that its tip glowed in the breeze, then he suddenly leaned forward and slid his arm round Steve's neck, pulling his head back against the headrest. 'Do you know how hot a stogie like this gets, Steve?' he asked as he held the cheroot close to the other's ear.

Steve grabbed Declan's arm and groaned as the pressure on his throat increased.

'I can't actually give an accurate figure in degrees,' Declan went on, his voice now menacingly sibilant. 'But it's hot enough to frazzle the skin in your ear canal and might even make your eardrum blister and pop like a piece of popcorn.

From now on keep your shit to yourself, don't get arsey and do exactly what you're paid to do.'

Alistair had slowed down and watched Declan in the driving mirror. He had flinched when he saw the actor hold the cigar so close to Steve's ear, for he knew from experience that he was not one to threaten lightly.

By the time he turned the corner and the Jeep came into sight again, the Irish actor was leaning back languidly smoking his cheroot while Steve was sheepishly rubbing his throat.

'Relax, boys. We're here for a bit of recreation. This is going to be as easy as shooting fish in a barrel, so it'll be fun. The first one is already in the barrel, so then we'll take care of the others one by one.'

CHAPTER SEVEN

The Kyleshiffin police station was a converted pebble-dashed bungalow off Lady's Wynd, which ran parallel to Harbour Street. After his usual early morning training session, Ewan McPhee had changed into his regulation Police Scotland uniform, which all officers were now forced to wear instead of the casual blue Aran sweaters that they used to wear when they were just members of the Hebridean Constabulary. Ever since the amalgamation of all the forces back in 2013 they'd been obliged to wear black trousers, a matching black wicking top with a zip-up collar, epaulettes with numbers and rank and a utility belt with all the accoutrements of law enforcement. Ewan didn't mind it at all, but he was aware that some of his fellow officers resented it, especially when they had to wear caps and hats.

He opened the office and did a quick dust around and flicked through the duty book to see what was on for the day before heading through to the kitchen to brew tea for the others coming in.

He smiled to himself as he passed the room next to DI Torquil McKinnon's office. It used to be a broom cupboard, but had been fitted out as an office when DC Penny Faversham had been seconded to work on West Uist. She and Ewan had taken an immediate shine to each other, and after secretly dating for a while they had recently let it be known that they were together. With his duster he polished her nameplate on the door and felt a pang of remorse that it would likely be several days before he saw her again.

'Blasted drugs! What do folk want to be taking them for anyway, never mind taking up all her time over on Barra?'

The bell rang to herald the entry of someone into the front office. Shoving the duster in his pocket, Ewan strode through to be in attendance.

To his immense surprise he saw Wallace and Douglas Drummond, two of the local fishermen who were also special constables. They were identical twins and were even taller than Ewan. Both were wearing their fishermen's waterproofs and bobble hats, as they were not due on duty until later in the day. Between them they had a large lobster pot that was covered in tarpaulin.

'What have you got there, you pair of rogues? Don't tell me you've found Nessie's younger brother?'

The three of them habitually poked gentle fun at each other, which belied the mutual respect and affection they held for each other.

'Geography never was your strong suit, was it, PC McPhee?' asked Wallace.

'No, I hear that hammerology is his thing,' returned Douglas with a grin, referring to the fact that Ewan was the champion hammer-thrower and current Western Isles wrestling champion. 'Although I understand he's still a hammer-chewer, he's hoping to become a professional when he grows up.'

'The jokes never get any better, you scunners.'

'We've brought you a wee present because we know you'll be missing DC Faversham.'

Ewan felt colour rush to his cheeks and shook his head in mock disdain. Then he scowled as they hoisted the lobster creel onto the duty desk counter. 'Och, not on there. What's in this smelly thing anyway?'

'Something that shouldn't be in a lobster pot, Ewan,' returned Douglas, signalling to his brother.

Adopting the manner of a dignitary unveiling a statue or a plaque, Wallace pulled back the tarpaulin with a flourish.

'Good Grief!' Ewan exclaimed, recoiling from the sight and taking a step backwards. 'A dead bird! It reeks.'

'Aye, that's precisely what it is. It's a white-tailed eagle, what you might call a sea eagle.'

Ewan looked bemused. 'But how did it get into a lobster pot? They don't dive deep, do they?'

Wallace resisted the opportunity to make a joke at Ewan's expense. 'We put it in there. We found it on one of the beaches of the Cruadalach Isles yesterday. We keep a stack of creels there and sometimes lay them down close by. Can you think of a better way to carry the poor thing here?'

Ewan covered his nose with his hand and wafted the air with his other. 'Och, did you have to bring it here? Now take it away before it stinks the station out. What will Morag Driscoll say when she comes in?'

'Not so fast with the take it away, Ewan McPhee,' said Wallace. 'You ken fine that Morag will want to know about anything that falls within our jurisdiction.'

'And this is a police matter, if poisoning is the cause,' interjected Douglas. 'Just like the buzzard last week, remember? We would have brought it in yesterday, but as you know we were out all day.'

'What makes you think it was poisoned?'

'Well, look at it. It doesn't look all that old, so it's not going to have just died on the wing. No, we reckoned it had landed on the beach to have a meal. It's all stiff and was on its back with its feet in the air.'

Wallace pointed at its feet. 'Apart from that, we saw its prints in the sand. It was making a right mess. We think it was staggering about in circles, then maybe had a fit and keeled over.'

'And there were the remains of a crab carcass close by that it had been feeding on,' Douglas added. 'It really stank, so we think it happened a couple of days ago. Maybe we should have brought it too, but we didn't want to risk handling it.'

'We thought we had to assume it had been poisoned.'

'You are right, of course,' Ewan agreed, rubbing his chin. 'It'll need to go to SASA. I hadn't put the two together straight away.'

The station door opened and a tall silver-haired lady of about seventy, dressed in a tweed suit and a silk shawl patterned with Egyptian hieroglyphs strode confidently up to the counter.

'Poisoning? Did I hear one of you twins mention something about poisoning?' she demanded authoritatively.

Ewan and the two special constables-cum-fishermen instinctively stood to attention, just as they did whenever confronted by the woman they had known all of their lives and who had taught just about everyone of their generation on West Uist.

'You're up awful early, Miss Melville,' Ewan remarked as he tapped the counter with his knuckles to signal the twins.

'Good morning, Miss Melville,' Douglas snapped, as Wallace was about to pull the tarpaulin over the lobster creel to hide the dead bird from sight.

'Stop!' she commanded, peering over his arm at the large dead creature. 'Oh dear, dear, dear,' she added with the disapproving tsking noise that they all remembered so well from their school days. 'And you think the magnificent bird was poisoned, you say?'

'They just brought it in from the Cruadalach Isles, Miss Melville,' Ewan said as he lifted the counter flap and signalled for the twins to bring the creel through to the rest room. 'We'll be sending it for analysis to the laboratory at SASA, the Science and Advice for Scottish Agriculture.'

Miss Melville nodded as Wallace and Douglas carried the creel through. 'Ironically, it's about poison that I've come here myself.'

Ewan stared at her with raised eyebrows. 'Poison, Miss? Who and what?'

The former schoolteacher opened a prodigious handbag and extracted a letter. 'That's what I want you to find out, Ewan McPhee. It's a poison-pen letter.'

'Oh, not this Mungo again,' Ewan said with a frown of annoyance.

The twins stopped with the creel between them.

'The scunner is beginning to be a real pain in the —' Douglas began, but thought better of finishing when Bella Melville turned her head sharply. Her expression was enough to rebuke him.

'Yes, but it's not just the poison that I object to. I can cope with being called an old harridan who has poisoned the minds of the youth of West Uist for generations — after all, that was the crime they accused Socrates of, poisoning minds.'

Despite themselves, the three men smiled at the way their old teacher managed to slip in an educational snippet even when making a complaint.

'The rulers of Athens made the philosopher swallow poison,' the retired teacher went on. 'Well, Mungo says that it's about time someone either forced poison down my scrawny neck or wrung it like a chicken.'

Neither Ewan nor the twins were smiling any more.

After depositing the dead sea eagle at the station, the Drummonds went back out to their boat *Neptune's Trident* and sailed past the Macbeth ferry *Laird o' the Isles* as passengers and traffic boarded.

As usual they gesticulated rudely to Tam MacOnachie as he and Willie Armstrong supervised the ferry boarding and disembarkation process. Receiving Eggy MacOnachie's customary angry shake of the fist, they sailed out to sea to check on the lobster pots they had laid closer to shore.

Ten minutes later, they started to round the Wee Kingdom, a star-shaped peninsula with steep cliffs at the northern end that were home to thousands of fulmars and gannets. The ground gradually sloped down to sea level and became machair and then a sandy beach at its westernmost point. Further on, where the sands gave way to a shingle beach under the sheer cliffs, three successive basalt stacks jutted out of the sea. Atop the furthest one from the shore were the ruins of the old West Uist Lighthouse and the derelict shell of the keeper's cottage. An automatic beacon on the clifftops had been installed in the 1950s, making the old lighthouse redundant.

The string of red and yellow buoys marking their lobster creels came into view. A little way off the last buoy a small boat was anchored.

'That's Ross McNab's boat,' said Wallace, pointing to the Wave and Dive logo painted on its side.

'But there's no one in the wheelhouse or on deck. He's maybe down below.'

'Aye, we'd better go alongside in case he's got engine trouble.'

As they approached they saw what they thought was a seal surfacing. Then they saw the sunlight glint off the face mask, and it became clear that it was a diver in wetsuit and with an aqualung on his back.

Spotting them, he waved.

'*Madainn mhath*,' Douglas called out. 'We didn't see you onboard and thought we'd better check that you were all right and weren't stuck. We thought you were a seal.'

Ross McNab trod water and removed his mouthpiece. 'I appreciate your concern, lads. I'm just out doing some research. I hope you don't mind me looking at your catches in situ?' He held up an underwater camera.

'If we've got any catches in the creels, then we're fair happy,' called out Wallace.

'You've got a fair few lobsters and crabs,' returned Ross.

'And what are you taking pictures of them for?' Wallace asked. 'Are you going to make them famous?'

'I'm checking their health. It's part of the ongoing benthic study I'm making of the seabed.'

'You'll be working with Elspeth McLauchlan and the Wookies, then?' asked Douglas.

'Partly. I'm also doing research for the University of the Highlands and Islands. I'm an associate tutor in the marine biology department, you see.'

'And here is us thinking you were just a diving instructor,' cried Douglas with a grin. 'We didn't know you were a high-powered academic.'

'Neither high-powered, nor an academic,' Ross returned. 'I never finished my PhD, so I just do a spot of undergrad tutoring and teach those who want to dive. This freelance research helps me to keep my head above water financially.'

'And then you spend all your time keeping it underwater,' Wallace returned. 'So what is this benthic research?'

'It means seabed research. My remit is to collect specimens of micro-crustaceans and send them over to the lab on Lewis. The macro-crustaceans, that's the crabs and lobsters, I'm just photographing and counting. I'm gradually working my way around the whole island's coastline, so the university can build a map.' He shifted the camera into his other hand. 'It's with the university's permission that I can share some of the findings with the West Uist Coastal Ecology guardians. They are interested in gathering evidence of pollution of the seabed.'

'Pollution from the MacCondrum Salmon Farm, you mean?' Douglas asked.

Ross pursed his lips. 'It's possible there might be pollution, because as you know there are all sorts of possible issues with salmon farming. The waters round West Uist and the MacCondrum Salmon Farm, being a smallish independent farm, make this an ideal place to study any issues that may arise.'

'Ah, so you're not just a pretty face and hunky chap that teaches all the lassies how to dive?' said Wallace, with a broad grin.

'Not just lassies, Wallace,' Ross countered. 'I get the odd chap down below the waves as well.'

'Well, as creel fishermen we have our own views about salmon farming,' Wallace said.

'But as special constables with Police Scotland, we couldn't possibly comment,' his brother added, poking him in the ribs.

Ross laughed and sculled his way backwards to his boat. 'But maybe as fishermen off duty we could have an informal wee chat, over a pint or two?' He clambered aboard and started to shuck his aqualung. 'I'll be in the chair.'

'We'll take you up on the beer at least,' called out Wallace. 'But now we'd better get on and haul up these creels and check on our lobsters ourselves.'

As they chugged back to the first buoy to start the winch to raise the creels, Wallace sucked air through his teeth. 'Sometimes our other job feels like it puts a gag on us.'

'Aye, I know what you mean. If we said what we really thought, we'd be sure to upset some of our friends.'

'Pity we don't have the skin of a rhinoceros like Calum Steele,' Wallace said with a grin as the winch engine started to do its work.

'Nor an invisible skin like yon poison writer, Mungo,' his brother quipped back.

'But that's not funny, Douglas. Miss Melville is a tough old bird, right enough, but I think even she was rattled by that letter.'

'No, well maybe it'll be a case of giving him enough rope and he'll hang himself. Save everyone the bother.'

They started to bring up the creels and inspect their catches and were so occupied that they didn't see Ross McNab's boat head off towards Kyleshiffin harbour.

CHAPTER EIGHT

As Torquil headed back to Kyleshiffin, he spotted another motorbike with a sidecar parked in a lay-by up ahead. It was a distinctive Ural 750, which he recognised immediately as belonging to Henson Dingwall, the young owner of The Crow's Nest at the top of Harbour Street in Kyleshiffin. Going down through the gears he slowed and pulled in, to check that the chef was all right and not in trouble. He knew that he was a wild swimmer, having seen him many times swimming in the sea or in Loch Hynish, and he knew how cold and dangerous the water was at this time of the morning.

Releasing Crusoe's safety harness, he vaulted over the dyke and crunched his way down the shingle beach, the collie darting ahead.

I needn't have worried, he thought with relief when he saw the young man fifty or so yards ahead, leaning over a rockpool with a couple of buckets by his side.

Crusoe reached the chef before Torquil.

'I was worried you'd be in the water, Henson,' Torquil said as he climbed onto the rocks and made his way over, to find Henson making a fuss of the dog.

Henson was a young man in his late twenties with a short black beard and curly, shoulder-length hair held with a scarlet headband. In a way he looked like a dark-haired Bjorn Borg, the tennis player.

'No wetsuit today, Torquil,' he explained, 'so it's a foraging morning for me. I've got buckets of razor clams, cockles and sea anemones and I've harvested some great samphire.'

Lorna and Torquil had eaten several times at The Crow's Nest, the café that Henson had transformed into a bistro. It was well known that his daily menus were dependent on what he had foraged that day or several days before. His culinary creativity was said to be attracting the attention of food aficionados from near and far, and that awards were not far off.

'Not barnacle soup tonight, then?' Torquil queried.

Henson rose to his feet and laughed. 'No, but even if I had been getting barnacles, you'd not get them or many of the creatures I forage for on my menus the day I take them. I depurate them all for a couple of days in my tanks to get rid of any pollutants.'

Torquil pursed his lips. 'Not that our waters have much of that, though, Henson. We have no raw sewage going into the sea, and no industrial waste.'

Henson gave a thin smile. 'That's true, but most bivalves, be that barnacles, mussels, cockles or whelks are all great concentrators of metals and chemicals. That includes by-products of fish farming. I wouldn't want to be feeding fish poo that is concentrated by the wee things I bring into my kitchen. And I certainly wouldn't want to poison any of my customers with the drugs that find their way into the water and the seabed.'

Torquil hummed. 'You know, I always suspected that there was more to cooking than opening packets and reading instructions.'

'I don't believe that for a minute, Inspector. Your fiancée told me you are a dab hand in the kitchen.'

'Only what I have learned from my uncle. Have you caught many crabs today?'

'No, it's not a crabbing day for me. But again, I don't use the crabs from close in; I'd rather take the ones I dive for, for the same reasons. Some are not in great condition to be honest, so I'm selective. As I said, though, no wetsuit or snorkel for me today.' He shook his head. 'And it's not just the crabs that are not so well. I've seen more than a few dead gulls along this beach lately. I'm wondering if it's some virus or disease that's affecting them.' Then he laughed. 'But since I only cook seafood, they're no real concern to me.'

Crusoe had been sniffing around the buckets and he immediately returned when Torquil called him. 'I'll leave you to it, then Henson. I love your Ural, by the way. I've got a Norton and sidecar for Crusoe and my pipes.'

'I like the Ural, but I guess your sidecar smells better than mine. Mine's for carting buckets of seaweed and seafood.' He grinned and added: 'Although Sergeant Driscoll tells me that bagpipes can stink a bit, though. She said that more than once she's had to stop you from cleaning them in the police station.'

Torquil laughed again. 'Aye, I don't do that in the station anymore. But it's important to clean the whole instrument regularly. Oil for the drones and chanter and a seasoning mix for the sheepskin bag.' He tapped the side of his nose and winked. 'Like a lot of your recipes, I use a secret mix that's been handed down to me.'

'That'd be from the padre, I guess. I had heard that you have both been bagpiping champions.'

'Aye, he's taught me all I know about the pipes. I always put an old copper coin in the bag, which seems to help. I thought it was just an old wives' tale until I did some research. It seems it is the copper ions that are released and have an antimicrobial effect. And that's important because there have been more than a few cases of pipers contracting pneumonia from fungi and bacteria that can grow in the bag.'

'So where do you clean it now, at the manse? I'm guessing that Sergeant Golspie won't be too keen on the smell.'

'You would be right there. But speaking of Lorna and Morag, I gather you're going to be cooking up a special seafood dinner for them after their diving hen-do.'

Henson nodded. 'It's enterprising of them, so they'll need a special dinner. But don't worry, I'll take as much care of the ingredients as you do of your bagpipes. Any shellfish I cook will be well depurated to get rid of any toxins. I don't want to give any of the police food poisoning.'

'I'd appreciate that! I'd like her in one piece for the wedding. And poisoning is best kept for the crime novels.'

Calum and Cora had gone back to the *West Uist Chronicle* newsroom via Allardyce the Baker's. Before returning to their home they agreed to sketch out the copy for the next issue, having decided on their way back that it would be one of their specials coming in between the usual biweekly editions.

'So, are we leading with a piece about Declan O'Neil?' Cora queried.

Calum shook his head as he leafed through the mail that had been delivered while they were out. 'No, lass, the ferry fiasco is the big one. That should please you, since we'll now definitely need to focus on the salmon farming question now. This is a perfect lead-in to it, and since we both got the perspectives from both sides we can devote most of the front page to it and then give a double spread inside.'

'With lots of photos, of course.'

'Aye, that's my girl. And we'll include a picture of Declan and his party along with one of him in the Quicksilver band as a hook to get the readers to look inside. Then we can do a general interest piece on him, saying that the famous pop singer and soap star has come to the island. If we drop in a few wee red herrings, then we'll leave them salivating to read the big interview in the main paper later in the week.'

Cora had made coffee and set out butter rolls on their desks. Calum had as usual also bought one of Gordon Allardyce's mutton pies as an appetiser.

He tossed a letter across to her. 'One for you, darling. You'll recognise the way it's addressed.'

Cora caught it with one hand and glanced at the precisely written address. Slipping a fingernail under the flap, she opened it and drew out a neatly folded piece of paper. Her eyes opened wide and she wrinkled her nose in distaste. Then she smiled and held it up triumphantly. 'You're right. It's a personal letter from Mungo. He starts it, "Dear Witchy Bitchy"!'

Calum leaned back in his editorial swivel chair and munched on his mutton pie, relishing the gravy that oozed from it. 'Classic! Is it a juicy one?'

'I don't know if I'd call it juicy. It's filthy, though. He suggests that I must be a dirty witch to want to have sex with a stunted, short-sighted familiar like the editor of the local rag.'

Calum gave a snort of amusement. 'A familiar? Me? Does that mean he thinks I'm a sort of shapeshifter?'

Cora frowned at his lack of concern. 'There's more than that,' she said, her initial amusement replaced by a trace of anxiety. 'There's a threat here.'

'A threat, you say? Let me see.'

Cora crossed the room and laid the letter in front of him.

Calum read it silently, grinning at the reference to himself. Then he read aloud the last sentence. '*Watch that pretty nose of yours. If you keep poking it in people's business, you might get it broken — or worse! And it may happen very soon. You know that nursery rhyme, Sing a Song of Sixpence. The maid was in her garden and down came a blackbird and pecked off her nose. Keep your nose clean or I'll set the blackbirds onto you. That's a promise. Sincerely, Mungo.*'

Calum held up another letter, addressed to himself in exactly the same geometrically precise way, and similarly stamped and postmarked. He tore it open, pulled out the paper and read it with a half-smile. 'The cheeky teuchter! He starts mine "Dear Specky Short-arse".' He flicked the paper with the back of his forefinger. 'He's called me an illiterate hack who is punching above his weight.' He winked at Cora. 'I can't really argue with that. But then he says the world doesn't need any more of my lies. I should take care or someone is going to shove a copy of the rag that I edit into each of my...'

Cora covered her ears. 'I don't want to hear that, Calum.'

'I'm sure you get the gist, darling. He says the one down my throat will stop me breathing and the other will...'

'Calum! No more.'

'Well, essentially, it will occupy me so much that I won't be able to spout any more — body waste, I'll interpret it as — into my gutter press. He says he has two copies waiting to do the job.'

Cora bit her lower lip. 'That's disgusting and I don't like this at all, Calum. He actually said "that's a promise" on mine.'

Calum tossed the note on his desk and spread a dollop of marmalade on a butter roll. He took a bite and shrugged his shoulders as he chewed. 'He wrote that to me, too,' he said unconcernedly.

Cora shivered. 'But these are threats, darling.'

'Empty threats, Cora. Nothing more. I think I'll leave my article about him as it is. I've told the readers to just bin any letters they get from the old fool.'

Cora stopped with her mug halfway to her lips. 'Are you sure that's a good idea? Should we not report —?'

But Calum had suddenly snapped his fingers. 'No wait, I've a better idea. I'll just add a highlighted box in the article with an editor's letter from me to him, telling him that we're not wasting any more time on him. As far as the *West Uist Chronicle* is concerned, Mungo is dead! That'll settle his hash, the teuchter.'

'Could that not agitate him? He obviously reads the *Chronicle*.'

'Aye, maybe it will,' Calum replied as he chewed his butter roll thoughtfully for a few moments before scooping a trickle of marmalade from the corner of his mouth. Then suddenly he leaned forward and thumped his fist on the desk, slopping the coffee in his mug. 'Wait, though, I've got it! We'll put the letter from me to him in as I just said, but we'll say that we've received more poison-pen letters with personal threats. That is something the press will not tolerate. I'll tell him he's crossed the line now and the *West Uist Chronicle* is not going to rest until we have exposed him!'

His eyes sparkled behind his wire-framed spectacles as if he was seeing the headlines on the front page, running off the press like the papers in the Orson Welles' movie, *Citizen Kane*. 'Ha! The headline will be: THE CHRONICLE IS COMING FOR YOU, MUNGO!' He winked at her. 'Remember what I said earlier. Sometimes you have to backtrack on something you've written before and just be assertive. Well, that's what we are doing. We're telling him we'll take no more of his nonsense. And don't worry, darling. I'm here to look after you.'

With an exultant flourish, Calum dunked his butter roll in his coffee and then crammed the rest into his mouth, his cheeks puffing out like a hamster.

Cora watched him and felt as if her heart missed a beat as the image of Mungo's threat to Calum suddenly flashed before her mind. Part of her suddenly felt anything but safe.

CHAPTER NINE

Ewan had a big pot of tea brewing by the time Torquil arrived at the station with Crusoe at his heels.

'Have you had a play on the pipes, Inspector McKinnon? Are you ready for a cup of tea?'

'I did that, Ewan. And I'd welcome a —' Torquil began, only to stop when he saw the station sergeant come in with her hands on her hips.

'Favouritism, is it, Ewan McPhee?' Morag said with a pretend look of exasperation. 'The detective inspector saunters in after a nice ride on his motorbike and a practice on his bagpipes and he gets feted with tea. Meanwhile, some of us have been sorting out a blockade down on the harbour that was threatening to disrupt the whole island. Tea! The nearest I got to tea was a fiasco between the WUCE guardians and the MacCondrum Salmon Farm folk that Calum Steele is probably going to report as West Uist's answer to the Boston Tea Party.'

Ewan blushed and offered abject apologies. 'I'll bring you both a good strong mug of tea right away.'

'I was only kidding, Ewan,' Morag called after him. She kneeled to stroke Crusoe. 'At least Sandy went off in better spirits. It fair gave him a laugh to see Tam MacOnachie and Willie Armstrong all of a dither. Tam wanted his harbour cleared and Willie was worried about getting his mealie jimmies and sausages ready.'

Moments later, after Ewan returned and they were all sitting in Torquil's office with mugs of tea, Morag recounted the events of her early morning. Ewan was especially interested to hear that Declan O'Neil was on the island.

'Well, I met him and his gang as well in a snazzy convertible Mercedes,' said Torquil. 'I issued one of them with a RPW. I have the paperwork in my pipes case. It will need to go in the book and on the computer system.'

'So that's a black mark against them,' Morag commented as she sipped her tea.

'And then I saw Henson Dingwall when I was coming back. He told me you had complained to him about me cleaning my pipes here, Sergeant Driscoll?'

'Well, so I did. You were reeking the station out,' Morag replied. Then, turning to Ewan, she pointed an accusatory finger. 'Rather like you, Ewan McPhee, and whatever you've got under that tarpaulin in the rest room. What is it? It stinks to heaven.'

Ewan slapped the side of his head. 'Sorry, Morag, I was going to tell you when I gave the morning report. The twins brought in a dead sea eagle they found yesterday on a beach out at the Cruadalach Isles. They think it was poisoned, so I was going to get in touch with the Science and Advice for Scottish Agriculture.'

'We'd better look at it in a few minutes, Ewan,' Morag said.

Ewan ran a fingertip round the rim of his mug. 'I might as well tell you this as well: Bella Melville came in first thing while the Drummond boys were here and she saw the dead bird.' He told them about her letter and the little lesson she had given them about Socrates. 'This Mungo is getting to be a nuisance.'

'He is indeed,' replied Torquil with a frown. 'In fact, I received one this morning and so did my uncle. They are bagged up in my pipes case there, too. It's worrying if this nutcase is starting to make actual threats.'

'Miss Melville didn't look worried.'

'She wouldn't show it,' Morag put in.

The phone went in the main office and Ewan excused himself and went through to answer it. They heard him expostulating loudly, then a few moments later he ran through to them. 'It's an urgent call from Rab MacQuittie, the gaffer at MacCondrum Salmon Farm. The boat has just arrived at the farm; they were delayed getting out of the harbour, as Morag just told us, and they've found Arran MacCondrum himself. His body was floating in one of the pens and they pulled him out. He's drowned himself.'

Doctor Ralph McClelland, one of Torquil's oldest friends, was the local GP and police surgeon. He had been in the middle of a morning surgery at the Kyleshiffin Cottage Hospital when he got the call from Morag. When he explained to the patients in the waiting room that he was being called to an emergency at sea, they all accepted the news sanguinely and resigned to call back in the afternoon.

Torquil took the helm of the *Seaspray*, the West Uist police catamaran, while Ralph and Morag sat behind on the way out to the MacCondrum Salmon Farm.

The rains had stopped a couple of hours before and the sun, after a brief period of exposure, had once again disappeared behind a leaden sky.

A mile out from the west coast, the barge with its cabin came into view. As they approached, they saw two boats were moored to it. One Torquil recognised as the *Betty Burke*, Arran MacCondrum's old boat which was a familiar sight in Kyleshiffin harbour. The other was the salmon farm crew boat. Closer still they saw the ten large circular fish pens with their enclosing nets, all linked by pipes and a walkway leading from the barge.

'There's a lot of activity,' said Torquil.

Morag and Ralph stood up as he slowed down and coasted to the barge. Rab MacQuittie and Marie Urquhart were standing waiting at the top of the ladder and the other four men of the salmon farm crew were standing round a body lying on the deck.

'I'm glad that you've all come,' Rab said. 'This is a tragedy that's been waiting to happen. We've all been worried about Arran for a long while now. His behaviour has been — erratic.'

'Did you check his pulse?' Ralph cut him short as he mounted the ladder onto the barge deck.

'We pulled him out, Doctor McLelland,' Marie interjected. 'It took four of us. Rab, Gordon, Micheal and Nialghus got him out of the water while Hector and I got the first aid kit and the defibrillator from the office.'

Ralph nodded at her and shook his head sadly. 'I wish I was seeing you under better circumstances, Marie. I was sorry that your mum died. She had worked for my surgery for a good few years.' Seeing her eyes well up, he nodded again then knelt by the body and opened his bag to pull out a stethoscope. While he did his examination, Torquil addressed the crew. 'You pulled him out from where?'

Marie was visibly shaken and had started to tremble. 'From pen two. He had cut the netting and thrown himself in, it looks like.'

'How do you know that?' Torquil asked. 'Could he have just fallen in?'

'Those nets are really strong, Inspector,' said Micheal, a sandy-haired young man of about the same age as Marie. 'No, he cut them. His knife was lying on the walkway, along with an empty.'

'An empty what?' Morag asked.

'An empty whisky bottle,' volunteered Gordon, a tall man in his mid-thirties with a wispy beard and moustache. 'It took all of us to drag him out. The fish were upset and some of them looped through the hole in the net. We saw at least six escape, so we patched it up when we had got him out and after we had —' he looked embarrassed before he finished — 'made sure he was dead.' He shook his head sadly. 'Poor Arran!'

Ralph had opened the waterproofs and saw that underneath the braces of his bib trousers had been unhooked and his shirt and jumper had been pulled up, exposing his bare chest. 'Did you shock him?' he asked over his shoulder.

Rab nodded. 'Aye, Marie is first aid trained, and we all had attended that course on CPR that you gave us, Doctor McLelland.'

Marie shivered. 'As I said, Hector and I got the kit while they pulled him out of the water. When I looked at him, he was pulseless and not breathing. His skin was frozen and we didn't know how long he'd been in the water. I tried to clear his mouth before I started cardio-pulmonary resuscitation. We did the chest compressions for a few minutes, then we used the defibrillator.' Her eyes welled up and she swallowed hard. 'After we gave up, I pulled his waterproofs down over him again.'

'I don't think there would have been much hope,' Ralph said, again over his shoulder as he used an ophthalmoscope to peer into Arran MacCondrum's staring eyes. 'He has cattle trucking of the blood vessels on his retinae, an absent cornea reflex and absolutely no life signs.' He checked the time on his watch and rose to his feet and faced Torquil. 'I can confirm that he is dead, I am afraid.'

Marie clapped her hands to her face and let out a cry of anguish.

Torquil knelt down and ran his hands over the dead man's waterproof clothes. He delved inside them and a few moments later pulled out four largish, heavy rocks. One was in each jacket pocket and two were in the front chest pocket of his bib trousers. 'Not the usual things you'd have in your trouser pockets,' he said, laying them on the deck beside the body. 'It looks like he was using some weights to help him to sink.' He looked at Ralph. 'So, what do you think about the cause of death?'

Ralph wound up his stethoscope and returned it to his medical bag along with his ophthalmoscope. 'I think it's clear that he drowned, Torquil, but it's not for me to say any more. It'll be a case for you to report to the Procurator Fiscal.'

'Indeed, which means we need to investigate further. Morag, can you arrange the things? We'll need to bag everything up and tape off this portion of the barge and the pen where he drowned.'

Rab let out a howl of despair. 'But the farm? What about the fish? They need to be fed.'

'We'll see what we can do with the minimum of disruption, Rab,' said Morag, still comforting Marie, who was now gently weeping.

Hector spoke out for the first time. 'The rifle, Marie. You didn't mention the rifle or what we found in the cabin.'

Marie nodded and took a couple of deep breaths to calm herself. 'I'm sorry, of course. You'll see soon enough, but I was just focused on getting the defibrillator and the first aid kit. He had smashed all of the computers and the consoles. His rifle was lying on the floor. It looked like he had used the butt like a hammer. He must have gone berserk.'

'What was he doing with a rifle?' Torquil asked.

'Seals!' Rab replied. 'He was always obsessed with them getting through the nets and we — that is, he — would sometimes come out to shoot any he found. Ever since his father's time, the farm has shot the number we've been legally allowed to. And it's not illegal, is it?'

'Not yet,' Torquil replied, 'but it will be soon, I am thinking. Pressure from animal rights groups is mounting.'

Morag patted the bag slung over her shoulder. 'I'll go and start taking pictures in the cabin, Torquil. Then I'll tape it off and give Ewan a call to set things in motion.'

Ralph had been making notes in a small book. 'Well, I've put the time of certification of death. I'd say he's been dead some hours, but it would be for the official pathologist to say more. Difficult to assess because he'd been immersed in this freezing cold water, which makes the signs hard to read. Once you've taken photographs, I'd suggest that we take the body back to the cottage hospital mortuary until the Procurator Fiscal's office decide what they want to do. It will certainly mean a post mortem examination.'

'We could take him back in our boat?' suggested Gordon.

'Or maybe Arran would have liked it if we took him in the *Betty Burke*?' Michael said.

'Thanks, lads, but I think we had better take him in the *Seaspray*,' Torquil replied. 'While Morag looks at the cabin, I'll have a look over his boat and the rest of the farm just to make sure there is nothing else of significance. If he ended his life himself, then there may be a note somewhere.'

'As the police surgeon I can make a preliminary examination of the body back in the hospital,' Ralph interjected. 'I'll take blood for alcohol levels and also for routine biochemistry and toxicology. The sooner I do it, the better.'

Torquil nodded at his friend and then turned back to face Rab. 'We'll also need to look over his house. I think he was single and lived on his own, is that right?'

Rab did not reply immediately but darted a glance at Marie and the rest of the staff. Then he nodded. 'Aye, he lived on his own, even if he wasn't always alone.'

'You'll be able to give me his address?' Torquil returned.

'He lives in … I mean, he lived in the tall thin house at the end of Kirk Wynd. You know, the one with a ship's anchor by the side of the door? It won't be locked; he only used such modern things as keys when he was inside!'

Torquil made a mental note to find out what Rab had meant, but he did not feel it appropriate to ask at that juncture. They would be taking statements from all of the staff in due course. There was something he wanted to clear up in his own mind first. 'Why do you think he was out here on his own?'

Rab pursed his lips. 'He often went off on his own in the *Betty Burke*. He might end up here, or go to the hatchery. He could polish off a quarter or a half bottle, no bother.'

'There was a completely empty bottle here, you said. Could he have had that?'

'Your guess is as good as mine. It may only have had a drop left in it.'

'He smelled strongly of alcohol, despite the water.'

Marie suddenly cut in. 'We have to tell him, Rab.' Then, turning to Torquil, she went on, 'He drank when he was finding life difficult. If the business wasn't running the way he wanted.'

'What was there to go wrong? It's a profitable salmon farm, isn't it?'

Marie blew air through her lips. 'There's always trouble with a salmon farm these days, Inspector. Sergeant Driscoll here will tell you about the pantomime we had with the Wookies at the harbour this morning. They blocked the ferry because we had a delivery come over by lorry.'

Rab nodded. 'And as I said, he was obsessed, maybe paranoid is a better word, about the seals. We had another net broken by seals the other day. It doesn't matter what you do, if there is a rich food supply, they'll find a way of damaging the pen nets.'

'We've been trying to persuade him to get underwater sonic scarers,' said Marie, 'but he just calls it new-fangled nonsense and insists that the only way to deal with seals is to cull them. He is a total technophobe and doesn't use email, social media or anything. It took ages to persuade him to get a decent mobile phone that took text messages.'

'But like you just said, the Wookies and all those pressure groups are going to get the government to outlaw shooting them,' said Gordon. 'We think that's what he was here to do last night, Inspector.'

Morag called out from the barge cabin door. 'The rifle's here, all right, Inspector. Not fired, though.'

'There could have been something else bothering him,' said Nialghus, the member of the staff who had so far stayed quiet. 'A woman, I am thinking.'

'Tell me more,' urged Torquil.

Nialghus shrugged his shoulders. 'He was a single man and never went out with anyone publicly, but every now and then he seemed to have a spring in his step.' He looked embarrassedly at Marie, then said, 'Well, it was like he'd had his oats, if you know what I mean.'

'And then he seemed proper lovesick,' agreed Gordon. 'You know, distracted, and he started wearing more aftershave and that. But we only think so, because it wasn't something you were allowed to ask him about.'

'Aye, just a feeling, you know,' Nialghus added.

Torquil held his hands up and looked at all of the staff. 'Do any of you know anything more? Anything at all?'

'It may be nothing,' Rab volunteered after a moment's silence. 'But number two was his favourite pen, you know. It was the first of the modern ones that we put in. Up until then, we had the old wood-framed square ones that his father and uncle had used when they started the farm. For some reason, that pen was his favourite.'

'That sounds a little quirky, if I may say,' said Torquil.

Rab gave a curt nod of his head. 'Arran could be odd, right enough.'

Everyone looked across at pen number two where they could see the fish leaping, their silver bodies arcing through the air to cut through the water with resounding splashes.

'I'm afraid that we'll need to take advice from the Science and Advice for Scottish Agriculture and maybe also the Scottish Environment Protection Agency,' Torquil went on. 'At this stage I'm not sure how finding a dead body in a salmon pen will affect the fish. They may not wish them to be used for human consumption.'

Rab recoiled in horror. 'That would mean they'd have to be destroyed. There are maybe twenty thousand fish in that pen.' He shook his head. 'What would Arran MacCondrum say about that?'

The cottage that had been prepared for Declan O'Neil and his party was a stone-built single-storey dwelling surrounded by gorse and wildflowers perched above the trout stream that ran down to one of the numerous ponds, or small lochs as Frazer called them on the Cruikshank estate.

'I understand that you'll be wanting to give us a shooting test, is that right?' Alistair asked, once Frazer had overseen one of the estate workers unloading their luggage, including fishing rods, wet weather gear and one set of golf clubs.

'That's right, sir. I need to check that you are competent shots. It'll only take a short while on the targets. Perhaps later this morning, after you're settled in.'

'Sure, why not?' said Declan. 'I think you'll find that we're all fairly competent. And Alistair fixed up the hire of the guns, is that right?'

'That is correct, sir. I've got 20 gauge shotguns for you all, that's quite enough for shooting fowl.'

'What cartridge size?' Declan asked.

'We use our own 29 gram six and a half shot, which gives an excellent pattern and a good balance of shot and punch. It's ideal for the rough shoot. I assume you know that as with most estates these days, we use bismuth shot rather than lead, and fibre wads instead of plastic. All good for the environment, of course.'

Steve snorted derisively. 'Pah! The world has gone mad over this politically correct nonsense. It's PC this and PC that these days. We're not allowed to poison the ecology with lead, but we can pepper our prey with bismuth.'

Frazer looked uncertain how to respond. 'Well, it's just the way it —'

'The way it should be,' Declan interceded. 'We're all for that, aren't we, lads?' He patted Steve on the shoulder, leaving his hand there for a moment. 'Of course, Steve is more a fishing enthusiast than a shooter,' he added with a grin.

'Aye, and we've got you booked for fishing in the trout river, too,' Frazer said, smiling at Steve. 'You'll get a fine catch on our waters.'

'Any chance of catching salmon?' Alistair asked, picking up one of the fishing magazines on the coffee table and thumbing through its pages.

'Ah, sadly not. Twenty or thirty years ago we could have accommodated you with salmon, but not anymore. We used to have our own fishing ghillie.'

'I hear that lots of rivers in Scotland don't have salmon anymore,' Declan remarked.

'Funnily enough, I read an article about that before we came here,' said Alistair. 'It said aquaculture was responsible for a decline in both salmon and trout.'

'Why was that, Alistair?' Steve asked.

'Sea lice, it said. The farmed salmon are prone to it and the concentration of sea lice affected wild sea trout and wild Atlantic salmon.'

Frazer shook his head. 'I am not convinced. You see, we have brown trout in the rivers and in Loch Beag here on the Cruikshank estate. It's true that we don't have the salmon anymore, but our brown trout have thrived. I think that's because we look after them better than we used to do with the salmon.'

'Was the ghillie you had no use?' Steve asked.

Frazer turned sharply and stared at him for a few moments before shrugging his shoulders. 'Maybe so. I look after the fishing and the game along with an assistant keeper. Our ghillie twenty-odd years ago was — less diligent, shall we say.' He smiled and added: 'He liked a dram too much.'

Alistair looked puzzled. 'How come the brown trout are thriving?'

Frazer nodded. 'It's a personal view, but I think it is because our brown trout are looked after so well and have plenty of food that our river and loch numbers have risen. That has seen the sea trout numbers fall. You see, sea trout and brown trout are actually the same species. We make sure there is enough food for the brown trout in our waters so there is less need for them to migrate to the sea to feed.'

Declan grinned. 'Interesting, and that makes sense. You clearly know your stuff about trout, Frazer. You don't get that knowledge overnight, I'll guess. How long have you been the head gamekeeper here?'

'Twenty-five years. Since I was twenty-three.'

'And you're happy here?'

'The Cruikshanks have been good employers and this is the best estate on the island. I think you'll enjoy your stay with us.' He looked at his watch. 'So perhaps if I call back in an hour we can go down to the gun room, fix you up with your guns and then head to the targets?'

When he had gone and the three were left alone, Declan went over to a drinks cabinet that was liberally stocked with spirits. He poured three large whiskies.

'So, what did you guys think of him?' he asked.

Alistair had opened a thin briefcase and pulled out several named files. He selected one with Frazer McKenzie's name on the front and opening it, placed it on the coffee table so that the others could see his photograph and the typewritten notes beside it.

'I think we're on the right track,' said Alistair.

Steve tossed back his whisky and sucked air through his teeth as the spirit hit his stomach. 'I agree, but he might need a bit of persuasion.' He opened his money belt and took out one of the sachets of white powder he had shown them earlier. Clearing a space on the coffee table, he started to sprinkle three small heaps of powder in front of each of them. Producing a pen knife he worked on each to break down any lumps then teased each into a line. 'I even brought a straw for each of you,' he said, producing three already trimmed drinking straws from his belt.

'I got in touch with the first target a couple of times,' said Alistair, accepting a straw and sitting forward. 'He's going to go overboard for us, trust me. Old Ciderman also said that one of his agents is on the island and has been preparing things. He'll make contact tomorrow, probably.'

The other two laughed. Then Steve closed a nostril with a finger and inserted the end of the straw up the other and snorted his line.

'Overboard! I like it,' said Declan, sipping his drink rather than touching a straw. 'You can have mine, right enough. You know I'm trying to stay off the stuff. And you two should take care, too.'

'Okey-dokey, Mother,' said Alistair. Kneeling in turn and mirroring Steve, he snorted his line up his straw. He rose and beamed. 'We share yours, Declan Goody-two-shoes.'

Declan rolled his eyes and continued. 'So, we'll begin on the others next.' He slid another file out and put it on his knee. 'I'll take this one and then we can see if I was right, Steve?'

'What do you mean?' Steve asked as he split the remaining line with his penknife.

'About him being related to that police inspector,' Declan replied, opening the file on his knee. A moment later, he grinned. 'Well, what do you know, they look as if they could be related and he's into classic motorbikes, too. And he's a golf nut, as we already know. I think I'll have fun meeting this old boy, the Reverend Lachlan McKinnon.'

CHAPTER TEN

Like many people on West Uist, Conn MacVicar had several jobs. Not only did he work a croft, but he was also a competent plumber as well as being the porter at the cottage hospital. The latter meant that he pretty well did all the moving of patients, the transporting of samples and, calling on his plumbing skills and ability with a screwdriver, he undertook any odd jobs that the nursing staff needed doing when he was on hospital duty. His portering duties often involved taking bodies to and from the hospital mortuary.

Morag had arranged via Ewan McPhee for Brian MacVicar, Conn's nephew who had recently taken over a carpentry and undertaker's business in Kyleshiffin, to meet the *Seaspray* at the harbour, bringing with him a temporary coffin to transport the body to the cottage hospital. Because of their relationship and Conn's experience, he often also assisted his nephew who was a qualified funeral director, in laying out bodies, embalming and helping at funerals.

In the mortuary, without any fuss or the usual banter between them that they enjoyed, because they both knew the deceased, they soberly transferred the body from the temporary coffin to a gurney before Brian took his leave.

Ralph McLelland had phoned through and told Conn to make the old post mortem table ready as he wanted to examine the body in his capacity as the police surgeon.

As always whenever he was on mortuary duty Conn had changed into blue scrubs and white wellingtons and was standing almost at attention when Ralph opened the door using the electronic security lock.

'Ah, Conn, a sad business,' said Ralph, who had also donned scrubs, but was wearing white theatre clogs rather than wellingtons. 'I have DI Torquil McKinnon and Sergeant Morag Driscoll with me.' He lay a small digital camera on the bench by the wall next to a neat pile of metal basins and specimen jars.

'Good morning, Inspector McKinnon and Sergeant Driscoll,' Conn said.

'Conn, as you know, we have identified the body as Arran MacCondrum,' said Torquil, waving aside further formality. 'He was pulled out of the water of one of his pens at the salmon farm.'

'But aren't they covered with strong nets to keep the salmon in?' Conn ventured.

'His knife was found on the walkway round the pen,' said Morag. 'It looks as if he cut his way in. He was wearing his heavy waterproofs as you can see, and he'd weighted the pockets with rocks.'

'I think he'd been in the water, partially or totally submerged for at least a few hours,' said Ralph.

'Aye, I'd believe that, right enough,' said Conn. 'I'm no doctor, but both Brian and I thought he was heavier than either of us would have expected. His lungs will be full of water, I've nae doubt.'

Ralph put on a surgical gown and pulled on a pair of rubber gloves. 'Well, let's get him undressed and I'll make a preliminary examination. Would you take pictures, Torquil? The camera is by the wall.'

'I'll get his clothes and bag everything up,' said Morag. 'If it's okay, I'll go through them all back at the station.'

Torquil nodded agreement.

'I can hardly believe it of him,' said Conn as he and Ralph peeled off the clothes from the dead salmon farmer. 'I wouldn't have thought he was the type to lose his bottle and do that.'

Ralph clicked his tongue. 'It takes courage to end your life. But we can't make any assumptions. It will be up to Inspector McKinnon and his team to investigate and for the Procurator Fiscal to finally make his determination.'

He handed the heavy waterproofs to Morag. Torquil started to take photographs of the body.

'See the shrivelled wrinkling of the skin of his hands and feet? Typical washerwoman changes that you get when the body's been in water a long time.'

'There is still a smell of whisky,' Torquil said out loud. 'Despite the water.'

Conn shook his head. 'Arran liked his whisky, right enough. I've shared space at the bar with him enough times. But I'll tell you one thing. He never had it with water. He always said water drowned it and if he drank a watered whisky it would kill him. Looks like he was right after all,' he added with a click of his tongue.

No one laughed.

After checking his emails and doing the bit of administration that couldn't wait, Frazer McKenzie had gone off on his rounds in his Jeep. Conscious that the party were wanting some shooting, he wanted to make sure that there would not be any nasty surprises when they went out with him the next day. There had been too many such unexpected shocks for him lately.

Looking for dead birds on the moor was never easy, covered as it was by so much gorse and bracken. Being aware of the way nature worked gave him a better chance than the uninitiated. Buzzards and crows would give a clue eventually, as would swarms of bluebottles if he got close. Yet if one fell in the thickets, he had little chance of finding it.

It was imperative that poisoned birds should not be found on the estate. Not if he wanted to keep his job. No, the only way was to find any and bury them quickly. He had the spade ready in the back of the Jeep.

Turning a bend on the track, he recognised an old green Hillman Imp parked near an outcrop of rock. It belonged to Annie McConville, a widowed lady of seventy-odd years who was something of a local celebrity in the Western Isles, known both for her vague eccentricity and for the dog sanctuary that she ran single-handedly. She often took a pack of her dogs for exercise on the Cruikshank estate moors and never made a secret of her disapproval of shooting. Rather than argue with the lady whom he had known all his life, Frazer had initiated a system whereby warning flags were flown at entry points to the estate on days when any kind of shoot was on. So far, that had worked.

Further along the trail he saw her and four of her dogs. He breathed a sigh of relief, for sometimes she could have up to a dozen.

She was kneeling on the ground in the heather with the dogs gathered round her. Frazer coasted to a halt and got out of the Jeep.

His heart sank as she rose to her feet, holding a dead bird by its feet.

'Ah, it's you, Frazer McKenzie. You'll not be happy to see that I've got a dead hen harrier here.' She raised it to her face and sniffed. 'Poisoned, I'd say.'

'Aw, hell!' he blurted out, and then quickly excused himself. 'I'm sorry, Miss McConville. I mean, I'm sorry to see one of these gorgeous birds has died. But you can't tell if its poisoned.'

Annie sniffed. 'It smells bad, and I know when I'm seeing a bird that's suffered. I can tell, you know. I have a special connection with birds and animals.'

'I'll take it off your hands, Miss McConville, since it died on Cruikshank land.'

'You'll do nothing of the sort, Frazer McKenzie. You're a gamekeeper and without meaning to offend you, this has to be reported immediately to the authorities.'

'It is my responsibility,' he returned sternly. 'If you will let me have it.'

He took a step towards her and immediately the large German Shepherd growled and bared its teeth. A small West Highland terrier standing beside it snarled and two medium-sized mongrels barked.

'Haud still, the lot of you,' said Annie. 'I'll take it myself, though, Frazer McKenzie. I'm going to the police station myself, actually. I've had another letter I need them to see.'

'A letter, you say?' Frazer asked, unable to keep a trace of anxiety out of his voice.

'A poison-pen letter,' said Annie emphatically, moving back in the direction of her Hillman Imp, holding the dead bird at arm's length in her gloved hand. 'It's from that scunner Mungo and he's got to be stopped.'

Frazer stood helplessly aside and watched her and her canine bodyguard retreat to her car. He cursed silently. He knew that there had been two pairs of hen harriers on the estate moors, and he had already buried one male. This female one that Annie McConville had was bad news any which way. He just hoped it was the mate of the one he had already disposed of.

'Dammit! And now the bloody woman is going to report another of those letters. Well, she's right there. That Mungo will have to be stopped, one way or another.'

Morag had come straight back from the cottage hospital and updated Ewan, who had been busy with SASA, to whom he had reported the dead sea eagle. According to their instructions, he had intended bagging it up prior to sending it off on the next ferry, but Crusoe had held him up.

'He's been intrigued by the smells in the rest room, Morag,' Ewan explained. 'You know what dogs are like with dead birds. He created a lot of noise when I shut him in Torquil's office, so I had to let him out and he came straight back to see what I was doing. I had to wrap the tarpaulin round the creel with the bird in it and put it up on the table tennis table out of his way. If the lads are right and it's been poisoned, it could be a serious matter.'

'Aye, it needs bagging up and getting off,' Morag replied, wafting her nose with her hand. 'It does pong a bit, and I'd like it out of my station as soon as possible. That's a good job for you.'

Ewan nodded, unsure of what he was going to use to bag it up. 'You've had a rotten morning, Morag, what with the Wookies and the ferry and all. But I'm right sorry to hear about Arran MacCondrum. I can hardly believe he'd do something like that.'

She patted his big shoulder. 'I'm afraid life is like that. You never know what is going on in someone's life or how low they can be feeling.'

'Was he depressed, do you know?'

Morag shrugged. 'Like most folk on the island he was on Doctor McLelland's books, but he doesn't recall seeing him professionally for years.' She frowned. 'I can't say I relish going through his clothes,' she said, pointing to the heavy-duty clinical waste bag that Conn MacVicar had given her to take the deceased's clothes back in. 'I didn't like seeing his naked body, but at least it wasn't a post-mortem I had to attend.'

'Will he need that?'

'Aye, but I'm guessing it will be in Stornoway. We'll have to get Brian MacVicar the undertaker to take him over from the cottage hospital. It will be up to the Procurator Fiscal.'

The bell in the front office sounded and Morag raised her eyes ceilingward. 'Talk about being saved by the bell. Why don't you put on the kettle, my wee darling, and I'll see who our latest customer is?'

'Aye, I'd rather that than do the undertaker thing with this dead bird,' Ewan said with a thin grin.

'You can do it afterwards,' Morag replied over her shoulder as she went through to the counter. 'Oh, just one thing. Until Torquil comes back and gives us the all clear to do so, let's not say anything about Arran MacCondrum.'

'Aye, mum's the word.'

A cacophony of canine sound greeted her as Annie McConville came in with her four dogs.

'Wheesht, Nero and Walt,' she said firmly to the two youngest dogs. 'Take a leaf out of Zimba and Sheila's books.' Then, turning to Morag, she held up the dead bird. 'Have you a good strong bag, Sergeant Driscoll? I'm thinking you'll be wanting to notify the authorities that I've found a dead hen-harrier up on the Cruikshank moors. Its poisoned, I'm pretty certain of it.'

Crusoe had come scampering through on hearing the dogs on the other side of the counter. He began to bark and immediately set off the others again.

Ewan came running through. 'Crusoe, will you stop —'

Morag immediately turned to him and held up a hand. 'Remember what I just said, Ewan. Remember that magic word that begins with M.'

The big constable nodded. Then, seeing Annie McConville holding the dead bird by its feet, he let out a groan. 'Oh, not another one!'

CHAPTER ELEVEN

Torquil had ridden the Norton Roadster to Arran MacCondrum's house on Kirk Wynd and parked opposite the great anchor. As Rab MacQuittie had said, the front door was unlocked so he let himself into a small vestibule with numerous waterproofs hanging from hooks. It smelled strongly of the sea.

He reached inside his leather jacket and took out a pair of examination gloves and pulled them on.

Then, pushing open a door, he found himself in a sitting room and was surprised when his nostrils were immediately assailed by the smell of fresh flowers. From what he knew of the salmon farm owner, he did not think he was the type of man who would buy flowers.

The room was in darkness and he made his way gingerly to the windows and drew back the curtains. Grey light crept into the room, revealing it to be a simply furnished sitting room, with every wall covered in large multi-photograph frames as well as an assortment of single photographs.

A cursory look gave the impression that it was a museum dedicated to salmon farming. Early pictures were in black and white or were crude polaroid shots of the MacCondrum Salmon Farm. Closer inspection revealed a chronological arrangement on three walls, with the space between the two main windows devoted to family pictures.

Torquil recognised pictures of Inver MacCondrum, Arran's father and his brother, whose name he couldn't recollect, in the early days when they only had two square wooden pens instead of the ten modern round ones they now had. Then there were pictures including Arran as a young man and still others more recently taken showing the staff that had been there this morning. And in many of them there was the *Betty Burke*, the boat that had done the MacCondrums such good service over the years.

Other walls showed the gradual construction of the hatchery building on the coast and the various tanks inside it where they bred their young fish and nurtured them to maturity. Then there were more recent ones of the installation of all the modern technical equipment. Lifting frames away from the wall, he noted that there were handwritten notes dating the various stages. Once again he recognised the current staff, especially Rab MacQuittie in pictures at the farm, and Marie Urquhart, who seemed ever-present with an electronic tablet and clinical white boilersuit at the hatchery.

'Your life is all here, isn't it, Arran?' Torquil mused aloud. 'The salmon farm was everything to you, it looks like.'

A glass-fronted cabinet was full of glasses and miniature bottles of assorted malt whiskies, and a sideboard had a salver on which were several empty decanters. He pulled out the stoppers of each in turn and sniffed. 'All long gone, I think. You liked your whisky a lot.'

Going through the door he entered a dining room, which clearly had been used as his office. An old typewriter was surrounded by baskets containing bills, invoices and ledgers. A jam jar was crammed full of biros and pencils. Torquil spent some time going through the various documents, but found nothing suspicious.

In a wastepaper basket he saw shreds of a typewritten letter and a torn-up envelope. Picking out the pieces, he assembled them and saw that under a letterhead labelled The Ciderman Consortium was a curt, business-like sentence: *Dear J Partner, the consortium representative will call on you this week to collect your final payment. Failure to respond will result in proceedings. Sincerely, Ciderman.*

'Interesting, Arran. And just what sort of consortium were you consorting with?' Torquil had the image of an irritated Arran MacCondrum ripping the missive up and tossing it in his waste basket. He photographed the assembled letter and envelope.

An empty bottle of whisky and an empty glass beside it sat on the window ledge. Torquil unscrewed the top and sniffed first the bottle and then the glass. 'Still smells strong, so I'd say Conn MacVicar was right. You didn't like water in your dram. Maybe you finished it after you'd thrown that letter away.'

The smell of flowers was stronger here and he followed the scent through into a hall, checking first the kitchen, which was empty, utilitarian and tidy. But the smell of flowers was not there. Following his nose he mounted the narrow staircase to a landing where he found the bathroom and shower, then a spare bedroom and a sort of dressing room with spare waders, boots, southwesters and umpteen bobble hats.

'But you didn't sleep here, did you Arran?' he muttered as he took another flight of stairs from the end of the landing. There he found the large bedroom with a garret window that looked out above the neighbouring rooftops with a fine view of the sea.

On the covers of a king-sized bed lay a bunch of wild flowers.

Torquil bent down and sniffed them. 'Sweet geranium, palmarosa and lavender. Not from any florist, but all from the machair and fairly recently picked. Now, surely you didn't pick them and leave them before you went out, whenever that was.'

Pulling back the duvet, he noted the rumpled cover sheet. 'Restless sleeper, were you, Arran?' he muttered. Then he stroked his chin pensively. 'Both pillows rumpled, too.' He bent over them and sniffed and sniffed again all over both pillows. 'And that's a different scent. Perfume not aftershave or cologne. So you shared your bed with someone recently, didn't you? Someone sweeter smelling than yourself, I am thinking.'

After replacing the duvet, he checked the small stack of paperback books by the bedside and then the drawers of the bedside tables. There were tissues, packets of unopened condoms, breath-freshener, a tube of lubricant gel, a couple of packets of Fisherman's Friends lozenges and a lip balm.

Under the bed, he found two envelopes. Both were handwritten in a recognisable style. They were very similar to the ones he and his uncle had received that morning. As he opened them one by one, he found that each letter had obviously been crumpled up and then flattened out and put back in its envelope.

He placed the letters on the bed next to the posse of flowers and read them. 'So Mungo really didn't like you or your salmon farm, did he, Arran?' he mused. 'You are a nasty bugger, aren't you, Mungo?' And then looking at the flowers, he added, 'But who are you, the bringer of flowers? And why? Had you shared his bed? And if so, when?'

Calum and Cora joined the throng in the police station as Annie McConville was explaining to Morag the purpose of her visit apart from the delivery of the dead hen harrier, which she had plonked on the counter in front of Ewan.

'Something will have to be done about this Mungo!' said Annie. 'That's two of these poisonous things I've had.'

'Phew! Maybe something needs doing about the smell in this station, Sergeant Driscoll,' said Calum. He laid a copy of the *West Uist Chronicle* on the desk. 'An advance issue for you, as usual.'

Morag forced a smile at Calum and then gave Cora the slightest of winks before returning her attention to Annie, who was still remonstrating with her dogs. She was determined not to give the journalists any information about the drowning until she spoke to Torquil.

'Did I hear the name Mungo being mentioned?' Cora asked above the din. 'Because we have something to report.'

'A dead bird. That's the smell, is it?' asked Calum, spying the dead hen-harrier on the desk.

'Poisoned!' said Annie McConville over her diminutive shoulder. Then with an authoritative slap of a hand on the counter: 'Wheesht, the lot of you.'

Silence was instant for a moment, broken immediately by Calum, who had pulled a spiral notebook out of a pocket of his yellow anorak. 'Poison, you say, Miss McConville? How do you know that?'

'I ken fine a poisoned creature of the Lord, Calum Steele. You can quote me on that, too.'

'It's the second today,' Ewan said with a groan. A sharp look from Morag made him regret his words.

'The second, eh?' Calum quickly returned. 'What was the first?'

'It was a sea eagle that the Drummond lads found out by the Cruadalach Isles. It looks like it was poisoned, too and we're—'

He stopped short when Morag gave him another sharp look and shook her head.

'Take a picture of it, Cora,' Calum said before quickly turning to Annie. 'Where did you find it, Annie?'

'On the Cruikshank moors when I was out with these four. I ran into Frazer McKenzie and I told him he couldn't have it. It needed reporting.'

'You saw Frazer?' Morag asked her.

'I did, and I wasn't taking the chance of him getting rid of it. I know about gamekeepers and what they get up to protect the moors for their rich absent landlords. That's why I brought it here, along with these other bits of poison. As I said, you'll have to do something about this Mungo.'

'I thought you mentioned Mungo,' said Cora. 'We need to report him too, don't we, Calum?'

The newspaper editor grimaced. 'Well, we need to inform you that we are going to unmask the venomous toad. That's my promise as the editor of the *West Uist Chronicle*.'

Morag put her hands to her ears and then slapped the counter with both hands. 'Enough! One person at a time. You are all talking over each other. Calum and Cora, Constable McPhee will deal with you while I talk to Miss McConville.' And then putting her hands together and making a quick diving gesture, she quietly mouthed to Cora, 'See you at the next lesson.' In return, Cora put her fingers and thumbs together to make pretend goggles and put them in front of her face before smiling and giving a thumbs-up sign.

'Oh, don't fret, Sergeant Driscoll,' said Calum, ignoring the signing between them and adopting his most solicitous tone. 'Look, we're happy to wait, aren't we, Cora? Why doesn't Ewan, I mean Constable McPhee, take care of this smelly dead bird and we'll just wait our turn and talk to him when he's ready?'

He winked at his girlfriend as she demurely put her mobile phone in her pocket. Good reporter that she was, he knew that she had taken the opportunity to get a good shot of the poisoned hen harrier.

Standing without interrupting any further, they listened as Annie McConville told Morag about the poison-pen letters she had received and the personal threat to her and her dogs in the most recent one. Calum knew that Annie would be more than happy to talk to him if he tracked her down later for further news comment.

Morag noticed the editor smugly waiting, but was ever more determined not to tell him about the drowning.

Frazer was surprised at how competent all three of the party were at the targets. He had expected the actor to be a decent shot, but they all certainly knew how to handle a shotgun and seemed quite happy with the bismuth cartridges the estate used.

'There were one or two useful things that my public school taught me,' said Steve Rollinson after the gamekeeper had locked their guns away again and complimented them all on their skill. 'Shooting was one of them, but you'll have to get to know me better to know the others, Sherlock.'

Frazer gave a thin, humourless smile, clearly discomfited by the tall man in walking shorts and all those friendship bands. He seemed over-enthusiastic and more hyper than he liked to see. His habit of fondling the friendship bands like he was stroking a pet he found unsettling.

'And I learned on my uncle's estate in Norfolk,' volunteered Alistair quickly. 'Mainly pheasant there, of course.'

Frazer wondered if they had taken something along with the whisky that he could smell on their breath.

'Watch out, your silver spoon may fall out of your mouth,' jibed Steve.

Declan winked at Frazer. 'As for me, it was shooting rats with an airgun on the farm in the old country when I was a kid. Then after I left the band and started acting, I had a couple of lessons to make my resumé look good. That was when I took up kick-boxing as well, which was fortuitous and helped land me the part in *Leave them to the Caretaker.*'

Steve sniffed. 'Actually, I think we had something to do with it, too.'

'Well, thankfully you'll not have to kick anyone here on West Uist,' returned Frazer. 'And shooting as well as you all do, I'm sure we can provide you with a good morning's shoot tomorrow.'

'We're looking forward to it, Frazer. And I'm planning to shoot a few birdies on your local golf course this afternoon.'

'It's not a game that ever appealed to me, sir.'

'I suppose not. Well, maybe you should take a leaf out of our book and broaden your horizons. That's what we're doing.'

'We might do a bit of diving while we're here, too,' said Steve.

'Aye, there is a diving business on the island, the Wave and Dive School.'

'Cool, and we want some good food,' said Alistair. 'I saw when I was researching this trip that there's a good seafood restaurant in Kyleshiffin.'

'Ah, that's The Crow's Nest. It's a youngish chef who's making a name for himself. Not just seafood I heard, though.'

'Can you recommend it, Frazer?' asked Declan.

Frazer shook his head. 'I'm more of a game man myself, sir.'

The actor laughed and patted Frazer's arm. 'Aren't we all, my man? Until tomorrow, then.'

As Frazer reached for the door of the gun room to let them out, Alistair asked, 'What are the postal services like between here and the mainland?'

Frazer looked puzzled. 'The post? Er — not bad. As good as can be, considering everything has to come in and go out by the ferry. It's Royal Mail, but if it's something special we can always arrange something with a delivery firm if you like. We use a firm called —'

Alistair waved his hand. 'No need. I was just wondering if folks round here thought they got a good service. Got their mail delivered on time.'

'You never know if you've got a big surprise in the post, eh, Frazer?' said Declan.

'A lottery win — or something,' added Steve.

Completely nonplussed by the question, Frazer nodded. 'It's fine.'

Suddenly, the letters that he was carrying in his inside jacket pocket and their contents almost seemed to give him an electric shock.

CHAPTER TWELVE

Crusoe was delighted to see Torquil when he lifted the counter flap and came through the gap. He gave a short bark and then sat wagging his tail.

'He heard you arriving on the Norton,' Ewan informed him with a grin. 'He seems to know the difference between it and the Bullet.'

'He should do, he's been on both often enough,' Torquil replied. 'Has he been any trouble, Ewan?'

'Not a bit. He's had an exciting morning, what with Annie McConville coming in with Zimba, Sheila and those two new ones. I think they are her better-behaved dogs.'

Morag came through with a mug of tea in one hand and a shortbread biscuit in the other. 'I'm glad to see you, Torquil. I found some interesting things when I finally got a chance to go through Arran MacCondrum's clothes.'

Torquil nodded and held up his piping bag. 'I've brought a few interesting things myself. Come through to my office and if Ewan could see if there's any tea left in the pot, I wouldn't mind a mug.'

'Coming straight up, sir,' said Ewan with a mock salute.

Minutes later, Torquil was looking at a plastic see-through wallet containing a blue paper envelope and alongside it a smeared piece of writing paper where ink had run.

'It's from Mungo,' Morag said. 'It was soaking, of course, but I dried it as best I could above the electric ring. You can still read it, though.'

'It looks as if it's been crumpled up. I can see wrinkles in it,' Torquil said, taking out a magnifying glass from a drawer. 'So, let's see what Mungo says.'

He lay the plastic envelope on the desk and slowly read out: '*Dear Farmer Mannie, I've given you enough warning. It isn't natural to farm in the water and cage all those creatures. I'm going to destroy you, bit by bit. I'm going to send a really hungry and clever seal to open all your pens one by one and let your harvest free. And I'm also going to make sure the eggs in your shack don't hatch anymore. You're losing your harvest, your clutch of eggs and everything. Just one question to answer, Farmer Mannie, which do I come for first, the fish or the eggs? Wait for my text. Sincerely, Mungo.*'

'It sounds like the usual sort of Mungo letter,' said Morag. 'Except it's a bit more threatening. Sinister, I'd say.'

Torquil opened his piping bag and from it slipped on a pair of rubber gloves, then took out the letters he and the padre had received and the ones he had found under the dead man's bed. 'That's mine and Lachlan's, and I found these two from Mungo under Arran MacCondrum's bed. The first says, "*Dear Farmer Mannie, you've been spreading wild oats for far too long. I know who with and when you committed your crimes. You are going to pay and soon everyone will know, too. If I were you I'd start praying, because soon you're going to be cropped properly. Sincerely, Mungo*".'

Torquil picked up the other letter. 'This is the more recent of the two. Listen: "*Dear Farmer Mannie, you and yours are nothing more than a pack of fornicating fish folk. I know exactly who you've been sleeping with and I'm giving you due warning. I'm telling on you all in two days' time. You are going to be gutted soon, Arran MacCondrum. I guarantee it. Sincerely, Mungo*".'

He looked up at Morag. 'They are pretty threatening, aren't they? He's threatening to tell someone about an affair and he also seems to be threatening to destroy his business.'

'Do you think Mungo is turning from just being malicious into a blackmailer, Torquil?' Morag asked.

Torquil pursed his lips. 'That's a possibility, though he hasn't mentioned anything about payment or given him any way out.'

'What do you think of the writing, Torquil?' Morag asked.

'It's impossibly neat and none of it is joined up. It's clearly done with a stencil and a fine nibbed pen. Probably a draftsman or an artist's pen. Proper ink, anyway.'

'Is it one or two lassies he's been sleeping with?' Ewan asked.

'Assuming it is women,' Morag said.

'Rab MacQuittie implied that he entertained at his house and only ever locked the door when he was inside entertaining someone,' Torquil replied. 'And Nialghus and Gordon said they had suspicions, but no one ever saw him with a local woman.'

'Maybe he had call girls visit him?' Morag suggested.

Torquil nodded. 'Every possibility has to be considered.' He told them about the rumpled bed and the flowers on the covers and the smell of perfume on the pillows. 'I also found a torn-up letter from some organisation called The Ciderman Consortium. I brought the pieces back in an envelope and I'd like them carefully put together and put in another plastic envelope. I already took a photograph of them and I'll send it to you to add to the files. It said a representative of this consortium would call on him to take a final payment. That may or may not be of any significance. Did he have anything to hide? The thing is, would any or all of these letters have been enough to push him over the edge if he was depressed? The strange thing is that Ralph had no knowledge of him being depressed. He was on his books, but never consulted, so he certainly wasn't on antidepressants.'

Ewan hummed. 'Excuse me, Torquil, but shall I go and get the rest of Mungo's letters that came in at various times this morning? I was going to show them to Morag first, but it's been so hectic.' He left the office and returned shortly after with a tray, which he lay on Torquil's desk. It contained several different sized envelopes along with an unused pair of rubber examination gloves. All of them were addressed in geometrically exact handwriting and all had stamps and Royal Mail postmarks.

'There is one from Bella Melville,' he said, pointedly. 'One from Tam MacOnachie the harbour master, another from Neil Buchanan over on the Wee Kingdom, another from —'

'Okay, Ewan, I'll have a read,' Torquil said with a smile.

'I was just going to say one each from Calum Steele and one from Cora Melville. They were in when Annie McConville brought in the dead hen harrier.'

'I'll tell you about Annie in a minute, Torquil,' interjected Morag. 'Let's have a look at these Mungo letters first.'

Torquil nodded and gingerly picked up the first letter addressed to his old teacher, Miss Melville.

His eyes widened as he read it. '...*and it's time someone poured poison down that scrawny neck of yours. Or wrung it like a chicken.*' He frowned. 'Nasty. Accusing her of bullying kids when she was teaching.'

He read each of the others in turn, carefully holding them at the very corners with his gloved hands so as not to contaminate any of the paper.

'Have you —?' he began.

'I photographed them first, Inspector,' Ewan replied. 'I've printed copies of them all and have them in a separate folder for you.'

'Good man. Did they all bring them in this morning?'

'Tam MacOnachie's came yesterday afternoon. The others came today.'

'Miss Melville's reaction would have been interesting, especially after the accusations in her letter.'

Ewan gave a humourless laugh. 'She was more concerned about the spelling, I think.'

The bell from the front office rang and a voice called out. 'It's only us.'

A couple of moments later, Wallace and Douglas came in, both now dressed in their specials uniforms.

'*Mo chreach*! We just heard about Arran MacCondrum,' said Wallace.

'What a shock. We'd never have thought it of him.'

Over the next few minutes, Torquil and Morag told them of the results of their investigations at the salmon farm and Arran MacCondrum's house.

'And we've just been going over some of these letters folk have brought in from Mungo.'

Torquil took out the large manila envelope that he had put his and Lachlan's letters into that morning. 'I have two more, Ewan, one to me and one to my uncle Lachlan, so please copy them afterwards for the Mungo file, too, then we'll need to get them all off to forensics on the mainland. We'll see if they pick up any prints, or clues that will lead us to him. How many of these poison-pen letters does that make now?'

'Altogether now, eighty-three, sir. This Mungo has been busy these last few weeks. The malicious scunner.'

Torquil nodded, tapping the manila envelope. 'Aye, he's got a twisted mind right enough. It's been a while since he was causing a nuisance. It seems that he satisfies his craving for mayhem after a while and then goes quiet. Something seems to have rattled his cage this time, though. He's sending letters all around the island.'

'Folk are getting suspicious of neighbours again,' said Morag. 'Calum Steele may make it worse, though.' She held up the advance copy of the *West Uist Chronicle* and opened it to the page with a bold headline: THE CHRONICLE IS COMING FOR YOU, MUNGO! 'Just look at that. Here's an article saying he's personally going to unmask Mungo.'

'That's Calum for you,' replied Torquil. 'He revels in anything he thinks will sell papers. Yet in fairness, he's had several letters himself. They attack his writing, but he takes that as a compliment.'

'He was just the same at school,' said Wallace. 'Always the practical joker and mischief-maker.'

Torquil blew air through his lips. 'Aye, him and you two as well. But this isn't a joke.'

'It is not,' agreed Ewan. 'Cora was a bit rattled by the letters she and Calum received this morning. They are what prompted him to write that piece.' He pointed to the last see-through envelope containing the letters side by side.

'I can see why,' Torquil said after reading them out to the others. 'These are blatant threats. We need to track Mungo down before Calum goes stirring things up any more. So, Ewan, can you fish out all the past files we have on Mungo?'

'I had a look already, boss. We have them going back well over thirty years.'

'Good lad. It's a start. Right then, let's get on. Anything else?'

'Aye, there is,' said the twins in unison. They looked at each other, then pointed at one another. 'You say —'

Wallace shrugged and told Torquil about finding the sea eagle on the Cruadalach Isles.

'Aye, Ewan told us all about it,' said Torquil. 'And about Miss Melville's poison-pen letter.'

'But Annie MacConville also brought in a dead hen harrier that she found on the Cruikshank estate,' Ewan told them. 'And she brought in a letter, too.'

'That's three birds, then,' said Wallace. 'The sea eagle, the hen harrier and that buzzard last week.'

Torquil sat back and drummed his fingers on the desk. 'Maybe there are more. Henson Dingwell said that he'd seen a few dead gulls on the beaches lately. If that's the case, we really do need to find out if they have been poisoned, and what with.'

Morag bit her lip. 'It couldn't have anything to do with the emamectin the Wookies are concerned about, could it? They use it to kill off the sea lice that feed on the salmon.'

The twins looked at each other, then Douglas snapped his fingers. 'We saw Ross McNab this morning. He was diving near our creels, filming the crabs and lobsters and taking samples from the seabed. He's doing a benthic study, I think he called it, with the University of the Highlands and Islands.'

'Aye, he's working with the Wookies,' Wallace added.

'They had placards this morning with all sorts of anti-salmon farming messages. One said to stop shooting the seals.'

Torquil looked round the others. 'Arran MacCondrum had taken a .308 rifle with him to the salmon farm.'

'But he hadn't fired it,' Morag said. 'He just used it to smash all the technology in the barge cabin.'

Torquil frowned. 'I'm not liking any of this, folks. Poison-pen letters, poisoned birds and now a salmon farmer has committed suicide. We know that he had received some of these letters, and that the Wookies folk are implying that the salmon farm is harming the seabed and endangering the seals. I have a bad feeling about it all.' He sipped his tea, which had gone cold, then grimaced.

'Sorry, boss, shall I get you another mug?' Ewan asked.

'No!' Torquil replied emphatically. 'No time for that. We've got three things we really need to get to grips on. The poison-pen letters, these dead birds and the Arran MacCondrum conundrum.' He pointed to Ewan. 'Get all files out for me along with all the photographs and get the actual letters ready to go off to forensics in Stornoway. I'll give Lorna a call and see if she can liaise there to help speed us up.' He looked at the twins. 'Before we get these birds off to SASA, we want to see if Henson Dingwall was right about there being dead gulls. Can you two go out to the beach near St Ninian's, go down by that layby above the rock pools and bag any carcasses you find? Wear gloves, of course.'

Ewan gathered the mugs onto the tray and he and the Drummond twins left to start on their allotted tasks.

'Shall I get onto the Fiscal's office, Torquil?' Morag asked.

'No, leave that to me. I'll explain that we've got more investigations to do. But you could make another couple of calls for me.'

'Sure, who to?'

'Firstly, to SASA and SEPA to find out what the situation will be with the salmon farm. If those fish are considered to be contaminated or unable to be released for consumption, that's going to be a big story and who knows what repercussions it will have? They certainly can't be released and we cannot make any decision on it, but tell them that we did decide to let the crew feed all of the fish as usual anyway.'

'I'll emphasise that we thought it would be cruel to leave them unfed,' agreed Morag. 'But of course, Calum will certainly want to know about it all. He'll be fizzing when he finds out that there has been a fatality at the farm that we didn't tell him about.'

'Don't worry about Calum. The second call is to Penny Faversham. I think we're going to need help with some of our enquiries. Ask her to come back on the next ferry. Tell her I need her.'

'That'll please Ewan McPhee.' Morag rose and turned to go, then paused. 'But what did you mean by the Arran MacCondrum conundrum?'

'The rifle, Morag. If Arran wanted to commit suicide, and he had a rifle powerful enough to kill a seal, why didn't he just use it on himself?'

CHAPTER THIRTEEN

After discussing the case with the Procurator Fiscal, Torquil had telephoned Rab MacQuittie to tell him that the question about the salmon in pen number two had been referred to both SASA and SEPA and that he needed to look over the hatchery as part of the ongoing investigation into Arran MacCondrum's suicide.

Rab said that Marie Urquhart would meet him there, as Marie was the senior fish technician with responsibility for the hatchery. They had all agreed that after the shock discovery of the owner's drowning, they should take the rest of the day off and go home once they'd fed the fish and repaired the net. Accordingly, they had all gone back in the crew boat. Marie would drive to the hatchery and he had taken the *Betty Burke* back to Kyleshiffin and would go on to the depot to check on the delivery from that morning.

After taking Crusoe for a quick walk, Torquil headed off to the harbour and took the *Seaspray* catamaran out to the west coast of the island. The MacCondrum hatchery could be easily reached by road, but the sea approach was relatively quick and he wanted to feel the sea air and the wind on his face to help him to think.

He moored up on the hatchery jetty next to one of the salmon farm boats and walked up the ramp to the door of the large corrugated building. Pressing the intercom, there was a buzz and a few moments later he heard the mechanically distorted but recognisable voice of Marie Urquhart. A clicking noise followed as the door was electronically unlocked and swung open.

She met him as he came through the vestibule. She was wearing a clinical white boiler suit with a hairnet over her purple dyed hair. Her eyes were red-rimmed as if from crying. He noted that she was no longer shaking, but she still looked pale and deeply upset. Despite that her voice was controlled, as if she was able to go into trained scientific mode.

She rubbed her left temple. 'Excuse me if I seem a bit spaced out. I get migraines and with this shock I'm trying to stave one off.'

Torquil took a moment to accustom his eyes, for the great warehouse space was shaded, with muted slightly orange light from special lamps along the walls. There were rows of various shapes and sizes of tanks with overhead lines of pipes linking them and everywhere the sound of pumps and running water.

'You must take care of yourself. Perhaps you should be lying down in a darkened room instead of still being at work?' he suggested.

'I'm better when I'm busy. And I like it here. It feels comfortable.'

Torquil nodded. 'I have never actually been inside the hatchery before, Marie. I hadn't realised it would be so laboratory-like.'

'Well, it's specialised work that goes on here, Inspector,' she replied. 'As a qualified fish technician with a master's degree in sustainable aquaculture, Arran made me responsible for updating a lot of the things we do here. I couldn't refuse, and it meant more money.' She held up the tablet she was working on in her hand and pointed around her. 'But I understand what you say. Folk are usually surprised when they come here, just as you were. So, let me give you a quick tour. The first thing folk notice is the lighting. You see, light in the ultraviolet part of the spectrum can be deadly to salmonid eggs, so they have to be kept in the dark in those special covered egg baskets you see over there. They have revolving discs and we extract dead eggs.'

She led him on to troughs which were also covered to provide shade. 'Over here we have the alevin sections, which also have to be light protected. There are four square boxes in each trough in this incubation system.'

'And the water flows through?'

'That's right. It flows under the upstream ends of the boxes, through perforations in the base and through other perforations at the downstream end from one box to another. Each trough can hatch twenty thousand eggs. And these are our smolt rearing tanks,' she said, continuing to explain the various processes and the procedures involved. 'The ambient temperature is so important and with the tailored temperature control system we have installed, we know that every single tank has the right temperature for the fish to thrive and develop in a controlled way.'

'You can control their development?' Torquil repeated.

'Certainly, at every stage from fertilised eggs to alevins, fry, parr and then smolts temperature is critical. Too high and they grow too fast and too slow and they don't develop enough.'

'I vaguely remember those terms from the biology classes, but I hadn't realised that you could control development.'

'Aquaculture is a real science, Inspector McKinnon. In the wild, the Atlantic salmon leave the sea and come upriver to their spawning grounds, after their physiology has adapted to living in freshwater. So, the eggs are laid in freshwater and they live in freshwater all through their different stages until they become smolts, when they are ready to migrate back to saltwater as adults. Their growth is subject to the temperature changes in the rivers. As you know, our climate varies a lot and the average time in the rivers in the wild for the juvenile fish is two to three years.'

She pointed around the hatchery as if to summarise. 'But here, with our controlled environment, we reduce that time to six to twelve months. Then we're ready to transport them out to the pens at the farm. We oversee everything, right up to when they change from freshwater to saltwater creatures.'

'So, all of these troughs and tanks at that end of the hatchery contain freshwater and those with the mature smolts have saltwater?' Torquil asked. 'It must be quite a feat coordinating everything.'

Marie nodded curtly and pointed to a large tank into which a steady flow of water fell from a high intake pipe. 'That is one of the main intake tanks for the freshwater. We measure everything by hand every few hours.'

'But it has no eggs or developing fish in it?'

'No, it is simply the freshwater checking tank,' Marie replied, noting some of the readings on her tablet and checking the gauges on the tank. Then: 'We normally have two or three staff running this hatchery during the day, but today there is just me and I'm only going to be here as long as it takes me to make sure all is as it should be.'

'I can see that there is masses to do,' Torquil said, committing all that he had seen to memory, which he supplemented by taking numerous pictures on his iPhone.

'Absolutely, the nutrition and the water environment are all geared so the physiological development transitions smoothly. We monitor it during the day and the computers and the automated systems do it at night.'

'And you can do all this yourself?'

'As I said, we have two or three of us here and we have a rota among the crew. But we always have a qualified fish technician, which is either myself or two of the others.'

'How often did Arran come here?' Torquil asked casually, dropping the dead owner's name in for the first time.

'More often than anyone, probably,' said Marie, without any obvious hesitation. 'He came on his own a lot. He talked to the fish, you see.'

'Really?'

'His father and his uncle did that too,' Marie replied. 'Not from any scientific reason, you know, just sort of habit. They believed that salmon farming was more an art than a science. It was like they could encourage them to grow by magic or by letting them know they were around. Arran used to say a good farmer walks his fields, but he walked his pens and kept an eye on his young ones.' She shook her head. 'Maybe to you it sounds weird, but Arran MacCondrum had his own way with things.'

'And you don't think it is an art?'

Marie shrugged her shoulders. 'Generally, it is advised not to make the developing fish aware of human presence, but it seemed to work for him. Perhaps call it experience rather than an art.'

'Did he do anything else when he came here, or did he just walk around the tanks and talk to the fish?'

Marie pointed to the closed cabin at the far end of the hatchery. 'He'd go and sit in the technician's station there and complain about the computers. Shall I show you?'

As Torquil nodded, she led the way to the enclosed cabin and opened the door to show all its computers and high-tech equipment. Apart from swivel chairs at the work console, there was a couch and a coffee table with a neat pile of magazines.

'We monitor everything from here,' Marie explained. 'We check oxygen saturation levels, water pH, temperature and the flow rates in all of the complex hydraulic systems. And we monitor the nutrients for every stage of development. As I said, temperature, light, and water quality are all critical.' She patted the clean console and gave a pained frown. 'Sometimes we have found an empty bottle here after he's been at night. He'd sleep on that couch.'

'It's all building the picture of him for me,' Torquil mused. 'But it's another conundrum.'

'Excuse me?' Marie returned. 'He drank, is that what you mean?'

'He's a bit of a puzzle, Arran MacCondrum,' Torquil replied. 'He runs a sophisticated salmon farm with all this gadgetry and yet he sounds like a bit of a technophobe.'

'You can say that again,' Marie said, pursing her lips. 'Fortunately, Rab and some of the others persuaded him to let me make some adaptations. They said he needed dragging into this century, otherwise, the business —' She left the sentence unfinished, but her shrug left Torquil in no doubt as to what she meant.

'And so, I understand that he was single and had no relations left. What is going to happen to the business? Does he have any partners?' Torquil thought of the torn-up letter from the Ciderman Consortium.

Marie looked slightly taken aback. 'Didn't you know? He had partners. A couple of years ago, things were tight and he sold shares. We all have some. And he also sold a large number to some consortium that he kept us in the dark about.'

When Torquil had left the hatchery and walked down the ramp to the jetty, his eyes fell on the rocks from which it was constructed, and the wall that bordered it. Like every schoolchild that passed through Miss Annie Melville's tutorage, he knew that the stone was Lewisean gneiss, some of the oldest rocks in Europe. But it wasn't the geology that interested him. It was the gap in the dry-stone wall that formed one edge of the jetty. Three or four rocks were missing.

And they looked similar to the heavy stones they had found in Arran MacCondrum's waterproofs.

He reached inside his jacket for his iPhone and took several pictures.

The smell of the dead birds had defied air fresheners and candles, so Morag had gone out to Maclean and Sons the ironmongers for some polystyrene boxes and heavy-duty bags, then to Willie Armstrong the butcher for some ice to pack in bags to go around the carcases. She and Ewan had just finished and were ready to get them off to the ferry when Calum Steele phoned her to give her a lambasting about not telling him about Arran MacCondrum's demise. Before she could give any explanation, he rang off in high dudgeon.

Then the Drummond twins returned with another tarpaulin-covered creel. Between them they hoisted it onto the station counter.

'Torquil's hunch was right, Sergeant Morag,' said Wallace.

Douglas whipped the tarpaulin back. 'Thirteen of them in all. A right assortment of gulls for you, but mostly terns.'

'We went right along the shingle beach to make sure we didn't leave any carcases in case they are all poisoned,' Wallace added. 'You never know if carrion or birds of prey pick them up —'

'If it proves to be poison, then this is really bad news,' said Morag with a shake of her head. 'And if it is, what poison is it and how did it get there?'

'Ah, then maybe you should expect a call from Calum Steele. He and Cora were off on his Lambretta scooter as we were coming in and they stopped to ask us what was in the creel.'

Morag rolled her eyes. 'And you told him — what, exactly?'

'We told him we had thirteen dead gulls.'

'Then he laughed like he had another of his scoops,' said Wallace.

'But he didn't thank us,' said Douglas. 'Instead, he just made a sarcastic remark about the way the police stuck together to keep the press in the dark. Cora tried to say something to him, but he just made an angry noise then they zoomed away in a cloud of blue smoke. He needs to get that scooter fixed.'

'He had called me a short time ago,' she told them. 'I knew he would when he got wind of the drowning. I'm guessing he'll burn Torquil's ears about it, too.'

Morag sent them back to MacLean and Sons and then to Willie Armstrong for more boxes, bags and ice. Then, while the twins went for showers in case they had been in touch with poison, she and Ewan made up the other dead bird parcels.

Since the birds case had been allocated to Ewan and he now considered them his territory, she left him to phone SASA on the station phone while she called them independently on her mobile to enquire about the salmon in pen number two. It was then that she found herself on a merry-go-round of being sent from one person to another at SASA, listening to various pieces of canned music until she finally was given an answer. That was that the person who could advise about the salmon in pen number two was out of the office and she would be called back.

Her call to DC Penny Faversham was another matter. She was more than pleased to know that her boss Torquil wanted her to return from Barra. She had been unable to find any evidence of cuckooing and Morag could tell that she was keen to see the big red-haired Constable Ewan McPhee.

Torquil was on his way back in the *Seaspray* when his phone went off and he answered it to hear the irate voice of Calum Steele shouting at him.

'A friend, I thought you were, Torquil McKinnon! Why did you not tell me that Arran MacCondrum had drowned? Me, Calum Steele, the editor of the *West Uist Chronicle*, the premier local newspaper in the whole of the Outer Hebrides — a laughingstock you've made me, because I had to find out about our local salmon farmer's death from one of my paper lads. It's all round Kyleshiffin, but who finds out last? Me!'

'Calum, hold on.'

'Hold on, you say! That's what you've done and that's what you got Morag Driscoll and Ewan McPhee to do. Hold onto the news. Some friend.'

'Calum, there are times when —'

'Times when I despair. Cora sends her love to Lorna, by the way, and looks forward to the next dive lesson.'

The phone went dead as Calum hung up on him.

'Calum Steele, sometimes you can be a —' Torquil began as he stared at the screensaver picture of Lorna that had appeared. He smiled at it, then he suddenly felt a cold shiver shoot up his spine. 'Aye, you can be a real firebrand, Calum,' he said slowly. 'But just sometimes you can shine a light in the darkness. You genius!'

He immediately typed in a number.

CHAPTER FOURTEEN

Morag was feeling pleased that the station now smelled more wholesome when she answered Torquil's call. He listened as she told him of the discovery of more birds and the packaging and efforts to make the station smell less offensive.

'Are you still listening, Torquil?' she asked, putting the phone onto speaker mode. 'It sounds really windy out there.'

'Aye, breezy enough to blow the clouds away. I'll be in soon and I need to look over Arran MacCondrum's clothes and everything that was with him when he was found.'

'I'll lay them out all ready. Anything else?'

'Aye, chase Ralph McLelland for me. I tried to ring him but he's not answering. I need to pick his brains.'

Calum opened up the throttle on the Lambretta as they took the road past the great locked gates that blocked the entrance to the drive leading up to the Scottish baroque Dunshiffin Castle on their way towards the Cruikshank estate. It had been the home of the MacLeods, the lairds of the Dunshiffin estate before becoming an institute and then being boarded up.

'Did you need to be so rude to the Drummonds, Calum?' Cora shouted into his ear, when she thought enough time had passed for him to calm down.

'Ach, they'll understand. I was angry with the police tactics. They were in uniform so they got the rough end of my tongue. That's fair enough and it'll teach them a lesson.'

Cora was silent for a few moments. 'What lesson, Calum?'

'To be square with me. Just like they should be square about the wedding and not gang up on me with Ralph McLelland and

Ewan McPhee about Torquil's stag-do.' He grunted. 'Not that Torquil's any better. He's the ringleader, the top cop who ordered non-cooperation.'

Cora gasped and slapped his shoulder. 'Is that what was behind it? Calum Steele, you are a ... a...'

'A wonder! Aye, I suppose so.'

She slapped his shoulder again, then followed it up with a noisy kiss to his yellow anorak. 'But seriously, it's worrying, isn't it? All those dead birds.'

He reached down and patted her now interlinked hands about his waist. 'Course it is. If they've been poisoned, then it could get into any food chain. Dogs, cats, crows, all of them could end up dead. That's why we have to publicise it on all our sites right away and in the next issue. It is our duty to protect the public.'

'Before the police get the toxicology back?'

'We cannot wait. If they've been poisoned, then someone's behind it, either deliberately or not.'

'Like who?'

He grunted. 'Much as I hate to think it, maybe the salmon farm. That emamectin they use, like the Wookies were saying this morning, it's poisoning the sea creatures as well as the sea lice.'

'But it's not supposed to affect other animals or birds. I looked it up already.'

'No, but what about crabs or lobsters or other shellfish that are washed up and decay on the beaches? What do all these gulls, cormorants, and gannets feed off? We need to investigate that.'

'So why are we not heading there or to the depot? Why are we heading this way to the Cruikshank estate?'

'We'll check the depot later. I'm fed up with being put off, so we're being pre-emptive about the other story. I want to pin Declan O'Neil down.'

'And what am I going to do?'

'You're going to find out from his agent and producer exactly what they are doing here on the island. I've had a wee think, and I don't think it is really to scout out a location for a TV show.' He looked over his shoulder and tapped the side of his nose. 'Brains and journalist's sixth sense, darling.'

Morag and Ewan had removed the net and covered the tennis table in the rest room with a polythene sheet. On it they laid out all of the clothing that Arran MacCondrum had been wearing when he was pulled out of the salmon pen. His waterproof bib and brace trousers, a jacket, boots and hat, and also his jeans, socks, shirt and jumper. They were all still damp, despite having been wrung out into a bucket. A large jar contained the water from the bucket in case it was going to be needed.

Beside these were the empty whisky bottle, the heavy-duty knife, the .308 rifle and the contents of his pockets, apart from the letter she had put into the file Torquil had already seen, along with the other poison-pen letters from Mungo. Also, in case he wanted it, Morag had asked Ewan to place the whole poison-pen folder containing the duplicated letters on the table, too. Finally, in a line at the bottom of the table she had laid the four rocks that had been removed from the pockets of both the jacket and the inner chest pocket of the bib trousers.

Doctor Ralph McLelland had been on his rounds but picked up Morag's call requesting that he come to the station. He came straight away.

'That's excellent,' said Torquil, seeing the West Uist team gathered round the table tennis table, drinking tea. He patted Crusoe, who had greeted him effusively before obediently pattering through to return to his basket in Torquil's office. 'Ralph, this is good of you to come in off your rounds.'

'Not a problem,' Ralph replied. 'Is something bothering you, Torquil?'

'Several things are niggling me, actually.'

Ewan pointed to the big teapot and as Torquil gave him a thumbs-up sign, he poured a mug of tea for him.

'Did you find out something at the hatchery?' Morag asked.

'Maybe. That's why I want to have a confab about the drowning. So let's all gather round and look at what we've got.'

Morag volunteered, 'His clothes, his gun, the empty whisky bottle and these rocks.'

'That's right,' said Ralph. 'I was there on the salmon farm barge when you took them out of his waterproofs.'

'It makes you cringe to think of him using them to make himself sink,' said Ewan.

'I know,' said Torquil. 'As you all know, I have a personal horror of drowning.'

The others were silent, but all nodded understandingly.

'But this is what I found at the hatchery,' he went on, pulling out his iPhone and showing them the pictures of the jetty wall and the gap that he had photographed. 'I'd say that these four rocks will probably fit in there like a jigsaw. I think that's where he got them from.'

'So, you think he had planned it, boss?' Wallace asked. 'Kept them ready on the *Betty Burke*?'

Torquil did not reply. Instead, he picked up and opened the folder and selected the duplicate of the one that had been found on Arran MacCondrum's body. He read it out. 'Note that last sentence. "*Wait for my text.*" That surely means a text on his phone.' He pointed around the table. 'So where is it?'

'Maybe it's on the *Betty Burke*?' Wallace suggested.

Torquil shook his head. 'There was no phone on it, nor at his house.'

'Maybe it fell into the salmon pen?' Morag said.

'That's possible, or maybe he threw it away. But for now, it's noticeable by its absence.' He touched the rifle. 'This niggles me, too. If he wanted to commit suicide, why not use the rifle that he had with him?'

'He was drunk, by the look of that empty bottle of whisky. Maybe he was not thinking clearly,' suggested Wallace.

'And he may already have planned to drown himself, hence the rocks,' said Douglas.

Torquil turned to Ralph. 'He looks as though he drowned himself, that's right, isn't it, Ralph?'

'It looks like it.'

'But can we be sure?' Torquil spread his hands out towards the table. 'I've got too many questions here.'

Ralph stared at him with narrowed eyes. 'The post-mortem should tell, Torquil. I'm not sure when it will be. Brian MacVicar hasn't arranged to collect the body to take it over to Stornoway yet. It'll take a bit of time to organise.'

Torquil's lips formed a tight line and he clicked his tongue. 'I'm going to call the Procurator Fiscal in a minute and try and get the post-mortem done urgently tomorrow morning. My question to you, Ralph, is if the Fiscal and the official pathologist agree, could you go and assist at the post-mortem? And maybe you could liaise with Lorna in the station? Speed things up a wee bit. I'll give you her direct office number.'

Ralph lifted his mug of tea and swirled it around before taking a gulp. 'I will, if you tell me what exactly you are thinking.'

'Isn't that Frazer McKenzie's Jeep?' Cora said in Calum's ear as they went slowly along the track, taking one of his shortcuts on the Cruikshank estate. The land undulated and was covered in gorse with large swathes of bracken and heather.

'Aye, and that's Frazer himself over there, I think. He'll not like us going across his blessed shooting moor on the scooter. But hello, what's he doing?'

'He's digging something. Out here?'

Calum rode up to the Jeep and stopped. 'Off you get, Cora, and have your camera ready.'

As they advanced on foot towards the gamekeeper, Cora started taking surreptitious pictures by zig-zagging behind the newspaper editor, as if she was walking to avoid tussocks on the track.

'Calum Steele! What're you doing here?' Frazer snapped, as he stood up and came towards them with hands held up as if to bar their way.

'We've come to see Declan O'Neil.'

'Well, you're on private land and well off the proper estate road.'

'What are you doing, more to the point?' Calum asked, bypassing the gamekeeper. 'Digging, I see.'

Ahead of them by the spade that Frazer had dropped to the ground there was a hole, and beside that two large square turfs that he had laid aside.

'Come back here. That's none of your business.'

'Photographs, Cora,' Calum said, turning swiftly to face Frazer. 'It is everyone's business — the *West Uist Chronicle*, the public and the police — when we find a number of birds of prey being buried.'

'Stop that! No pictures allowed here.'

Cora ignored him as Calum stood irresolutely in the gamekeeper's way.

'An eagle, a couple of buzzards and I don't know what the other two are,' said Calum. 'They should all be reported — they will all be reported, both to the public and to the police.'

Frazer had pulled off his deerstalker hat and ran a hand through his hair. 'It's not ... it's not what you think.'

'Poisoned birds, like the hen harrier that Miss Anne McConville took into the police station this morning? I hate to think why a gamekeeper would be found burying birds of prey unless he didn't want anyone to find them. Especially if they were poisoned.'

'I didn't — I haven't —' Frazer blustered.

'Maybe you should just tell the police and show them the actual bodies.'

'Please! I am not responsible for this. My job will be —'

'Call them now, that's my advice,' said Calum. 'We've got the geo-location for this, so I'll be passing that on to the authorities as well.' He turned to Cora. 'Come on, Cora, we've got an appointment. And then we've got to get some news stories out in the digital issue of the *West Uist Chronicle*.'

Neither of them saw Frazer staring daggers at them as they walked away.

'You'll regret this, the pair of you. I promise that,' the gamekeeper muttered.

Back on the Lambretta, Calum steered the way back onto the main estate road just in time to see the O'Neil party's cream-coloured Mercedes disappear round a corner on the way out of the estate.

'Dash it all, where are they off to?' cried Calum. He turned round in the road and set off in pursuit, but failed to catch sight of them again.

'Shall we check out the depot, then?' Cora shouted.

'Good idea! We've got one bird in the bag, might as well see if we can get another,' he chuckled.

But much to their chagrin, the MacCondrum Salmon Farm's depot was locked up and deserted, so they could not take that story further forward. Instead, intent on picking up yet more copy before they went back to the office, and since Calum's stomach had started rumbling again, they headed for The Crow's Nest for sustenance and so that Cora could make contact with Henson Dingwall about the feature she planned on him and his cuisine.

As usual, the little bistro café was full. All sorts of pleasing aromas greeted them as they entered and were shown to a table by Amy Reid, one of several local girls who had been eager to work in the up-and-coming Kyleshiffin bistro-café.

To their surprise, they saw Alistair Pitcairn and Steve Rollinson already eating. At a corner table they also saw Ross McNab and Elspeth McLauchlan deep in conversation.

His ears pricked as usual, Calum sat and listened to the conversations that emanated from the surrounding tables. Not surprisingly, a lot of it was about the tragic drowning that morning of Arran MacCondrum.

'Hey, Calum Steele, why has the *West Uist Chronicle* not kept us informed?' a diner at a neighbouring table barked out.

'We are working on it, Murdoch. We've got news on it in the next digital issue if you check it up in a couple of hours, as well as some other alarming news.'

'What about? That Mungo devil and his poison-pen? He's written to me,' Murdoch replied. 'Lies! All lies, but it's upset my lassie here.'

His wife nodded emphatically. 'I'm upset all right. Just as long as they are lies, Murdoch Finlay.'

'And he wrote to us!' came another raised voice from the other side of the café.

'Aye, we're reporting on that, because I'm going to unmask the scunner,' Calum said boldly. 'Just give us time. But we have other news that could well make the national television.' He tapped the side of his nose. 'If all our readers would be patient, you'll see it on the digital issue and in one of our specials.'

A large man sitting at a table on his own near the window banged a glass down noisily. 'That poor soul, Arran MacCondrum. Badgered, he was, and now he's gone and done it.' He raised his hand to attract Amy Reid the waitress's attention. 'Bill please! I've lost my appetite having to share space with agitators.'

Elspeth McLauchlan turned in her chair. 'Was that aimed at me?' she demanded.

Amy stood in the middle of the café, uncertain of whether to advance to the man or not.

'If the cap fits — Wookie!'

Elspeth rose from her seat but was beaten to it by Ross McNab, who stomped across and stood arms akimbo, looking down at the seated man.

'You are being offensive to my friend in at least two ways. I think an apology is in order.'

The man gave a slow smile and rose to his feet, at least six feet four or five, and looked down challengingly at Ross.

'I apologise to no one.' He pulled out a wad of cash from a pocket and peeled off a few notes. 'That's far more than I've eaten. I won't be giving it more than a one star, I'm telling you. It's not half as good as the food in the Bonnie Prince Charlie, not that it's up to much either. You keep whatever change is left, lassie. I'm guessing you don't get paid much in this dive.'

Ross glared at him as he walked past him and left.

A moment later, Henson Dingwall came through from the kitchen, wiping his hands on a towel. 'Is everything all right, ladies and gentlemen?' he asked, looking around the café. 'I thought I heard raised voices.'

Amy suddenly burst into tears, went running past him and pushed through the swing doors of the kitchen. Ross McNab quickly explained to him about the diner's sudden outburst.

'It all kicked off when Calum Steele came in,' said Murdoch Finlay. 'It's always the same when he shows up.'

Henson raised his hands apologetically. 'Ladies and gentlemen, I am so sorry. Please, order whatever main course you would like. They are on the house, and if you've already had one, then choose a dessert with my compliments.'

Calum smiled and rubbed his hands together. 'Let's have a look at the menu, Cora,' he said softly. 'Don't waste an offer like that.' Then, raising his voice, 'Did you know the man, Elspeth?'

'Never seen him before,' she replied.

'I think I have seen him about a few times,' Calum returned, before leaning across the table and whispering to Cora. 'Did you get a photo? I think that chap might have done us a favour. Henson is bound to give you total cooperation after that.'

Cora was stowing her smartphone away. 'Of course,' she returned in a hushed voice. 'I also saw him wink at Declan O'Neil's pals as he went past them.'

CHAPTER FIFTEEN

Lachlan had locked himself away in his study all morning, working on mundane parish matters and planning his next sermon, so he was ready for a few holes of golf. The telephone call to arrange nine holes came at just the right moment as far as he was concerned.

At the arranged time, with his bag over his shoulder, he crunched across the gravel path from the St Ninian's manse and let himself out of the wrought iron gate, then crossed the road and mounted the stile that led directly onto the ten-acre plot of undulating dunes, heather and machair that he and several other local worthies had transformed into the St Ninian's golf course. For a golf aficionado like himself it was perfect, seeing as how St Ninian's Church was three holes away as the crow flies.

The ground was damp after all the rains and there was a patchy ground mist, but the course would be by no means unplayable. He took a moment to take off and wipe his spectacles.

A man was waiting on the first tee by the honesty box.

'*Latha math*,' Lachlan said. 'You will be Mister O'Neil, I am guessing.'

'Declan O'Neil. I've heard a lot about this golf course of yours,' he said, walking to meet him and shake hands. 'I heard you've got solar-powered electric fences around the greens.'

'That's correct,' Lachlan replied. He pointed down the fairway where sheep were ambling about, grazing on grass. 'We have a tractor that comes whenever one of the farmers has time, but our sheep there are natural mowers of fairways. The rabbits excavated the bunkers over many generations and we just extended their work.' He grinned as he pointed out the tee they were standing on with its white tee boxes, and the tee-mats some distances off with red and blue tee boxes. 'We've only got six holes, but each one has three tees, as you can see, so you can play a full eighteen or any combination.'

'Ingenious!'

'And as you'll have seen from the scorecard, each of them has a name in Gaelic and in English.'

'Can't wait to start. Nine holes will do me. And as an Irishman, I have to ask if you'd like to make it interesting. A pound a hole.'

'I like a bit of extra interest. My handicap is a shaky eight these days.'

'Mine is sixteen, but it's always been wobbly.'

'Then I'll give you four shots over the nine. Shall I show you the way?'

Lachlan noticed the expensive bag and top-of-the-range clubs along with a battery-operated trolly, quite at variance from his old canvas pencil bag containing just seven clubs. 'You won't be offended if I cover my ears when you hit the ball with one of those tin can monstrosities that folk play with these days? As a traditionalist I play with a good old wooden brassie and spoon, which will be two and three woods to you, I think.'

Placing his ball on a tee and taking out his spoon, he made a couple of quick practice swings and then struck the ball down the right side of the fairway. It gradually curved towards the left in a neat draw to land and roll down the centre of the fairway, well over two hundred and twenty yards.

'I recognise the name, Declan,' Lachlan said as he pulled his old briar pipe from his top pocket and started filling it from a yellow oilskin tobacco pouch. 'And your face is very familiar.'

'Maybe you've seen me on the old box,' said Declan, pulling out a hybrid club and swinging freely. 'I'm an actor and I used to sing a bit.'

'Ah, now I have you,' Lachlan replied.

They watched as Declan's drive sailed down the fairway and then sliced to the right, landing in one of the pot bunkers.

'You'll find it a good test of golf,' Lachlan said, lighting his pipe and picking up his pencil bag. 'And if you have a mind to see our church, I'll be popping in there afterwards.'

Their meal over and their appetites sated, Calum and Cora had discussed in hushed tones their immediate plans. As soon as Elspeth and Ross or Alistair and Steve called on Amy Reid, who had recovered her composure and was again waiting tables, and asked for their bills, they would ask for theirs. Calum would then waylay the first couple to leave, and Cora would do the same with the other. If, on the other hand, Henson Dingwall emerged from his kitchen again, Cora would effusively compliment the chef and buttonhole him for her interview.

There were three potential stories to follow up and good reason to ask, since the news about Arran MacCondrum's demise was flying around already and they were about to publish and make it known that birds on the island had been poisoned.

As it happened, Alistair and Steve called for their bills first and Calum was able to follow them outside and engage them in conversation, while Cora stayed to settle their bill.

'We're actually on our way to an appointment,' said Steve as Calum stopped them outside the café.

'No Declan with you?' Calum asked.

'Clearly not,' returned the tall man, unsmilingly.

Alistair was more amenable. 'We are seeing one of the councillors at the — let me see if I can pronounce this — the *Comhairle nan Eilean Siar.*'

Calum beamed. 'Ah, the Western Isles Council. There is an office on the first floor in the Duncan Institute. That's the pink-faced building further down Harbour Street. That's this street, of course. It will be Councillor Charlie McDonald you'll be seeing.'

'That's the chap,' replied Alistair. 'He's the local man on the Sustainable Development Committee?'

'That's right. They look after crofting, fishing, conservation and tourism. It'll be the tourism if you're here scouting out a location for a television show?' Calum asked innocently.

'Now, why would you think that's why we're here — what was your name again?' asked Steve.

'Calum Steele, the editor of the *West Uist Chronicle,*' Calum replied, immune to the other's sarcasm. He produced cards and shoved one towards each of the two men. 'And we're the folk to see about publicity.' He shrugged. 'I was hoping to catch Declan. I saw you all leaving the Cruikshank estate earlier.'

'He's playing golf,' Alistair said quickly before Steve came out with another cutting remark. 'I'm sure he'll ring you about that interview. But we really better be off, time is short.' Once they were out of earshot, Alistair whispered, 'You need to be careful, Steve. We don't want to upset the local press. They could make things awkward if we are rude.'

'He seems a twerp, just like that blooming police inspector who gave me that bit of paper,' said Steve. He winked and tapped his belly. 'Not to worry, though. Old Mother Hubbard's cupboard is filled again.'

Alistair hushed him. 'Careful, Steve. Best not to broadcast it. You never know in a community like this. There may be other folk related to him close by. Like the old guy Declan is playing golf with right now.'

Lachlan knew a bandit when he saw one. Someone who protected a higher handicap than they played to so that they could win money and trophies. Declan O'Neil was such a golfer, though he didn't see him as someone who wanted to win cups at his local golf club under false pretences just to put in a cabinet and show off his prowess to his house guests. No, he had him sussed as having fibbed about his handicap for some ulterior reason. And that reason wasn't so he could win. Lachlan knew when a shot had been deliberately mishit so that he could lose the hole. He suspected what was going to happen when they arrived at the ninth green.

They had played nip and tuck, each winning a hole then losing the next to arrive on the ninth tee all square. Both reached the elevated green in two shots and Lachlan putted up to six inches with his first stroke.

'That's a gimme,' said Declan.

'Thank you. So you have one putt for the win, two for a half.'

'Tricky distance,' said Declan, putting to four feet.

'A wee bit too far for a gimme, I am afraid,' said Lachlan.

'I wouldn't expect it,' Declan returned. He marked his ball, cleaned it, then placed it down again and lined up. He putted and the ball just missed the outside of the hole and rolled two feet past.

They shook hands and Lachlan replaced the flag. 'A good, fun game. Thank you,' he said as Declan handed over a pound coin. 'Would you care to come into my boss's office?' he asked, pointing towards the church.

'I don't mind if I do, Lachlan. I've something I'd like to ask, and you are the man best suited to answer me and, I hope, help.'

Lachlan smiled. The golf game had been neatly played and engineered to let him win, and think he had done so despite having to give away stokes. That, he suspected, was to get him in a good mood and soften him up, so he would be amenable to whatever the Irish actor was about to soft-soap him about.

'Of course. We'll go in and take a pew, then you can ask me. After you.'

Cora did not receive the same brusqueness as Calum had. Indeed, Ross and Elspeth both seemed happy to see her, especially as she was on her own. They sat down at her table on their way out while Amy went off to get the card machine for Cora to pay her bill.

'I'm so looking forward to diving the wreck of the *SS Lister*, Ross,' she enthused.

'You're diving to that?' Elspeth asked in surprise. 'Couldn't it have unexploded bombs or things like that?'

Ross laughed. 'No. It was a tramp steamer, which means it was a merchant vessel involved in what they called the tramp trade.'

Elspeth frowned. 'I've heard the name in old black and white movies. Wasn't *The African Queen* with Humphrey Boggart a tramp steamer?'

'It was,' Cora replied. 'I've researched them. So too was the boat in *King Kong*. Tramp steamers shuttled unscheduled cargo from port to port. They would load whatever cargo had the best profit margin to a port where that cargo was needed. Then they would take whatever cargo needed to be hauled from this new port of call. That's how they often ended up with an assortment of weird goods.'

'Which the *SS Lister* apparently had,' Ross went on. 'I've been down a few times and it will make a good first wreck dive.'

'Which is what I want to talk to you about,' said Cora. 'Calum is quite happy for me to write a feature on your diving school. I've been taking pictures of the girls as you've been teaching us and it would be good to show the stages through our certification and then to the dive itself. It should give you free publicity, if nothing else.'

Ross's handsome face lit up. 'That is brilliant. And I'll take lots of underwater pictures of you all. Your surface camera and smartphones will be no use down there.'

Cora let out one of her nervous giggles. 'I must confess to being a bit apprehensive as well as excited about the wreck dive. I know all the girls are, too.'

'You'll be safe with me,' said Ross. 'I'll look after you all.'

Elspeth stared curiously at him for a moment, then turned to Cora. 'Ross takes incredible underwater pictures. I told you this morning about the benthic studies that he's doing for the University of the Highlands and Islands, which they are making available to the WUCE guardians.'

Cora smiled at Amy as she arrived with the card machine and the bill. 'Calum, my boss, is a great one for leaving me to settle up,' she explained as she popped in her pin number. Then, fishing out a tip for Amy, she waited while the waitress tore off the receipt and left them. She went off to another table just as Henson Dingwall came out of the kitchen carrying a tray laden with a shellfish banquet, one of his specialities for a young couple who were enjoying champagne and seemed to be celebrating something.

'This is just between us,' Cora went on conspiratorially, 'but we were also planning a feature on the salmon farming issue.' She shook her head. 'But I think we'll maybe have to put it on hold after the tragedy today.'

'Why is that?' Elspeth asked coldly. 'I mean, I'm sorry to hear about Arran MacCondrum's death, but surely this is a part of the whole issue? Salmon farming is dividing the island, it's causing ecological havoc and now it looks as if it has contributed to someone taking their own life. The WUCE guardians have been campaigning along with other groups around the islands on this for ages. It's about time someone listened and took us seriously.'

'I'm taking you seriously, and perhaps you are right,' Cora returned, hesitantly, 'but I'm guessing there will have to be a Fatal Accident Inquiry.'

'There will, undoubtedly,' agreed Ross. 'And it will in itself raise the issues to see if there is a cause somewhere.' He shrugged his shoulders. 'Who knows, maybe there is more to it? Maybe he'd received one of these poison-pen letters? Nasty damned things they are, too. I had one myself.'

Elspeth darted a concerned glance at him. 'So have I, but I binned it.'

'In retrospect, maybe I should have shown mine to the police,' Ross said.

'Or let us see it,' Cora volunteered quickly. 'As Calum said, the *West Uist Chronicle* is going on the offensive with this Mungo and is going to unmask him.'

Ross smiled, then prepared to stand. 'I'll think about it, Cora. But I'm afraid I have to be off. Can I give you a lift, Elspeth?'

'That would be grand,' she replied, rising with him and taking her leave of Cora.

Cora was left on her own for only a moment. She was putting her credit card away and looked up to see Henson Dingwall coming through from the kitchen again, with another tray with the utensils and special cutlery needed for the shellfish banqueting couple. She had wanted to catch him, but didn't want to appear too pushy. She had already secured one feature about the diving and had gathered an interesting perspective on Arran MacCondrum's demise from Elspeth McLauchlan. She thought she might be tempting divine providence by trying to get another feature agreement, but to her surprise Henson was advancing directly upon her with an uncertain smile on his lips.

'Ah, Cora, I was hoping to catch you alone,' he said, placing his hands on the table and leaning on them. 'Amy told me about that imbecile that was causing trouble here. I hope it won't, er —'

'Won't what, Henson?'

'Won't find its way into the *West Uist Chronicle*. I mean, bad press can cripple a business like this. I have to be so careful. Indeed, I am so very careful.'

'Of course, I know that. And everybody loves your food. That's why Sergeant Lorna Golspie is having her hen-do celebration dinner here.'

'Not everyone loves my food, Cora.' He reached into his apron pocket and pulled out an envelope. Cora recognised the geometric addressing. 'I overheard you talking to Elspeth McLauchlan and that diving chap about poison-pen letters. A lot of my customers seem to have had them, and now so have I. He says he's going to destroy me and my café.'

'Perhaps you should let the police see it?'

'I thought maybe you and Calum might want to use it. You know, if you are going to expose him.'

Cora wondered whether the guy who had caused the trouble could have some connection with the poison-pen letters. She decided not to mention that she had managed to take a picture of him.

'Of course, Henson. Calum and I will read it together, so that we don't handle it too much. You never know, this could be the thing that leads us to him.'

Gingerly taking the letter, she slipped it in her bag. As she did so, she felt a disquieting shiver run through her. She was unsure whether she was as keen as Calum on investigative journalism. As Henson opened the door for her to leave and she stepped into the gathering mist, the contents of her own poison-pen letter played on her mind.

Henson had said Mungo meant to destroy him. The language he was using seemed to be getting more and more violent.

She wondered if Calum and she might be playing with fire.

After a long day, Torquil was glad to ride the Norton back to the manse with Crusoe sitting alongside in the Charnwood Meteor sidecar. The smell of cooking greeted him as soon as they opened the front door. After seeing to Crusoe, he went upstairs and phoned Lorna to exchange their news and confirm with her that all of the documentation and liaising with the Procurator Fiscal's office had gone smoothly. Then they exchanged their usual endearments before he bade her goodnight and came downstairs again to join Lachlan in the sitting room, where they sat and chatted over a much-needed pre-dinner dram of Glen Corlin.

Lachlan was shocked to hear about Arran MacCondrum's drowning.

'I had been busy all morning with my sermon about spitefulness. You can guess what inspired that, I'm sure.'

'Mungo and his letters?'

'Precisely. By the time I had finished with the church accounts and various parish bits and pieces, I was ready for a few holes and lo and behold, I was phoned up by a chap who turned out to be a celebrity who wanted to play nine holes with me.'

'Declan O'Neil would be his name, I presume?'

'The very man. He's an actor and used to sing a bit, he told me.'

'Apparently he did more than just sing a bit. He was in a boyband called Quicksilver and he's now in a soap. I had a run-in with him and his agent and producer early this morning, after I'd been out at The Piper's Cave. I thought I recognised him, but I didn't fully twig him until Frazer McKenzie told me.'

'Interesting, well, it was only himself that I saw. He's a good golfer, but he lied about his handicap. All a subterfuge to soften me up so he could make a proposal.' Lachlan grinned as he swirled his whisky in the glass. 'It was not the sort of proposal the Lord is used to hearing in my church. He's here representing a consortium of business folk.'

'A consortium? Did he say what it was called?'

'No, not that I remember. But he said they have a lot of money behind them and have big plans to establish themselves on West Uist. They want to buy Dunshiffin Castle for one thing and turn it into a hotel.'

'Interesting. And what sort of proposal did he make to you?'

'St Ninian's Golf Course. They want to buy it and develop it into a real eighteen-hole course, beef it up, lengthen it and put in bigger pot bunkers, and divert a stream through it to give it water hazards. You know, like the Swilcan Burn at St Andrews or Jockie's Burn at Carnoustie.'

'But that's outrageous!' Torquil returned in disbelief. 'It would ruin the character of the course.'

'He said they want it to have the same sort of Fife feel as the Askernish Golf Club on South Uist. As you know, it was built by Old Tom Morris as an eighteen-holer back in the nineteenth century, but in the 1920s after the Great War it declined and it became nine holes, the rest just being left to get overgrown. Then in 2005 they rediscovered the "lost course" and made it into a super-duper one that golfers come from all over the place to play. He says this consortium want to do the same here. It would go well with Dunshiffin Castle if it's made into a hotel and conference centre.'

'And that would be an end to the pay and play honesty box. They'd hoik up the prices and turn it into something that the locals couldn't afford.'

'My sentiments entirely, but that's why I think he was trying to soft-soap me. To strengthen their case.'

Torquil sipped his whisky and stroked Crusoe, who sat down by him and put his chin on his knee. 'But surely the golf course is on common land?'

'It is indeed. It is crofting common grazing land, so the St Ninian's golf course is there thanks to the crofters who permit it to be used as such. And that is why the sheep and cattle graze freely on it, except for the greens that we by and large protect with the solar-powered electric fences and cut with a real mower. Cattle in particular would churn up the greens in no time. As golfers, we allow free drops of the ball if you end up in a hoofprint or a cow plop.'

'So it can't be bought by this consortium?'

Lachlan finished his whisky. 'No, but there may be ways and means. Declan told me his pals were going to see Charlie McDonald at the *Comhairle nan Eilean Siar* office. He's one of the councillors on the Sustainable Development Committee. Since it comes under crofting, and I suppose also tourism, the things this consortium is talking about will be right up his street.'

'And if he brokers some sort of deal, it could help him politically,' said Torquil. 'He's an ambitious man and has his sights on becoming a Member of the Scottish Parliament.' He finished his whisky.

'Come away through,' said Lachlan. 'Let's have dinner, and then you can tell me more about Arran MacCondrum's drowning.'

Torquil clicked his tongue. 'I'll tell you what I know. But it's what I don't know that worries me.'

That night, the man calling himself Mungo was busy writing more letters into the small hours, the time when all of the research came together and the creative juices flowed.

It was hard work using the stencils with gloves on, but it was so very satisfying.

Just as it had been a satisfying day.

After completing each letter and carefully putting it in its envelope with the special sterilised and prepared instruments, Mungo inspected it and applied the specially prepared stamps with the care of a surgeon.

Then, stacking them in the receptacle in readiness for despatching, everything was done with the utmost care to avoid even the slightest chance of any letter being traced back. Only then was there time to relax over a drink.

Just one drink, though. The lesson had been learned about drinking. One could relax, but more than that could make one sloppy. That's when mistakes could be made, and Mungo could not afford to make mistakes.

Watching the old boy drink himself to death should have been enough to put one off alcohol. But it seemed true that alcoholics were born alcoholics. It was just a matter of time before they escalated, became dependent and then everything went to pot. That was what had happened to the old boy. There had been no necessity to take on his care, especially as he had never had much of a part in Mungo's life. None that was remembered, anyway.

It had been curiosity more than anything. If he hadn't been likeable, that would have been it. In the lucid moments the jokes could tumble out, along with all the hard luck tales. But it was the information about his wife, who became his ex-wife after the divorce, that was of greater interest. And about the kid. The other kid, that was. The one that had died without having lived.

That was the way he had described the stillbirth.

He had dissolved into tears, feeling genuine sorrow for all that he had cocked up.

Then he had talked about Mungo. Now, that was really fascinating, if it was true. But then, why shouldn't it be true? Why would he lie about his own parent? The image he created was romantic in a twisted sense. A bit like the Scarlet Pimpernel, or any of the superheroes in the American comics. An ordinary person, an upright member of the community in daily life, but an avenging soul by night. Okay, perhaps not avenging, but 'a writer righting wrongs.' Yes, that was good. A writer with a writing box, accumulating all the sins, peccadilloes, crimes and all the hypocritical secrets of the sanctimonious bastards who thought they were better people.

Mungo — a great name, that — after St Mungo the patron saint of Glasgow, the home of the brother and sister. Of course, the Mungo who'd inherited the writing box from the distant relative was no saint. Never pretended to be. It had started as a little hobby, writing those little letters.

But what a great way of getting even, of exerting power and hitting the bastards where it hurt, without any repercussions whatsoever. That was the genius of it.

And that was what the old boy admired about the parent, since he had fallen so far. He had screwed everything up and had to leave the island. But he knew that Mungo protected his back, got back at them all, while enjoying putting so many cats among so many pigeons.

Then the old boy died, a horrible way to go, bleeding to death like that and drowning in his own blood as well, until he was given that last little nudge. The legal process began soon after that and then eventually, and very unexpectedly, the old barrel key arrived with a note to expect the treasured possessions that it would unlock. A week later, the writer's box arrived.

Reading the diary was compulsive. Mungo truly had a writing talent. A talent used to such effect over the years with the little hobby that developed into a sort of crusade.

But it was the diary that put everything into place. Explained the growing up in Glasgow, under the guardianship of the one thought to be his grandfather. Rich as Croesus he was, thanks be to St Mungo. Except he wasn't his grandfather at all, but his grand uncle. It explained too about the old boy's alcoholism, his constant absence. His perpetual grief, bitterness and failure in life.

It planted the seeds of fury which germinated into a plan. Total revenge. Annihilation of the bastards for what they had done. They would reap the rewards of the sins. The writing box with all its secrets, like Pandora's box, would be opened and used again.

It had taken time, planning, money, a great deal of manoeuvring and then planting. Like a great cuckoo. And one by one, the eggs would be tossed out of the nest.

Careful now. No more to drink. Let the anger smoulder unseen by anyone. Let it just be Mungo's secret for now.

Dirty bastards, all of them.

But some dirtier and guiltier than others.

Now, one down and so many more to go.

CHAPTER SIXTEEN

The post-mortem on Arran MacCondrum was scheduled for nine-thirty in the morning, so Ralph McLelland had travelled over on the last ferry of the day with Brian MacVicar and the coffin. Sergeant Lorna Golspie herself had rushed through all of the documentation so that Brian could get the body into the mortuary in good time.

Forensic pathology was one of the smallest specialties in medicine, so as a former consultant himself Ralph knew Doctor Hamish Hamilton, the official pathologist attached to the Procurator Fiscal's office, very well. And since Ralph had explained the deep concerns that Inspector Torquil McKinnon had about the case, Hamish Hamilton had no qualms about them performing the post-mortem together.

Hamish was a big burly man with a barrel chest, a mane of shaggy ginger hair and a matching spade-like beard. A graduate of Aberdeen University who looked as if he might be handy tossing the caber at the highland games, or supplying the power at the back of a rugby scrum, yet he had good surgical skills and an incisive brain. It was common knowledge among the profession that he was destined for a chair in forensic pathology in the not too distant future.

The two doctors dressed in surgical scrubs, heavy plastic aprons and surgical gloves stood on either side of the body lying on the post-mortem table. Hamish had made the usual Y-shaped incision from each shoulder down to above the suprasternal notch of the breastbone, and from there right down to the pubis. He had then used a scalpel and forceps to cut through the layers of skin, fat and muscle, to expose the ribcage and to incise the abdominal cavity. He then reflected the walls to show the abdominal contents underneath the peritoneum.

Ralph had then used a rib cutter to cut through all of the ribs and the intercostal muscles between them on each side, so that the whole front of the ribcage could be removed like a shield to expose the heart and lungs.

'Well, my first impression is that the lungs are still full of water,' said Hamish, reaching into the thoracic cavity to feel the turgor of the lungs. 'I suggest that since you have these specific questions from your inspector chum, you remove the heart and lungs and make your examinations. Feel free to use the side room with my microscope. Florrie, my mortician assistant, will write down the weights of the organs on the whiteboard as you call them out to her.'

'I appreciate all this, Hamish,' said Ralph. He smiled at Florrie, a blonde-haired young woman whom Hamish had introduced as a marathon runner vegan. Given her choice of career as a mortician, her commitment to veganism and fitness did not surprise him in the least.

'No problem, Ralph. Meanwhile, I'll carry on with the rest of the post-mortem and we can amalgamate our findings for the report. So, I'll examine the abdomen and start removal of the intestines and intra-abdominal organs.'

'It sounds a good plan,' replied Ralph, selecting scissors and forceps before feeling down the trachea to cut through the cartilage and connective tissue under the thyroid gland. 'There are certainly a few oesophageal varices,' he reported as he dissected the trachea.

'He was a drinker, you say?' said Hamish as he incised the peritoneum and examined the liver. 'Well, by the looks of his liver, it's pretty fatty, although not yet cirrhotic.'

'I took bloods yesterday for alcohol and toxicology levels. I'd be surprised if we don't find a really high level of alcohol. There was an empty whisky bottle near where he was pulled out of the salmon pen.'

As the lungs and heart came out of the thoracic cavity, some frothy, pink fluid exuded from the open trachea.

'Pulmonary oedema and water. And the lungs weigh a heck of a lot more than you'd expect.' Ralph took the organs to the side bench while Hamish continued to operate. Florrie assisted him in the weighing before he laid them on the large board prior to his dissection.

'Are you going to use a Gettler test, for what it's worth?' Hamish asked over his shoulder. 'And a diatom test?'

'Aye, and as well as that, I'm going to do his strontium, iron and electrolyte levels from both sides of the heart.'

'Have you got samples of the water?'

'I brought some that was wrung out of his clothes by the local sergeant, Morag Driscoll.'

'Florrie, will you get all these off to the lab and ask for the results as matters of extreme urgency?' Hamish said as he began to loosen the intestines.

Ralph stood straight. 'Before I do that, though, I'd like to canulate his sphenoidal sinuses and see if I can aspirate anything. Then I'd like to use your microscope while the lab gets to work on the electrolytes and trace elements analysis. I'll also need to look at the lung histology.'

Florrie stopped at his shoulder. 'Whenever you are ready, just let me have the lung samples you want examining and I can take them straight through to get the lab to prepare them and take microtome sections.'

Ralph thanked her and selected an aspiration probe. Leaning over the head, he inserted it into a nostril and then gradually advanced it into an anatomical place deep inside the skull called the spheno-ethmoidal recess, where the ethmoidal sinus communicated with the deeper sphenoidal sinus that sat near to the pituitary gland underneath the brain. Then he advanced a tube into it, attached a syringe and gradually pulled back the plunger to draw out a clear fluid. Florrie held out a sample tube for him to deposit the fluid sample into, then took it away to label it.

'Now to look at the heart and lungs and get all these samples off.'

'Well, good luck with this,' said Hamish. 'Folk always think that diagnosing drowning is easy, when in fact it's one of the hardest things to be specific about. I know, I read that paper you wrote in the *Journal of Forensic Medicine* before you threw it all up to go back to being an island general practitioner.' He sniffed. 'You lucky sod!'

Lorna had driven over to the mortuary on receiving Ralph's call just before lunchtime. She had attended many post-mortems in her career, two of them performed here in Stornoway by the ebullient Doctor Hamish Hamilton, but she had not enjoyed them. The smell of blood, body fluids and the all-pervading odour of disinfectants and formaldehyde, coupled with the locked doors, the refrigerators and the low temperature of the place all made her feel how vulnerable humans were. Seeing a body extinct of life being dissected in order to determine the cause of death seemed so clinical, so soulless, yet she knew it was so important.

She had met Arran MacCondrum on a few occasions when she was in Kyleshiffin and did not relish seeing him on the mortuary slab. It was with some relief that when she rang the outer bell, she was greeted by the smiling Florrie who led her inside the building and into an office where Ralph and Hamish were already seated, joking and drinking coffee.

'Hello again, Sergeant Golspie,' said Hamish, jumping up and pulling out a chair for her. 'We've got a preliminary report and the Procurator Fiscal has given us permission to share it with you, considering the urgency of this case.'

'Was it simple drowning, then?' she asked.

'It's not simple anything, Lorna,' said Ralph as he made her a coffee. 'Torquil said he wanted us to liaise with you.'

'That's right. And I'll pass it on to him.'

Hamish gave a Father Christmas laugh. 'Chinese whispers, Sergeant!'

'Oh, call me Lorna, please. What do you mean, Chinese whispers?'

'Right-ho, Lorna. I mean explanations of complicated things can get distorted if they are passed on along a chain of people. In forensic medicine, we try to be as precise as possible. That's not always as precise as we would like it to be, because often there is not an absolute answer. We often have to make a diagnosis of exclusion.'

'I'm not quite sure what you mean,' Lorna replied, sipping her coffee.

Hamish proffered a pack of jammy dodgers, which she declined with a politely raised hand. 'Take drowning. We have several tests but not one of them is specific. You might think that water in the lungs gives you the diagnosis. But not necessarily. If a body is immersed post mortem, some water will seep in and get into the lungs and stomach. It is often a case of finding a body in water and in the absence of other causes of death, we give an opinion that drowning is likely.'

'I see, I think,' she said uncertainly.

'Which is why we thought it would be sensible if we could talk to Torquil at the same time as yourself,' said Ralph. 'If you don't mind, we'll phone him now and put him on the speaker?'

Moments later, they were in contact. Lorna spoke first, refraining from using their usual sweet nothings and maintaining strict professionalism, which made Ralph, who knew them both so well, smile. 'Doctor Hamilton and Ralph wanted to avoid Chinese whispers by me transmitting what they said to me, because it's complicated,' she explained.

'Well, thank you, Ralph, and thank you, Doctor Hamilton,' said Torquil. 'Can you confirm that Arran MacCondrum drowned?'

'I'm going to let you talk to Ralph,' said Hamish. 'He's done the donkey work here on the lungs and heart. And when he was one of us, a forensic pathologist, that is, he wrote a much quoted paper on the subject.'

Torquil knew that Ralph had effectively given up his career in pathology when he'd come back to West Uist, but he realised that he knew little of the esteem that he had obviously been held in by his former peers.

'Without too much pathology gobbledygook, Torquil,' Ralph said, sitting beside the phone, 'the blood tests I took are back, and they showed he had a very high alcohol level. Consistent with having drunk a bottle of whisky over a period of hours.'

'He had liver damage and oesophageal varicosities,' said Hamish. 'Both are signs of chronic alcohol ingestion.'

'We found a lot of water in his lungs,' Ralph went on. 'But it is his heart that I wanted to focus on, specifically the blood in his heart. Hamish had the lab here run biochemistry on the samples straight away. First, I ran a Gettler chlorine test, which has just come back. This is a test where we compare the blood in the left ventricle of the heart with that from the right ventricle. We measure all of the electrolytes in the blood, sodium potassium, magnesium, strontium and chloride. Without going into the complex physiology and blood chemistry mechanisms, if the chlorine levels are lower in the right side of the heart, it suggests the person drowned in seawater.'

'Yes.' Torquil's voice was louder and interested. 'Go on.'

'But if the chlorine level in the left ventricle is lower, it implies drowning in freshwater. In this test, the level was much lower in the left ventricle.'

Hamish chipped in. 'This test was introduced in the 1920s by Alexander Gettler, the doyen of toxicologists. It was regarded as a definitive test for decades, but nowadays it is controversial.'

'So, what does that mean?'

'It is inconclusive in itself.'

'What about a diatom test — doesn't that help?' Torquil asked.

Ralph nodded. 'It helps, Torquil, but it too is not specific. But we've looked at iron and strontium levels, and they are not as high as we would expect if he'd drowned in the salmon pen.'

'So what are you saying — that we can't say anything conclusively?' Torquil asked, a note of frustration in his voice.

'Perhaps not quite that,' Ralph replied. 'We have four pairs of facial sinuses. They get blocked and infected if you get sinusitis. These are the maxillary sinuses in the cheeks, the frontal sinuses in the forehead, the ethmoidal at the root of the nose and the sphenoidal. The sphenoidal is the most posterior one; it is near the optic nerve and the pituitary gland. I syringed out water from his sphenoidal sinuses.'

'And compared it to the water he brought that had been wrung out of his clothes. Seawater, that is,' said Hamish, eager to contribute.

'Under the microscope, there was nothing much in it,' said Ralph. 'The seawater sample by comparison was full of algae, debris and fish scales. It was freshwater, Torquil.'

'You're sure?'

'Of this, I am. But although in the trachea samples of water there were fish scales and diatoms, the water I expressed from the alveoli in his lungs matched the water from his sphenoidal sinuses. There were no salmon fish scales. It's freshwater.'

Hamish was once again keen to chip in. 'Which makes the Gettler chlorine test very interesting, because it is indicative of freshwater drowning.'

'As are the strontium and iron levels,' Ralph added. 'As we say, it is not conclusive, since his body was found in the salmon pen, but if you were to ask our joint opinions...'

'Which I am,' Torquil said quickly. 'What do you think?'

'We think he drowned somewhere in freshwater,' said Ralph. 'I would say it is almost impossible that he drowned in a pen containing tens of thousands of salmon.'

'And that is just what I thought you would find,' said Torquil grimly.

Calum was feeling pleased with himself. He and Cora had produced a brand-new digital issue of the *West Uist Chronicle* as well as having loaded up several new articles on their website.

Calum had gathered all the gossip he could and wrote a piece of purple prose extolling the MacCondrum family and the contribution that they had made to island life, the local economy and the community. He had essentially discounted Cora's concerns about salmon farming and had implied a link with the WUCE guardians campaign. She had remonstrated, but he'd told her that it was important to get a reaction from the readers. They would use it to test their opinions in the reader's bag, then she could have free rein in the issue after that to put forward the WUCE campaigners' points of view.

Although he had not been told whether Arran MacCondrum had received any letters from Mungo, he suggested that if he had it would seem possible that he had felt badgered to take his own life.

He had followed it with an article on the poisoned birds of prey that they had caught Frazer McKenzie burying.

They had already had lots of comments and clicks to show that people had been reading.

'We'll soon have the special ready for printing, too,' Calum said with glee. 'This will also put a rocket under that Mungo. And then the piece I did on Declan O'Neil and his gruesome twosome should spark interest. Mark my words, they are here on some sort of business scouting trip. And if they were meeting with Councillor Charlie McDonald, it smacks of something to do with buying land. I tried ringing Charlie himself, but his new secretary just said he was unavailable for the foreseeable future.'

Cora pursed her lips. 'I'm not so happy about this Mungo thing, darling. Especially after Henson Dingwall gave me that letter. It said he was going to destroy him. When you think what he said he was going to do to us —' She shivered.

'He doesn't worry me, Cora. I can handle anything he throws at us.'

'But what if it isn't just words, Calum. What if —?'

The editor shoved his glasses up on his nose. 'Trust me, Cora.'

'But do you not think we should share it?'

'Who with?' he returned sharply. 'With the police? With Torquil, after he shut us out and didn't tell us about Arran MacCondrum? Well, you can see from the comments already that the poisoned birds article has had folk getting really angry.'

'I feel a wee bit sorry for Frazer McKenzie, though,' said Cora. 'The pictures are pretty damning.'

'Well, he shouldn't have been burying those birds. Even if he didn't poison them himself, he should have reported them.' He grinned at her. 'And since you think we should be reporting things, that's what we're doing, reporting them to the public.'

'But not to the police, Calum.'

He shrugged and folded his arms triumphantly. 'They can read it as well as anyone else.'

DC Penny Faversham was pleased to be back in Kyleshiffin. To be precise, she was glad to be back in the arms of Ewan McPhee in her broom cupboard of an office at the station. It was an opportunistic quick kiss and cuddle, as Ewan brought in some tea, and while Torquil was on the telephone.

She had meant to come over on the evening ferry, but her Mini Hatch, of which she was so fond, had sustained a complete smash up to its exhaust system courtesy of one of Barra's pot holes. She had been unable to get it fixed at such short notice and had had to leave it at the garage in the morning, travelling back in a battered old Fiat 500, the only vehicle available for hire.

'So, what's the emergency, Ewan?' she said, gently disentangling herself and stepping back to straighten her short auburn hair. She was five ten in height, but several inches shorter than Ewan. Dressed in jeans, trainers and a quilted anorak, she liked the outdoor life and often eschewed make-up and perfume, but prior to coming into the office she had applied a delicate squirt of Chanel Coco Mademoiselle and applied a new lipstick.

'It's the suicide of Arran MacCondrum, the salmon farm owner. Torquil isn't happy about it.'

'Morag told me a little on the phone. She said he'd asked Doctor McLelland to go over to Stornoway to assist at the post-mortem, and he wants me to do some enquiries. I take it there is no news on the post-mortem?'

There was a tap on the ajar door and Morag popped her head round it. 'Ah, you are back. Sorry you've had to come back before our next dive lesson, but I think we might be busy and need all hands on deck.'

Penny blushed on realising that the door had not been properly closed.

'Torquil is on the phone right now to Lorna and Ralph over in Lewis,' Morag continued. She pointed to Ewan's mouth. 'Nice shade of lipstick, Penny,' she said with a knowing smile.

The shoot had not gone as well as Frazer would have wished. Indeed, he didn't think it could have gone worse.

The three clients were individually accompanied by one of the Cruikshank estate's professionals. Frazer himself walked with Declan O'Neil, while Alistair Pitcairn and Steve Rollinson had an assistant gamekeeper each.

The game was there and the bag that each shooter took was relatively good, but Frazer's mind was not on it. He had been unsettled when Vincent McPhee, the young assistant he had allocated to accompany Alistair, had drawn his attention to the latest *West Uist Chronicle* digital issue when they had all stopped for the clients to have a sandwich and a drink at the Bothy, where he often took guests on shoots.

There had been shock among the gamekeepers that Arran MacCondrum had been found dead at his salmon farm. There was a post headlined: ARRAN TAKES A DEEP AND DEADLY PLUNGE.

The piece was fairly nebulous and showed a stock photograph of the salmon pens and an adjoining picture of Arran MacCondrum. It stated that further details would be made available later, but that it looked as if he had taken his own life.

It got worse as they scrolled down to the second story, which had three photographs of Frazer with his hands raised to the camera as if trying to block its view, and the hole with dead birds and one of his spade, all under the headline: PRAYING THAT BIRDS OF PREY BURIAL STAYS SECRET.

The article read:

This morning the editor and assistant editor were present at the Kyleshiffin police station when Miss Annie McConville brought in a dead hen harrier, which she stated she had found on the Cruikshank estate moor while exercising four of her dogs. She told us that she had refused to let the gamekeeper take the dead bird, in case it was clandestinely disposed of.

She told us, 'I ken fine when I see a poisoned creature of the Lord.' And everyone who knows Miss McConville will respect her knowledge.

PC Ewan McPhee also informed us that this was the second dead bird that had been brought in today. He volunteered that a sea eagle had been found out by the Cruadalach Isles by Special Police Constables Wallace and Douglas Drummond, both well-known local fishermen.

Initial speculation was that there could have been poisoning from eating a dead crab found near the MacCondrum Salmon Farm. These pictures of the Cruikshank estate's gamekeeper, Frazer McKenzie, showing three dead birds of prey pose the question, why are they being buried on the lonely moor and not reported to the authorities?

Vincent and his fellow assistant gamekeeper had tried to brush it aside as Frazer had declared it wasn't what they might think, just sensationalism on the part of their local gutter press.

Declan and his two colleagues had seemed to take little interest, and said nothing after Declan had joked about some of the bad press and fabricated news in the celebrity gossip columns about him. But once they were again on their own, the actor started to quiz Frazer about gamekeepers and the accusations that some had been proven to have poisoned birds of prey to protect their game.

'It's illegal, and I've never done anything like that.'

'More than your job would be worth?'

Frazer had grunted assent.

'So I expect you'll not like that article?'

'Calum Steele, the editor, is a nuisance. He bends the truth.'

'You do know that I'm a personal friend of your landowner?'

'I didn't quite know that —'

Declan's normal smiling expression suddenly changed and looked menacing. 'He won't like it if I get pissed off.' He raised his shotgun to his shoulder, spying a rising target. He fired and the bird stopped flying, plummeting groundward like a stone. 'And right now, reading that, I'm pissed off really badly. I hate poison and anyone who uses it.' He lowered his shotgun and stared at Frazer. 'Any type of poison.'

CHAPTER SEVENTEEN

The Drummond twins had come in by the time Torquil came off the phone. They showed Morag, Penny and Ewan the *West Uist Chronicle* digital issue and they were all discussing it when Torquil came into the restroom.

'Calum has been filling in the gaps between the facts with speculation as usual, Torquil,' Morag announced, swivelling her laptop round so that he could see the issue.

Torquil read the Arran MacCondrum post and shook his head in annoyance.

'But read the next piece, too,' Morag urged.

Torquil scrolled down and read the post. 'Gosh, it looks bad for Frazer if he actually was burying birds of prey without notifying us. Ewan, since this is your pigeon — no pun intended — when you get a chance, could you take a trip out to see him and investigate that? Better get the exact location from Calum, though.'

'Will do. Shall I make tea for everyone?'

Torquil nodded. 'But be quick. We've got some serious work to do here. Let's get that whiteboard up.'

By the time Ewan had prepared and poured out mugs of tea, Torquil had used a marker pen to write in bold letters at the top of the whiteboard: THE MACCONDRUM CONUNDRUM. Halfway down the board, he wrote the name Arran MacCondrum and drew a square round it. Beside it, he drew a cross.

He tapped the board. 'That is not a play on his name; ever since his body was pulled out of the salmon pen, there have been things that don't fit.'

'The rifle,' said Morag.

'Exactly. If he had a desire to take his own life and he had a rifle handy, why not do it quickly?'

Under the square, he wrote the word 'rifle' and a question mark. Then he wrote: 'missing mobile phone', and under that, 'rocks from hatchery jetty'. 'And we have this.' He added the words 'apparent suicide' and underlined them.

'Did the post-mortem support that, boss?' Wallace asked.

'It supported drowning, Ralph told me. But not drowning in seawater. And not drowning in the salmon pen. He was drowned in freshwater.'

'In a river?' Ewan asked.

'I don't think so,' said Torquil. He took out his phone and showed the pictures he had taken inside the hatchery. 'I think he died here. Possibly in the main freshwater intake tank there, near the technician's station.'

'So not suicide at all,' Morag said.

Under the list, Torquil added the words 'post-mortem'. 'Ralph and the pathologist are going to rush their official report through. We'll add the details here, but they are as sure as it is possible to be. Essentially, there is a test that suggests he died in freshwater, and the water from one of the sinuses near his eyes contains only freshwater and no fish scales or diatoms.'

'So, this was simple murder,' said Douglas.

'Nothing simple here,' Torquil said with a shake of the head. To the right of the whiteboard, he wrote the words 'poison-pen letters' and circled them. Again he added a question mark. Then he drew an arrow from the bottom of the list and wrote 'the *Betty Burke*'.

'Someone killed Arran MacCondrum by holding him underwater. We think that was in the hatchery. There is a cryptic comment in one of the other letters he had received. Mungo called his hatchery an egg shack. He said calamity was going to fall, either at the farm or the hatchery. Yet the *Betty Burke* was moored at the salmon farm, as if he had gone there on his own. The question is, how did that person, presumably the murderer, get away?'

'There must have been two of them!' Morag said, putting her mug down suddenly and spilling tea on the table. 'One took the *Betty Burke* and the other took another boat.'

'So, they both went back in this other boat, after dumping his body in the pen,' said Ewan. 'But there are an awful lot of boats on West Uist.'

Torquil nodded. 'Which means we have two very dangerous people loose on the island.'

After the shoot and going through the motions with their bag, Frazer left his three clients in the care of his two assistant keepers. Adopting a casual manner, he sauntered over to the estate office and, turning on his computer, brought up the *West Uist Chronicle* digital issue.

He felt his blood pressure rise as he looked at the damning article and pictures. With his head in his hands, he wondered what he should do. He couldn't ignore it, but his options didn't seem at all clear.

As if on autopilot, he started to check his emails and found to his horror that there were around a score with subjects about birds or poisoning. He scanned them one by one, feeling himself becoming more outraged at the tone of the writers, most of whom he either did not know or only had a passing acquaintance with. They had all read Calum's article and were angry. Some called for apology, others for explanation, yet others for his resignation or dismissal. The worst was a wish that he would be sent to prison for an indefinite period.

His first impulse was to phone the *West Uist Chronicle*, but after a moment's thought he felt that paying a personal visit might have more impact. He was angry, but worried at the same time. And the letters he carried in his inside breast pocket from Mungo were not helping at all.

And that bloody woman, Annie McConville. If she hadn't found that hen harrier corpse...

He reached into a pocket and pulled out his hip flask. He took a large nip. And then another. It helped take the edge of his anxiety, but only slightly.

What does that Irish actor mean? He's a good friend of the boss, Digby Cruikshank. Is he going to tell him? Surely he's not intending to blackmail me? Why would he? He must be loaded and I'm just a gamekeeper on his friend's estate.

The thoughts tumbled into his head, but again returned to Calum Steele's article.

But that wee busybody and his lassie, they've made it a thousand times worse. Why did they have to write that? I should bloody well —

His phone beeped and he fished it out. The message made him cringe.

DEAR POISONKEEPER,
SO YOUR SINS HAVE COME HOME TO ROOST. SEE HOW YOU HAVE HIT THE PRESS. I SAID I WAS GOING TO DESTROY YOU AND THAT EVIL ESTATE YOU LOOK AFTER. WELL, LOOK AT THE TROUBLE YOU'RE IN NOW. SPLASHED ACROSS THE NEWS. THE POLICE WILL BE AFTER YOU, POISONKEEPER. YOU'VE ONLY ONE CHANCE AND THAT'S ME, MUNGO. KEEP QUIET AND TALK TO NO ONE. WAIT

FOR MY NEXT MESSAGE IN ONE HOUR.

The gamekeeper stared at the message for a few moments, then took another swig of whisky. This time it did little to assuage his fear, but his temper started to rise again.

He went to the gun cupboard and took out his own 20 gauge Beretta Silver Pigeon.

'An hour! Time enough to pay a debt.'

Morag excused herself from the meeting, took the awaited call from SASA and was told that the official had discussed the case with her opposite number in SEPA and the decision still had to be made whether the salmon in the pen where the body was found would be considered safe for human consumption. The conversation, while not exactly monosyllabic, was not definitive.

'So, are you saying that the salmon farm will have to quarantine this penload?'

'That is the consensus opinion.'

'But not harvest them?'

'Not until we have investigated fully.'

'But meanwhile the farm can continue in operation?'

'At this moment, until an inspector visits and deliberates.'

'And what if the inspector condemns the fish?'

'Pet food is possible. They will still be able to sell it, just not so profitably as if it was destined for the human table. I'll email their office to tell them an inspector will be contacting them.'

'And what shall I tell the media if they contact us?'

'Well, they can contact us or SEPA, and we will tell them the official line.'

'Which is?'

'No comment until our inspector has investigated.'

When she popped her head round the door to report it back to Torquil, she anticipated that he would advise her to report to Superintendent Lumsden. Five minutes later, after a barrage of ire from Lumsden, she returned to the meeting.

'He wants us to do nothing except keep an eye on the farm and report to him when the inspector has been.'

'As useful as usual,' Torquil replied. 'But in fact, at this moment in time doing nothing but observing might be the best thing.'

He moved along the whiteboard and at the top wrote the word 'considerations'. 'So, what needs to go here?'

'Suspects,' said Penny, speaking up for the first time. 'But I'm not sure who should be there.'

'That's got to be anyone with a thing against the salmon farm,' added Douglas.

'The Wookies,' Wallace suggested.

'Correct,' Torquil agreed. 'But let's not use that nickname. It's a bit derogatory.' He drew an arrow from considerations and wrote and underlined the word 'suspects'. Under that, he wrote WUCE. Under this, he wrote Elspeth MacLauchlan, and one by one the other names that were called out.

'The WUCE guardians accused him of poisoning the seabed and killing the lobsters and crabs and all the smaller crustaceans with the chemicals and antibiotics they use to treat sea lice.'

'There is this mysterious woman — or man — you told us about?' suggested Morag. 'A lover, maybe.'

Torquil wrote the word 'lover' and followed it with a question mark. 'Is she the one who left flowers on his bed?' He added the word 'flowers'.

'Mungo!' exclaimed Ewan. 'Those letters he sent him were very threatening.'

Torquil added it. 'Indeed.' He circled the name 'Mungo' and drew an arrow linking it to the circle containing poison-pen letters. 'We'll need to come back to this in a while.'

'I'm thinking maybe add Ross McNab,' said Wallace. 'He was doing this benthic study thing of the seabed and the seabed creatures. He's friendly with the Wookies — I mean the WUCE folk.'

Torquil added the name, then underneath wrote 'salmon farm staff'. 'We need to look at all of them, since Marie Urquhart told me that they are all shareholders in the salmon farm, although Arran MacCondrum had maintained his majority holding.'

He reminded them about the torn-up letter he had found from the Ciderman Consortium. As he did so, he wrote the word 'consortium' and beside it the name 'Ciderman' in brackets and circled them. 'I am thinking this is the same consortium that my uncle mentioned to me last night. He played nine holes with that actor-singer Declan O'Neil. He said they were planning some business ventures on West Uist that include buying Dunshiffin Castle and the St Ninian's golf course. We'll need to check this out.'

Underneath, he wrote the names 'Declan O'Neil' and 'Steve Rollinson'. 'Steve is the one I gave a Recorded Police Warning to.' He briefly recounted his run-in with the trio for Penny's benefit. 'They are all staying at the Cruikshank estate,' Torquil went on.

'And Frazer McKenzie the gamekeeper is splashed across the *West Uist Chronicle* digital issue,' Wallace pointed out. 'There seem to be a lot of poisoned birds around. The sea eagle we found, the buzzard, all those gulls.'

'And the birds of prey he was burying,' Ewan agreed.

Penny looked troubled. 'There is something that stands out for me, boss.'

Torquil held out his hand encouragingly. 'Please, Penny. Speak.'

'Well, there seems to be a lot about poison here. Poisoned seabed, crabs, birds and letters.'

'Agreed. But are they actually linked?' Torquil asked. 'That we don't know, yet. But we need to find out. So here's where we can start to divvy out some interviews.' He sighed. 'Before we do that, I need to speak to Detective Superintendent Ross and put him in the picture, then the Procurator Fiscal — then the media. We have to make this an official murder investigation.'

'So, are you going to tell Calum Steele?' Morag queried.

'I meant I'd call Kirsty Macroon on Scottish TV, as she's always amenable and will give us a fair slot. But I suppose I'll have to let Calum know, too. Best to get him on our side rather than trying to score points against us.'

Henson Dingwall was upset when Amy Reid came in before her shift and handed in her notice. She had been a good worker, but he knew that she was quite a sensitive young soul.

'It was that man who created such a fuss,' she told him as he made her sit down with a coffee. 'He was just so angry, and I thought there was going to be a fight. I ... I didn't know what to do. I sort of froze on the spot.'

'Look, Amy, these things happen in the very best and most genteel of restaurants. The fact is that there are just some people who are born rude. I wish you wouldn't let one bad experience blight this.'

Tears welled up in her eyes. 'I've never seen grown men fight, and just the thought of it happening here...'

'But it didn't happen, Amy. Tell me exactly what occurred.'

She recounted it all to the best of her memory, which impressed him, for she could recall all of the customers, where they were sitting, what she chatted to them about as she took their orders and even what they had chosen to eat and drink.

'It was when Calum Steele and Cora Melville came in that it started. One of the customers actually said that, too.'

'Was it all about the food?'

Amy frowned. 'No. That all came at the end. It was when people started talking about poor Arran MacCondrum. The whole café was mumbling about it. Then someone sort of implied that the *West Uist Chronicle* should have known about it.'

'Aye, I'd heard the talk myself. Indeed, we were talking about it in the kitchen.'

'No one wanted anything with salmon in it,' Amy volunteered.

Henson nodded. 'Inevitable, if he drowned in one of his salmon pens. It's the association, I suppose.'

'Well, then it turned to this Mungo and these poison-pen letters folk have been getting. Even my auntie had one, and she's so prim and proper.'

'I had one myself, Amy. It's obviously the work of someone who's got a screw loose.'

'Calum Steele said they were working on it and they were going to expose him.'

'Did he now?'

'And then that big man kicked off. He said that Arran MacCondrum had been badgered and that he killed himself. Then he called me for his bill.'

'Badgered by who?'

'That was just it; he said by agitators and he didn't want to be here anymore.' She sipped her coffee. 'But he was saying this as if he knew Arran MacCondrum well.' She shrugged. 'West Uist is not a big place, but I'd never seen this man before.'

Henson took off his headband and ran his hand through his curly black hair. 'That's curious, right enough.'

'Everyone knows about the demonstration at the harbour yesterday, so maybe he's a driver or something. Anyway, Elspeth MacLauchlan, she's a big wig with the WUCE guardians — so is my cousin Sheila, by the way — well, she called out to him and asked if he was meaning her. And he called her a Wookie.'

'I think I heard some of this, but I was in the middle of a dish and it was time-critical, otherwise I'd have been through myself.'

'That was when Ross McNab, the Wave and Dive man — he was having lunch with her — he got up and confronted the man. It was scary.'

'But there was no actual, physical contact between them?'

'No, the big man threw down a lot of money and told me to keep the change. He was so rude about the food here and said it was only a bit better at the Bonnie Prince Charlie. It was as if he was trying to put your customers off eating here again.' She looked at him uncertainly. 'I didn't want his money, so I put it in the tips tray.'

Henson smiled. 'I thought it was bulging with money.'

'Then he just pushed past and left. That was when you came in.'

'After the excitement.'

'But I saw something else, Mister Dingwall.'

'Oh, what?'

'I saw him wink at those two men, agents or something, I think they are. I saw pictures of them in the *West Uist Chronicle*. They're visiting the island with Declan O'Neil. You know, from —'

'From *Leave them to the Caretaker*.' He smiled. 'As a matter of fact, the three of them have booked in for lunch tomorrow. Then they want to have a meeting with me.' He smiled at her. 'Look, Amy, please don't go. I guarantee there won't be any nonsense like that again. In fact, I'm going to find out if they know that big man and if they do, I want to discover what they're up to.'

Calum and Cora were both busily fielding emails and phone calls following the latest digital issue. Both the article about Arran MacCondrum's drowning and the piece about Frazer McKenzie had sparked intense interest, shock and a need for more information.

'Phew! We've opened a couple of cans of worms there, lassie,' said Calum, rolling up his sleeves and standing up to stretch. 'Let the answerphone just collect a few calls while we take a break and have a bit of a recap.'

Cora went through to the kitchenette and prepared coffee, while Calum opened a drawer and took out a notebook with his ideas for the forthcoming stag-do for Torquil. He was riding a wave of pride over the success of his articles, so although he was peeved with his best friend, he felt sufficient magnanimity to turn his mind again to organising something really memorable. He was determined that the lads should not be outdone by the lassies' hen-do arrangement for Lorna.

'Learning to dive and then hunting for underwater treasures,' he muttered to himself. 'It's like something out of *The Adventures of Tintin*. And then a feed by Henson Dingwall.

Surely we can equal that. I just need the others to toe the line and listen to someone who knows how to organise things.'

His mind ran over the things he had suggested and which Wallace, Douglas, Ewan and Ralph had either singly or unanimously rejected. They all wanted something physically demanding, whereas his ideas mainly involved beer and whisky and more traditional Scots fare.

He interlocked his fingers behind his head and wandered round his desk, stopping at the window and looking down.

It was then that he saw the man who had caused the rumpus in The Crow's Nest the day before. He looked furtive as he walked up the street, checking the various shops and business windows.

'Who are you? You're not local, that's for sure.'

Cora came in with two mugs of coffee and the biscuit barrel. 'What are you talking about, darling?'

'Him,' Calum replied, taking his coffee and nodding down at the street.

'Oh, it's that man from the café. He was so rude. And he winked at those two friends of Declan O'Neil.'

The man was dressed in an anorak, waterproof trousers and a baseball cap. He had a large carrier bag in his hand.

'He looks dodgy to me,' said Calum. 'He seemed to be trying to spot somewhere.'

Several vehicles went up the street.

'Look, that's Frazer McKenzie's Jeep,' he said, his interest suddenly piqued. 'He's parking. Not very well, though. A bit erratic and in a hurry.'

'Do you think he's going to come here?' Cora asked warily.

'Maybe. He's getting out, and that chap is going over to talk to him.'

They watched as the two men chatted and then they moved across the road together.

'I can't see them now,' said Calum, taking a quick gulp of coffee and then laying the mug down. 'But a good journalist doesn't just sit and wait. He goes and finds out. Come on, Cora.'

He grabbed his anorak and made for the stairs.

'What?' Cora began, but seeing Calum disappear down the stairs she followed suit and gulped a mouthful of coffee before getting her jacket and running after him.

Out on the street they looked right and left, but neither Frazer nor the other man was there. Instead, they saw Frazer's Jeep accelerating up the street, spinning the wheels as it did so.

'He's not himself, I can tell you that,' Calum said.

A flamboyantly dressed couple were walking towards them. 'That was Frazer McKenzie,' the man said. 'He should'na be driving. He looked half cut.'

Calum recognised the proprietors of the local art shop.

'We saw your article about him, Calum Steele,' the woman said pointedly. 'Either he's been poisoning birds, or you've driven him to drink.'

They passed by without further dialogue.

'Did you hear that, Cora?' Calum said, momentarily nonplussed.

But she wasn't listening. Her eyes were wide with horror, and she was gesticulating towards Calum's yellow Lambretta that was parked as usual in front of the *Chronicle* offices.

Hanging from the handlebars were two dead crows.

CHAPTER EIGHTEEN

After Torquil had made his telephone calls, he rang Morag, who brought all of the staff together in the restroom again.

'We have the go-ahead to make this official,' he told them. 'I called Lorna and she said that Ralph is on his way back to West Uist. He and Doctor Hamilton have given a preliminary post-mortem report to the Procurator Fiscal and to Superintendent Ross. Ian Gillesbie the Senior Scene Examiner will be coming, too. He'll be useful.'

'Ian is good to work with,' said Penny. 'He's an old pro.'

With the amalgamation of all eight of the Scottish regional police forces into the national Police Scotland, a Scene Examiner, a specially trained civilian employed by the Scottish Police Authority, was called in to collect evidence to assist the investigating officers with criminal investigations. Past experience had shown this to be of great value, as it gave a direct line with the forensics labs.

'And I also had a call with Kirsty Macroon and did an impromptu interview with her by phone. She's going to slot a piece into the next news bulletin announcing that we have a murder inquiry into Arran MacCondrum's death. She's going to get archival pictures to illustrate it.'

'And how did Calum react when you told him?' Morag asked.

'I didn't speak to him. He had his answer machine on, so I left him a message to call me.' Torquil clapped his hands. 'Right, we'll get started straight after lunch. I want to see how it comes across. So between then and now, I want to allocate jobs. I take it you have no objections, Morag?'

The uniformed sergeant shook her head and gestured for him to proceed.

'Wallace and Douglas, can you meet Ian Gillesbie off the ferry and show him the *Betty Burke*? It's in the harbour. I want him to go over it.'

'Of course, boss,' Wallace replied.

'Then, after that, take him out to the salmon farm on *Neptune's Trident*. I'm going to call the salmon farm now so the crew will know that it is officially a crime scene and that a murder investigation has been instigated. They'll all be in a state, I imagine, but as soon as you get there I want police tape round that pen number two. Also, the cabin on the barge should be sealed off with tape. Check with them the state of the computers in there. I want to know if any of their cameras, underwater or surface, picked anything up. If they haven't checked, then don't let them try until Ian Gillesbie has had a good look round, fingerprinted and photographed everything.'

The two special constables nodded.

'I'll be surprised if anything is caught on film. That's why the place was so trashed, rather than him going berserk.' Torquil turned to the station sergeant. 'Morag, since you dealt with the demonstration at the harbour yesterday, I'd be grateful if you could contact Elspeth MacLauchlan and the WUCE guardians.'

'What tack shall I take?'

'I would like to know how she and the others personally felt about Arran MacCondrum.' He turned to Penny. 'I'd like you to do some digging. Check with the post office. See if we can find out where these poison-pen letters were posted from. Look at all the letters in Arran's file and that torn-up letter from the Ciderman Consortium. See if you can find anything in any of them. There didn't seem much information on the

Ciderman Consortium one, apart from the fact that he was in some sort of trouble. Find out what that was, if you can. Then we want to know how Declan O'Neil and his chums are associated with it, if it is the same consortium.'

Penny made notes in her little black diary. 'Declan O'Neil? I'm surprised to hear that he's involved in a business venture personally. I thought these celebs sent their minions and got them to do these things.'

'That's another thing to find out. Do a background check on him and on both his two agents or producers or whatever they are.' Torquil pointed to the whiteboard. 'As I noted there, one of them, Steve Rollinson, has a Recorded Police Warning from me.'

'And it's been entered on the system,' said Ewan. 'So, what shall I do, Inspector? You said you want me to go out and have a word with Frazer McKenzie.'

'I do, but man the fort here first. While you are doing that, find out from SASA about the toxicology. It would also be good to find out about this emamectin the salmon farm uses against sea lice and if it is poisonous in any way to birds. Then, whether or not there has been poisoning, we want to know what Frazer McKenzie was doing when Calum and Cora photographed him and why he hadn't reported it to us.' He clapped his hands. 'Now, what about food? I'm starving, and it would be good if we can get something in while we watch the news. Then I'm going off to check over Arran MacCondrum's house again.'

Kirsty Macroon had gone through all the latest national news, then the scene behind her changed to a picture of West Uist.

'And now, I am afraid that we have an unpleasant bulletin just in from West Uist. The local MacCondrum Salmon Farm has been featured in the news several times in past years. Most recently, there has been controversy about the number of seals that they have culled, especially in view of mounting international pressure on the Scottish government to ban the practice and use such methods as underwater deterrent sonars.'

The scene changed to a distant shot of the ten circular salmon pens and the interlinking walkways all leading to the concrete barge and cabin.

'The body of the owner, Arran MacCondrum, a colourful local personality was found in one of the pens yesterday. Initial speculation was that he had taken his own life.'

A grainy photograph of Arran MacCondrum appeared. He wore full waterproofs and was holding a huge salmon in both hands.

'But now, following a post-mortem examination and investigation by the local police led by Detective Inspector Torquil McKinnon, there is considerable doubt about the cause of death. A murder investigation is underway. Earlier, I was able to talk to Inspector McKinnon on the phone.'

Then followed the brief interview put together with Kirsty asking questions in the studio then hearing Torquil's voice, slightly distorted due to the telephone connection. Subtitles accompanied it on half of the screen. It was skilfully done, with Kirsty allowing Torquil free rein to get the messages he wanted to get to the public across.

'...so we have very strong evidence that supports our belief that Arran MacCondrum was drowned elsewhere and his body was taken — probably on his own boat, the *Betty Burke* — to the salmon farm at night, where the net in one of the pens was cut open and his weighted-down body was lowered into the pen. Various artefacts were left to imply that he had committed suicide.'

During the interview, Kirsty had looked straight at the camera with a professional expression of concern, nodding appropriately. Then she asked: 'And have you any leads to the identity of the murderer?'

The distant telephone voice answered: 'We have a few lines of investigation. Significantly, we are looking for not one but two people who we believe were involved in this murder.' There was a pause, then he added, 'One thing I will say is that we have evidence that he was being threatened and possibly was being coerced.'

'We await further developments. Detective Inspector McKinnon, thank you for joining us.'

The scene changed to a cricket pitch and Kirsty went on with a sports report. In the restroom, Torquil signed to Morag, who turned off the small television.

'Let's hope it gets the murderer properly agitated,' Torquil said.

Morag frowned. 'It will have the effect of a bomb going off in West Uist, I think. I bet that Ewan is going to have a busy time manning that phone.'

And indeed no sooner had she said it than the station phone started to ring.

Calum and Cora had watched the news while eating pies from Allardyce the Baker's, a couple of mutton pies for Calum and a vegan one for Cora. As usual, whenever there was a big story going on, they received feedback on their paper or on the digital issue in whichever shop they went into. Gordon Allardyce, a ruddy-faced, middle-aged bachelor and a notorious flirt was sarcastic as usual to the editor, but geniality with a wink to Cora.

Since they had made their purchases before the news came on, they had fielded questions and comments about the suspected drowning of Arran MacCondrum and also about the piece on Frazer McKenzie and the dead birds.

Neither of them mentioned the dead crows they had found tied to the Lambretta, as it had been a point of contention between them and they had agreed to consider what to do about it.

Returning to the office and the pinging of the answerphone, they had intended to listen to the a messages after lunch. The bulletin with Torquil's interview caught them by surprise, as Cora was finishing her vegan pie and Calum had just taken a bite of his second.

'Murder! I don't believe it!' Calum bellowed, spraying pie crust in the direction of the television.

'That's horrible!'

'He didn't tell me about the drowning and then he didn't tell me that it's murder!'

'The poor man.'

'Threatened and coerced! On my back step a story like this and he didn't tip me the wink! Some friend.'

'Calum, I'm worried.'

'Aye, and I'm incandescent.'

'We should have a word with the police.'

'I'll give him words!'

'About the crows, I mean.'

He looked at her in surprise. 'Not on your life, Cora.'

She knew this was not one of the times for persistence. Instead, she smiled demurely and fluttered her eyelashes.

'Well, maybe I'll call after I calm down a bit,' he conceded, susceptible as ever to her charm.

The man calling himself Mungo had watched the bulletin but did not display any of the emotion that the revelation about the murder had stirred up.

So, the plods were not as stupid as he'd thought. That made it more exciting. Especially when Inspector McKinnon implied they had clues. Threatened and coerced, he had said. That was good. Everything was going to plan.

But for now, it was imperative not to risk betraying oneself. Best to just mirror the reactions of others when they heard the news. Yes, that was the way. But it was amusing to anticipate how the next ones would be received.

The urge to laugh was almost unbearable, but in case anyone saw, the feeling was suppressed. The ghost of a smile was all that anyone would have seen.

CHAPTER NINETEEN

Elspeth MacLauchlan worked at *Ionad dualchais uist an iar*, the West Uist Heritage Centre at the top of The Bonniegate, which was effectively the local museum, information centre and Gaelic book and giftshop all rolled into one. She had worked there for as long as Morag had been in the police.

There was no one in the centre except Elspeth. She was wearing a purple dress with a neat West Uist tweed jacket and was arranging a bookshelf. She turned upon Morag's entrance.

'Ah, I was expecting to see you sometime, Morag, or should I call you Sergeant Driscoll?'

Morag gave her a wan smile. 'If you are referring to your demonstration, Elspeth, you know that I had to be official when I talked to you. Morag will be fine for now.'

'So it's not an official visit, then? You're not coming to warn me as a representative of the WUCE guardians in case we stage another protest?'

'It's a semi-official visit, Elspeth. Have you not seen or heard the news?'

She looked quizzically at Morag and her hands went to fiddle with the lapels of her jacket. 'News? Has a decision been reached about what will happen to the salmon farm? I heard that the salmon may be condemned. That's not what we —'

Morag held up her hand. 'No, it's not that. It's been on the news today about Arran MacCondrum's death. We are treating it as a murder investigation.'

Elspeth gasped. 'No! I … I hadn't heard.' Her clenched hands rose to her mouth and she shuddered. 'That's not possible. I heard he drowned. He … took his own life.'

185

'Would you like to sit down? I can make you a cup of tea if you show me your kitchen.'

'No, I can do that,' she replied. 'Come through.'

Over tea and a piece of shortbread, Morag told her of the news bulletin and the fact that the post-mortem examination and other things had led them to conclude that he had been murdered and that at least two people were involved. 'Obviously, we are investigating everyone who may have had any sort of relationship with him. As the spokesperson for —'

'I am the chair of the West Uist Coastal Ecology guardians,' Elspeth interjected. 'And because of that, you think I may have had a grudge against Arran MacCondrum?'

'We are investigating all possibilities.'

'The WUCE guardians position is quite clear. We are concerned about the ecological damage that salmon farming is doing to the ecology, to the seabed creatures, the wild Atlantic salmon and the trout in the rivers. Sea lice proliferate in enclosed pens, and they try killing them off with these antibiotics and chemicals. Oh, they say they are using the wee wrasse fish in the pens to eat the sea lice, but yet they are still using vast amounts of chemicals. We've had benthic studies done by the University of the Highlands and Islands and —'

'Is this by Ross McNab of Wave and Dive?'

'It is. He's been given permission to help us. I often had contact with him.'

'But from what I've heard, this emamectin that they use isn't harmful to other creatures.'

'We think otherwise and worse, it's killing the bird population.'

Morag was making notes as they talked. She looked up. 'I have to tell you that we are investigating a number of dead birds in the area.'

'I saw that article by Calum Steele on the *West Uist Chronicle* blog about Frazer McKenzie. He implied that he'd been poisoning birds, but I'll wager it was something that those birds had eaten along the coast or from the beaches that killed them.'

Morag made further notes. She looked up again and tapped her pen on her notebook. 'We found certain letters, poison-pen letters on his person.'

'So he'd received some as well, had he? Who hasn't?'

'Have you, Elspeth?'

She nodded and rose to get her handbag. She opened it and took out two letters with the recognisably geometric address on the envelopes.

'May I take these? I'd rather they were opened forensically.'

Elspeth nodded. 'This Mungo has it in for lots of people, it seems. Do you think they could have driven him to —' Then she stopped herself. 'Oh no, if you think he's been murdered, then you won't think he was driven to kill himself.'

Morag slipped the two letters into the back of her notebook. 'What were your personal feelings about Arran MacCondrum?'

Elspeth started to fiddle with her lapels again. 'I … I was indifferent to him.'

'You didn't dislike him, or hate him?'

Elspeth stared at Morag, suddenly aghast. 'Hate him? No, how could I? We were once engaged when we were young. I loved him then, but these long years past I've just been indifferent. Until … until now, that is. Strange, but knowing he's been murdered, maybe I did still have some feelings for him.'

Morag lay down her pen and steepled her fingers under her chin. 'Tell me more, Elspeth.'

Torquil unlocked the front door and let himself into Arran MacCondrum's house. He had retained the key after his last visit. As before, the vestibule with its waterproofs and boots smelled strongly of the sea and of fish, but once he stepped through into the sitting room, he was aware that the smell of flowers was still very powerful. He determined that he would draw the attention of the Scene Examiner to the smell of those and of the fragrance he had detected upon the pillows in the bedroom. He wondered if it would be possible to bottle the smell somehow.

And, of course, the bedclothes would have to be examined for any stains and for DNA other than his.

Once again, he reached for a pair of examination gloves from his inside pocket and took care not to disturb anything more than necessary.

'Now, let's have a closer look this time, eh, Arran? Last time I was here, I thought you had put your life in pictures on these walls.'

Methodically, he started to photograph them all, knowing the beauty of the inbuilt digital camera that allowed each picture to be zoomed into. He would ask Ian Gillesbie to take more with his high power crime scene camera, but these would do for now.

Every now and then, he lifted the frames away from the walls to see if Arran had labelled who folk were in particular pictures. He was not surprised to find that he was meticulous with some, but others were just indecipherable scrawls or completely lacking in annotation.

As before, he formed the impression that one wall had been for the history of the salmon farm from the days of his uncle and father until the present, so he was able to put names to most of the more recent faces. So too with the wall space between the two windows.

A multi-frame was full of old polaroid pictures with Arran in his younger days, which looked like the first ones of him at the salmon farm on the first wall. Couples were in some and groups of young folk enjoying themselves in others. In one, there was a trio of young people, a woman and two men, the men with their arms about her waist and she with her hands on their shoulders.

'That's you, Arran, and Elspeth MacLauchlan, isn't it?' he asked the air. 'But who is that with you?' He looked closer and then lifted the picture away from the wall. It was one of the ones without names.

Then it dawned on him. A man of about the same age. He put a thumb over the top of the head to reduce the amount of hair. Then it was clearer. It was a young Frazer McKenzie.

'So, you used to hang out together, did you?' he said as he took a close-up to counter the graininess of the polaroid.

Next to it was another polaroid of another trio, and again Arran was one of the men but the other he did not recognise. And as before, the men had their arms about the woman's waist and she her hands on their shoulders.

'All bonnie folk, weren't you?' he said, looking for names behind, but frustratingly, it too was unlabelled. 'And it looks like you were friends together, because here's another of the two women and Arran in the middle. All smiling.' And again, the picture was unlabelled.

Underneath there was a picture of the three lads, Arran, Frazer and the other, each with a can of beer in one hand and cigarettes in the other. 'The Three Musketeers, eh?' he mused, thinking of himself, Calum and Ralph in their teenage days, when that was how they thought of themselves. Up for anything.

Finally, at the bottom there was a picture of all of the same young folk, but now two or three years older and the woman he could not place had a baby in her arms. He photographed the whole multi-frame and then turned to the images of the hatchery and took more pictures of them, focusing on the freshwater intake tank and the technician's cabin, just in case.

Satisfied that he had taken pictures of all the photographs, he mounted the flights of stairs again to the bedroom, where the floral and perfume smells were still strong. The flowers were still on the bed, as he had left them.

'Who brought those flowers to you, Arran? When and why?'

Ewan and Penny had been relieved when the others left the station on their various tasks. The phone calls gradually stopped coming in, and they were able to snatch a few moments to talk of personal feelings before Penny asserted herself with a gentle shove and a reminder that they both had important jobs to do. She closed her broom cupboard office door and started the process of searching for information about the Ciderman Consortium, first looking at Companies House Scotland.

Ewan had followed suit and telephoned SASA. He was informed that the birds had all been received and were undergoing examinations and testing.

After surfing the web and printing off all the information he could about emamectin and related drugs, Ewan turned his mind to Frazer Mackenzie. He tried ringing the Cruikshank estate office but was told that the head gamekeeper was not there. Rather than give it up at that point, he called Calum.

The newsman answered after a few rings. 'Is that you being sent to apologise to me?' was Calum's opening gambit.

'Eh? It's me, Ewan McPhee. What are you talking about, Calum?'

'An apology from the big boss, Detective Inspector Torquil McKinnon.'

'What do you want an apology for, Calum?'

'Because Torquil deliberately kept me in the dark. A news story like the local salmon farmer drowns himself, then —'

'He didn't, Calum.'

'I know he didn't! Now I know, but only because I watched the Scottish TV news and Kirsty Macroon told the world. But no one thought to tell the local newspaperman. A laughingstock, that's what he made me. I deserve an apology, don't you think?'

'But Torquil rang you and you had your answer machine on.'

'He what? He — just a minute,' Calum said, before Ewan heard Cora Melville's muffled voice in the background. Then: 'Oh, ah well, Cora is listening to our answerphone messages and just this minute got his. It's been pandemonium. Okay, so he left a message, but that doesn't change the fact that I didn't get it. And what exactly do you want? Is it another hare-brained stag-do idea?'

'It's about your poisoned birds story, Calum. About Frazer McKenzie. We are investigating it, because the Drummonds found a whole lot of dead gulls along the coast. I've sent all of them off to SASA for examination and we're waiting on the results. I think I need to get hold of these dead birds of prey, too.'

'Good idea.'

'I just wondered if you could tell me exactly where they were?'

'Out on the Cruikshank estate moors, Ewan. You'd never find it, I'd need to show you.'

'Well, could you?'

'Now, you mean?'

The phone went quiet again and Ewan pictured the editor holding his hand over it as he talked to Cora. A moment later: 'Aye, I'll lead you now. But it's trekking over the moor; you'll need to follow me. Cora's staying here, because we need someone to man the phones in case an important news story comes in.'

'I'll come over to you and then we'll go. Penny is back and she's got to be in the station, so she'll be able to look after things here, too.'

'Say hello to her for us and then get yourself over here. We'll leave pronto.'

Fifteen minutes later they entered the Cruikshank estate in tandem, Calum on the Lambretta and Ewan on 'Nippy,' his mother's old Morris 50 cc moped.

Calum looked back and pointed across the moor from the road. He shouted above the wind. 'We're going off road now, so watch out. It can be boggy and skiddy from now on.'

They turned onto a well-defined path, then soon went over what were more like sheep tracks. 'Shortcuts!' Calum cried as they went over the undulating terrain, cutting through large swathes of gorse, bracken and heather.

At last they found the place and Ewan coasted Nippy to a halt beside the Lambretta, both of which, like their legs, were now covered in mud.

'There, you can see where the turf was dug up and then replaced,' said Calum. Then with a grin: 'I take it you have an order to exhume this grave? Otherwise we're a couple of grave-robbers.'

Ewan dutifully smiled, took out the sack and the spade that had been protruding from the old canvas pannier and tested the ground with his foot. 'It's been worked recently enough.' He slipped the blade into the line of cut turf to elevate and then remove it. Then he started to remove soil. After a few minutes: 'There's nothing here. Either the birds have flown or Frazer has properly disposed of the bodies.' He shook his head and tsked. 'No bodies, no crime.'

Penny had been working steadily, every now and then answering the phone and dealing with any matter that she could or taking messages for Ewan or Morag.

She was just making a hot drink when the phone went again.

'Emergency,' an Irish voice said so loudly that she had to hold it away from her ear.

'This is the police station, DC Faversham speaking. What is your emergency, sir?'

'Get someone here right away. And an ambulance. I'm at the cottage at the Cruikshank estate. I'll do what I can … but … but I think he's dead.'

Then the line went silent.

CHAPTER TWENTY

Knowing that Ewan had gone off with Calum Steele to follow up on the bird story after he had been unable to contact Frazer McKenzie, Penny called Torquil.

'Any more details?'

'That's all. The phone went dead and it's a withheld number. I've called the Cruikshank office and they don't know where Frazer McKenzie is. They're getting one of the assistant gamekeepers to go over to the cottage, but she said she doesn't think he's first aid trained.'

'I'll be on my way. I'll try and raise Doctor McLelland; the ferry should have docked. If you don't hear from me in ten minutes, call the air ambulance from Stornoway.'

Ralph was with Ian Gillesbie and the Drummond twins on the harbour when he took Torquil's call about the emergency. Minutes later, Torquil came racing down the ramp on his Royal Enfield Bullet 500.

'Hop on, Ralph, and I'll take you to the cottage hospital to pick up the ambulance.'

Nodding at the bemused Ian Gillesbie and leaving him in the hands of the twins, they zoomed away. When they arrived at the hospital, Torquil phoned Penny to hold back on the call for the air ambulance as help was on its way.

Ewan answered Penny's call.

'Hi, my bonnie —' he began cheerfully.

She cut him short and quickly filled him in.

'Do you know where this cottage on the Cruikshank estate that they are talking about is?'

Ewan asked Calum and received an emphatic nod.

'Trouble?' the editor asked as Ewan hung up.

'An emergency of some sort. Torquil and Ralph are on their way, but every minute may count. Can you get us there?'

Calum was already mounting the Lambretta and poised to use the kick start. 'It's another shortcut, but it'll be very boggy. Follow me!'

Morag arrived back at the station to find Penny manning the counter and dealing with several locals while speaking on her mobile. The station phone was ringing, and Penny gratefully pointed to it as she spoke to Lorna on her mobile.

Seeing the uniformed sergeant, several of the folk started pestering her until she assertively shushed them with a slap on the counter and a withering look while she took the call.

It took some minutes, but eventually they were able to clear the office and talk. Penny explained the emergency that Torquil and Ewan were on their separate ways to, and that Torquil had told her that the Drummonds were taking Ian Gillesbie to the *Betty Burke*.

'That's all we need, with a murder investigation on our hands,' Morag said with a groan. 'I think strong tea is called for.'

'It gets murkier, though,' said Penny. 'That was Lorna. She managed to get the toxicology back on Arran MacCondrum. His alcohol level was sky high, but they also ran a complete spectrum and found traces of a poison. It's not one they were expecting at all.'

Torquil rode ahead on the Bullet and Ralph drove the West Uist Ambulance, an old camper van that been donated by a former laird and adapted at public cost. Upon arrival at the

Cruikshank estate cottage, they found the doors wide open and Calum's Lambretta and Ewan's Nippy parked outside.

Vincent McPhee, a second cousin of Ewan's, was waiting at the door to direct them in. He was ashen and obviously relieved to see them.

Ralph and Torquil rushed in to find Declan O'Neil standing and wringing his hands.

'There ... there ... help them, please!' he mumbled.

Two bodies lay on the floor. Calum was holding Alistair Pitcairn in the recovery position and was talking to him, telling him to stay with him. On the other side of a coffee table that was littered with upturned glasses, a half full bottle of whisky and the remains of some white powder and a couple of straws, Ewan was giving CPR to Steve Rollinson.

'Has he got a pulse, Calum?' Ralph asked with professional calm.

'Aye, but he's not hearing me. He's just frothing at the mouth and fitting every few minutes.'

'This chap isn't breathing and has no pulse,' said Ewan, as he continued to administer chest compressions.

'Keep going while I examine him,' said Ralph, pulling his stethoscope from his bag and listening to his chest while simultaneously checking for a carotid pulse. Producing a pen torch, he flashed it in Steve Rollinson's eyes and looked for a pupillary reaction. 'How long have you been doing chest compressions, Ewan?'

'I don't know. A few minutes.'

Ralph swept the frothy saliva from the patient's lips and made sure there was no airway obstruction. Cursorily he sniffed his fingers and then bent and smelled the mouth.

'Have they overdosed on cocaine?' Torquil asked.

'That and something else,' Ralph replied. He looked up at Declan and asked: 'Did you take any of that white muck?'

The actor shook his head. 'I had been out and came back to find them like this.'

'You were lucky,' Ralph said curtly. 'Torquil, I need to shock him. Run and get the defibrillator from the back of the ambulance. And phone the cottage hospital and tell them to stand by. Tell Sister Lamb I'm going to need all the hydroxocobalamin and thiosulphate that she has for two patients.'

Torquil was already on the move. 'Thiosulphate and hydroxy-what was that?'

'Just say thiosulphate and vitamin B12. And get the air ambulance on its way. I've got at least one patient I need to get to Stornoway pretty damned quick.'

After attempting to defibrillate Steve Rollinson three times and giving an injection of intracardiac adrenaline with a long needle and syringe directly through the chest wall into the heart, between them Ralph and Ewan lifted him into the back of the ambulance. On the couch on the other side, Torquil and Calum placed Alistair Pitcairn and again put him in the recovery position.

'Torquil, you can drive and I'll stay in the back and see if I can shock him again. His chances are slim, but I need to get the other patient to the cottage hospital. I've got an oxygen cylinder in the ambulance and I'll get a mask on him.'

'Ewan, you stay here and try to find out what the hell happened. I want it treated as a crime scene. You'll find some police tape in the pannier on the Bullet.'

'I'll stay, too,' Calum said.

'Calum, go easy on this — please,' said Torquil sternly as he opened the driver's door of the ambulance. 'And don't go putting anything on social media or anywhere until we have a clearer picture of all this.'

The newspaperman made a gesture across his mouth. 'I'm zipped until you say.'

'I think I need a drink,' said Declan, tremulously.

'Maybe we all do,' said Calum.

'Not from that whisky bottle or from anything in there,' Ralph said over his shoulder as he prepared to pull the door closed behind him. 'These guys have been poisoned.'

A moment later, the ambulance with its light flashing and the siren going sped off back to Kyleshiffin.

CHAPTER TWENTY-ONE

Conn MacVicar had been mobilised and was standing ready when the ambulance roared into the cottage hospital grounds.

'We've one deceased patient, but I need to get the other into the resuscitation room straight away,' Ralph said, getting out of the ambulance to help Conn with the trolley.

Torquil had driven fast while Ralph was occupied in the rear, trying to resuscitate Steve Rollinson at the same time as he was looking after Alistair Pitcairn. The doctor had given Alistair a hefty injection of intramuscular diazepam, the best drug he had in his bag, to try and control the seizures.

'They've both been poisoned with cyanide — mixed with cocaine, I've no doubt,' was as much as Ralph had said. 'You can smell the bitter almonds on both of them.'

Now was not the time to distract the doctor with questions, Torquil decided. But he accompanied them to the resuscitation room, which adjoined the small theatre where Ralph routinely performed minor surgery and where every month a consultant surgeon would visit the island to do a list of more complex laparoscopic surgery.

Sister Lizzie Lamb who ran the nursing side of the cottage hospital was there with a trolley set up with all the instruments he might need for intubation and an intravenous stand, ready to put up a drip. She adjusted the flow of oxygen and air to the mask over the patient's mouth and nose.

Ralph swiftly put on a gown, surgical hat and gloves. 'Did you organise the air ambulance?' he asked as he applied an elasticated tourniquet to the patient's arm preparatory to taking blood. That done, he inserted a small catheter into the vein, removed the tourniquet and attached the IV line to it.

'It's on its way,' Torquil confirmed.

'They'll need to take the deceased's body too. The procurator will want Hamish Hamilton to do a post-mortem fairly smartly. If I'm right and this is cyanide poisoning, it deteriorates rapidly after death and may be hard to trace.' He stood straight and pointed to the drip. 'I need fluids inside him and may need to intubate him if he stops breathing. Right now, that's all he has going for him.' He turned to Sister Lamb. 'Right, hydroxocobalamin first, then thiosulphate.'

As the sister drew the drugs up in separate syringes, he explained, 'This is not ideal, but the best I have. Hydroxocobalamin or vitamin B12 will convert some of the cyanide in his system to cyanocobalamin, which is relatively safe. The sodium thiosulphate I'm giving him will theoretically help by changing the cyanide into thiocyanate. Ideally, we want dicobalt edetate to chelate it.' He began administering the medicine via the IV tube. 'Sister, I'll want glucose in the drip.'

Ever efficient, Lizzie Lamb followed his instructions, watched by her staff nurse Helen Carmichael in case she needed help.

'Glucose is a natural counter to cyanide, Torquil,' Ralph said as he felt the patient's pulse. 'There's a theory that's why Rasputin survived so many of the attempts to assassinate him — because they put his poison in sweet pastries and drinks, which reduced its impact.'

Torquil stored the history lesson away. 'Would it be easy to get cyanide into cocaine?'

'It's in the literature. Potassium cyanide is a white sweet powder. It could easily be mixed up with cocaine powder.'

Torquil scowled. 'Which means whoever put it there and gave it to them was intent upon murder. Probably Declan O'Neil was the third intended victim.'

Ian Gillesbie had a lot of experience, but he had little knowledge about boats. Having Wallace and Douglas with him had been a considerable help as he examined, fingerprint tested and photographed the wheelhouse of the *Betty Burke*.

'I doubt we'll not be turning up much amiss here, lads,' he had said as they climbed aboard *Neptune's Trident* so they could take him out to the MacCondrum Salmon Farm.

When they arrived and moored up to the barge, they were greeted by the salmon farm crew.

'You will all have heard the news?' Wallace asked.

'Aye, we saw it on our phones,' said Micheal, running a hand through his sandy hair. 'It cannae be true.'

Gordon clicked his tongue. 'Suicide was bad enough, but being murdered…' He shook his head in disbelief.

The Drummonds and Ian Gillesbie climbed down onto the barge. Wallace introduced the senior scene examiner.

'We've to tape pen two off as well as the cabin, DI McKinnon said,' Douglas told them. Then, looking round the staff: 'Where's Rab MacQuittie and Marie Urquhart?'

'Neither of them are here. Rab's twisted his back and is laid up and Marie is lying in a darkened room with a migraine,' said Gordon.

'That's a pity, because we have to find out about the computers and cameras,' Wallace said with a frown.

'Well, I don't think you'll have a lot of luck,' said Micheal. 'Marie and Rab couldn't get any of it to work. The cameras won't work and the CCTV system is broken beyond repair.'

'I may be able to salvage something,' said Ian. 'Or if I cannot, the forensic lab boffins are a dab hand at it.'

The Drummonds set about taping off the areas while Ian set up a white pop-up forensic tent on the barge, fastening it by tying its guys onto various rings that ran the length of the boat. The staff disappeared down the walkways to the other pens and set about their usual tasks.

Ian was still busy working in the cabin when Torquil phoned Wallace. The tall special constable listened in disbelief to the DI's news and instructions. He signalled his brother over to him.

'We've to get back to Kyleshiffin and then get Ian out to the cottage at the Cruikshank estate straight away. There's been another murder and an attempted murder.'

Ewan had taped off the cottage with the roll that he'd found in the pannier of the Bullet, while Calum talked with Declan O'Neil and Vincent McPhee.

Briona Grant the estate office manager came over to see what all the commotion was about and offered to take them all over to sit in Frazer McKenzie's office, but Ewan vetoed the suggestion.

'The cottage and the whole area is a crime scene, and we must disturb nothing. It would be okay to sit in your office, though, Briona. I think Mister O'Neil could do with a tea.'

'A drink is what I need,' the actor protested. 'Those are my friends they've taken to hospital.'

'Tea or coffee only, I'm afraid,' Ewan said. 'Until we know more, I must follow Doctor McLelland's orders. No whisky and nothing from the cottage.'

'I wonder where Frazer is,' Briona said, leading the way across to the office.

'Well, he's probably still at the Bothy. He said he wanted to meet us there, when I phoned him before I got back here from Kyleshiffin.'

'He wanted to meet you there? Why?' Ewan queried.

'To show us something. He sounded a bit excited. Flustered, maybe. Not quite himself. You know how bad reception is over on this island of yours. No one ever sounds the same.'

'It was his phone?' Ewan ventured.

Declan nodded. 'Yeah, I have his number in mine and it showed his name.'

'He hasn't answered me at all,' said Briona, anxiously.

Ewan looked at Calum, who nodded. 'I know a shortcut to the Bothy. I need to talk to him about a couple of crows anyway.'

'Crows?' Ewan repeated, but Calum had already turned and was running for his Lambretta.

'I could take you,' suggested Vincent to Ewan.

'No, Vincent,' Ewan replied. 'You stay here with Briona and Mr O'Neil. I'll follow Calum Steele. Wallace and Douglas should be along soon with the scene of crime officer to photograph and check everything here. Tell them I'll be back as soon as I can.'

By the time he had mounted Nippy, Calum had already set off.

Mist had started to reduce visibility as the air ambulance touched down on the large painted H in the corner of the cottage hospital car park that was reserved for it. Emergencies requiring more specialist care than Ralph was able to offer were always transferred by air these days.

The paramedics were briefed by Ralph on the provisional diagnosis and the treatment given to Alistair Pitcairn. His fitting was under control, but his colour remained poor and his clinical state frail. Staff Nurse Helen Carstairs agreed to travel with them, to help with the IV drip and the oxygen and in case he started to convulse again. The paramedics understood that if his breathing rapidly deteriorated, intubation might be necessary.

Conn MacVicar had contacted his nephew Brian, who had gone straight to the hospital and helped load Steve Rollinson into a body bag before transferring him from the ambulance to the helicopter.

With the helicopter back in the air on its way to Lewis, Torquil felt the tiniest lessening of the weight on his shoulders. He called Penny at the station and told her that she needed to trace Steve Rollinson's next of kin so that they could be contacted, as they would need to identify the body and transport would have to be arranged.

Then Ewan McPhee called.

'Boss, you better come quick to the Bothy on the Cruikshank moor. Calum and I have just found Frazer McKenzie.' There was the sound of retching in the background. 'That was Calum just spewing up. Frazer has blown his brains out.'

CHAPTER TWENTY-TWO

The bothy had stood on the moor for over two hundred years. It was a simple stone-built affair that had once been a shepherd's dwelling, but most recently was just one of three stopping off and rest places on the shooting moor for the gentry and well-off shooting fraternity. It had been renovated to give it some modern-day comfort, while retaining its rustic functionality. It had a few easy chairs and a simple table in one room. The back room had a couch and next to that was a basic washroom and toilet.

The mist had fallen and partially shrouded the old building.

Frazer McKenzie's Jeep was parked outside, and when Ewan had pushed open the door of the Bothy he had immediately caught the coppery stench of blood. As he looked inside, he thought he had walked into a charnel house.

Ralph had driven Torquil back to the Cruikshank estate in the ambulance since there was a body and he was needed to pronounce death.

Calum was sitting on the ground outside, hunched up with his head on his knees, rocking himself from side to side. Ewan was by his side, trying to comfort him.

'I've never seen anything like that, Torquil,' Ewan said. 'I didn't touch anything, of course.' He looked pained. 'I'm sorry that fellow Rollinson didn't survive. Penny told me on the phone.'

Torquil patted him on the shoulder. 'You did as much as anyone could, Ewan.'

'Fingers crossed for Alistair Pitcairn,' Ralph added. 'Now, we'd better have a look inside.'

When Ralph and Torquil entered, they saw at once that there was no doubt what had caused the death when they saw Frazer McKenzie's body.

The gamekeeper was sitting sprawled back in one of the easy chairs with a shotgun between his legs. The barrel was still clutched in his left hand and his right thumb was still between the trigger guard and the trigger. His mouth was slightly open, but the top of his face and head had gone. The stone wall behind and the ceiling above had been splashed with blood and cranial contents.

'Nasty! It looks very much like he had the barrel in his mouth and fired,' said Ralph. 'The gas pressure would have been immense when the gun went off and his head virtually exploded.' He put his medical bag on a clean bit of floor and advanced to gingerly feel for a pulse. 'I still have to make sure there are no signs of life for the official record. And we'll need to wait for Ian Gillesbie to get here and record the scene before we look at his clothing.' He pointed to a hip flask on the table and underneath it a couple of letters.

Torquil looked down at them, but refrained from touching. 'It looks as if he had received some mail from Mungo recently. And if I'm not mistaken, there's a note with it. I can just see two words until we get them bagged up.'

'What's it say?' Ralph asked.

'It says, "Forgive me",' Torquil replied. He got out his phone. 'I'll need to get Ian here straight away. The scene at the cottage will have to wait.'

Penny had found herself acting as a command centre after she had spoken to Lorna on Stornoway, with phone calls coming and going from Ewan, the Drummonds and then Torquil.

She and Morag had been horrified when Ewan had phoned first and told them that after seeing the ambulance off with the patient and the body of Steve Rollinson, he and Calum had found Frazer McKenzie's body in the Bothy, where he had apparently called Declan O'Neil some time before to arrange to meet him there.

'It's a nightmare, Morag,' she said. 'Two murders, an attempted murder and now a suicide. Ewan said Calum is in a right state.'

'Our local newspaperman is maybe not as rhino-skinned as he thinks. But it's not the sort of thing anyone would wish to see.'

'He's saying to Ewan it must be his fault,' Penny said, biting her lip. 'Ewan doesn't know how to handle it, especially as he's feeling ill himself.'

There was the rumble of thunder, then moments later a lightning bolt flashed outside the window.

'And here's the rain again. At least it will reduce the number of folk walking in.'

The phone went again and Penny answered it.

'Hello, Cora,' she said, flicking on the speaker so Morag could hear.

'Penny, has Calum been in touch? I know he headed off with Ewan hours ago to check those dead birds we saw Frazer McKenzie burying, but he's not been in touch and he isn't answering his phone. It's not like him.'

Penny grimaced and looked helplessly at the station sergeant. The anxiety in their friend's voice was all too obvious.

Morag signalled to let her talk.

'Cora, I'm afraid there's been another — well, two major incidents.'

The journalist gasped. 'Is Calum —?'

'He's all right. Well, he's shaken up, but he's okay. Ewan is with him. Torquil and all the others probably are there too, by now.'

'Are they outside? They'll get soaked to the skin. Its pouring down now.'

'I don't have the details yet, Cora. But there has been another murder and an attempted murder, plus a suicide.' Morag paused for a moment to let her take it in. 'This is not for publication or transmission at this stage, though. Not until Torquil gives the say-so.'

'Understood. Go on, tell me.'

'Ewan and Calum found the two men who have been with Declan O'Neil. One is dead and the other needed to be resuscitated. He's been airlifted from the cottage hospital to Stornoway. They were both poisoned.'

'Oh God. I don't know what to say.'

'The second incident is also upsetting. Ewan and Calum found Frazer McKenzie in the Bothy on Cruikshank Moor. He's shot himself. That is as far as I can say.'

A strangled sob came from the other end of the phone. 'Oh no! I told Calum something bad would happen. And … and it has. It's all … our fault.'

In the background there was a sudden loud bang and Cora shrieked.

'Cora! What was that?' Morag called.

'That was the front door! Someone thumped it.' She hesitated a moment, then in a hushed voice: 'There's someone in the office downstairs.'

'Cora, stay where you are!' Penny said quickly.

'It's okay. I'm not … scared. I've got Calum's shinty stick. I'm going down.'

Morag and Penny heard her footsteps recede.

Then, loudly: 'Who's there? I'm coming down and I'm armed.'

There was another banging noise, the sound of footsteps on the stairs, then nothing.

'I'm going over to the *Chronicle*!' said Morag, grabbing her anorak from the peg.

'Me too,' said Penny, joining her and getting down a plastic poncho.

Moments later, they dashed out of the station into the pouring rain as another fork of lightning lit up the sky.

Ian Gillesbie had seen every imaginable crime scene and could not be flustered by anything. He was again dressed in his white boiler suit, mask and gloves. Almost as if he had entered his own bubble, he detailed every step of what he was doing into a hands-free headset microphone recorder, while Torquil and Ralph stood by. They too were wearing masks and did not move for fear of contaminating the scene. The smell of blood and cordite were unmistakeable.

The Drummonds, Ewan and Calum had taken shelter in the twins' old Bedford van as the rain lashed the windscreen and pattered on the roof.

Torquil watched and noted everything down in his own notebook as Ian meticulously photographed the body and the site with a sophisticated digital camera, using a high illumination lamp to get the best possible exposure on every shot. Then he took samples and bagged all the pulped brain tissue from the wall and ceiling and labelled everything, annotating a detailed map with exact measurements and flagged numbers of where everything was found.

'You don't do things by half on West Uist, Inspector McKinnon,' Ian said as he finally stood up. 'Once I finish here,

I'll get over to the cottage where you say the other body was found. Then I think you said I need to do Arran MacCondrum's house.'

Torquil tsked. 'Arran MacCondrum's house can probably wait until tomorrow. These two incidents are now the priority.'

'In the other incident that we attended before this, one man was dead and the other has been air-lifted to Stornoway,' Ralph volunteered. 'They snorted cocaine laced with cyanide. At least, that's my guess.'

'And if it's yours, I'm sure it will be right,' Ian replied. 'But could it have been an accident? Crooks will mix anything in coke. Baking powder, cement, talcum powder. Cyanide seems a bit like putting a bomb in an envelope.'

'That's what worries me,' Torquil said. 'A poison like that can't accidentally be used to bulk out some cocaine. I suspect it was intended to take out three people.' He briefly told Ian about Declan O'Neil and his companions. 'And they were supposed to have been called by Frazer here. He had something he wanted to show them, by the account Declan gave us.'

Ian sucked air between his teeth. 'Well, I'm all bagged up, and I've taken pictures of these letters and the note you were interested in. I'll email you them all straight through, of course, and I'll bring everything over to the station once I've been to the other crime scene. But you can see the letters in these see-through envelopes.'

'He must have been in a hell of a state to do that,' Ralph said with a grimace.

Ian nodded. 'Aye, the hip flask seems to have had whisky in it, and it's empty. Fool's courage, I reckon.'

'All in all, is there any doubt he took his own life?'

Ian tsked again. 'It's not for me to decide, Inspector, as you know. But I've taken all the measurements of the gun, an over and under 20 gauge Beretta Silver Pigeon. Only one barrel discharged, which of course you'd expect with its single trigger. It looks like there has been rapid exit from the mouth; his head was thrown back and exploded, lifting the top of his cranium off and splattering his brain on the wall and ceiling. There is GSR, that is gunshot residue, on his thumb and hand, where the trigger was pulled and the back spatter residue on the clothes is consistent with the shot to the mouth. I've got all the pictures, so the blood pattern analysis when the pictures are up and enlarged will tell more conclusively. My personal opinion is that there is no doubt, but the definitive conclusion is above my pay grade.'

Torquil nodded and looked at the see-through envelopes to read the letters and the note. 'All the note said was, "Forgive me". But what did he want forgiveness for? Was it this poisoning of the birds? It's time we found out who Mungo is and put an end to his poison. He's out of control and wreaking carnage.'

The *West Uist Chronicle* office door was unlocked and the stairwell was lit when Morag and Penny burst in.

'Cora! Are you okay?' Morag cried.

The journalist appeared at the top of the stairs with a shinty stick in one hand and a letter in the other. 'I'm fine. Come on up, I just had a delivery.'

The two police officers mounted the stairs. 'And what was the delivery? Was it just mundane *Chronicle* business? An order or something?' Penny asked with relief.

'Not quite. I've got the kettle on, or I can open Calum's filing cabinet if you'd like something a bit stronger after all this.'

'We're on duty, so no thanks,' Morag replied, reaching the top of the stairs and following her through. 'Tea would be better for me, please.'

'Ditto for me,' said Penny. 'And so what is the "not quite" message?'

'It's from Mungo. See what you think,' Cora said, leaving it on the desk while she went through to the kitchenette to make tea.

Without picking up the stencil-written message, Morag read it out loud. '*Dear Specky Short-arse and Nosy Nelly, remember what I said to you both about newspapers and blackbirds? Promises, promises. I always keep them. Sincerely, Mungo.*'

Penny looked at the sergeant questioningly. 'I haven't got up to speed entirely. But I assume —'

'Calum is Specky Short-arse and Cora is Nosy Nelly. They both received threatening poison-pen letters before about what Mungo would do if they didn't back off.'

Cora called through. 'Calum refuses to be threatened.'

'Where was this message, Cora?'

'It was on the welcome mat. That was the noise I heard. Mungo must have wanted to grab our attention. I had a peek out the door, but I didn't dare go further on my own, even with his shinty stick.'

'That was sensible,' Mora replied. 'You didn't see him, though? Or hear him?'

'No. The rain is hammering down, as you know.'

'Well, this puts a different complexion on the whole Mungo affair. He's getting bold and starting to crawl out from under his stone. The trouble is, we don't know where the stone is.'

Cora came out with a tray and three mugs of tea. 'These murders are terrifying. And you will know that Calum was upset that Torquil didn't tell him that he considered Arran

MacCondrum's death to be a murder. We had turned the answer machine on so didn't get his message.'

'Arran MacCondrum had been getting letters from this Mungo and so we're going to pull out the stops to find him,' said Morag.

'Calum is determined to unmask him, too. In fact, we've got a few letters that you probably need to see.'

'That will be good. We probably need to have a better line of communication,' Morag returned, accepting a tea. 'Once we've got a better idea about these incidents, we'll need to have a press release.'

'I can't wait to get Calum back safe here,' Cora said with a shiver.

Penny sipped her tea. 'And the same for me and Ewan, too. I just hope that —'

A sudden thud from downstairs, as if the door had been thrown open against the wall, was followed by the smashing of glass and then by a whooshing, whumping noise. The smell of petrol hit them, and there was a sudden flash as a fireball shot up the stairs. Then the downstairs door slammed shut again.

'That's a petrol bomb!' exclaimed Penny.

'We're trapped. That's the only way in or out!' gasped Cora.

CHAPTER TWENTY-THREE

The company of the other lads in the Bedford van had been enough to calm Calum down. There was none of the usual jovial banter, but that was to be expected given the sudden deaths and the horrific scene.

'A good thing it is that we had attended one of Ralph's CPR training sessions at the cottage hospital,' said Calum.

'Maybe I didn't do it well enough,' replied Ewan. 'Steve Rollinson didn't make it. You getting Alastair Pitcairn into the recovery position and talking to him must have helped him, though.'

'I did my best,' said Calum, his natural self-confidence returning with every minute.

'If it was cyanide like Ralph McLelland says, you did well to save one of them, boys,' said Douglas.

'I wish we could have a proper drink,' said Calum. 'Cora will be worried and my phone is out of charge.'

'If you feel more yourself and if the rain stops, you could get yourself off on your scooter,' said Ewan.

'I'll stay with you lads. You all need a bit support.'

No one mentioned that they all knew that even though he had been shocked and upset by what he had seen, Calum Steele was not going to miss a detail on what could be the biggest story of his career.

The three women ran to the top of the stairs.

'It was a petrol bomb and the entrance is on fire,' Morag cried out. 'Call Cailean Dunbar to bring the fire engine here straight away.'

'I'm on it!' returned Penny.

'We need to extinguish it immediately or we must evacuate somehow,' Morag said. 'Have you a fire extinguisher, Cora?' She looked round at the sound of running feet as Cora came with the large red cylinder.

'Gangway, Morag!'

'I hope it's not water, because petrol floats,' Morag cautioned.

'It's foam! I got it last week,' Cora replied as she raised her mobile phone in her other hand and took a picture of the flames as they licked upward to the hall ceiling.

Then she pulled the pin and broke the tamper seal before pressing the lever. A spray of foam shot out and she aimed it at the walls and then the door. There was much hissing and the flames increased temporarily as the petrol vapour rose and burned. Within moments, the flames were extinguished and the hallway was a mass of foam.

In the distance, the sound of the fire engine could be heard.

'I had Cailean advise me which extinguisher to get, and he showed me how to use it,' Cora explained, slightly out of breath. 'I thought we should upgrade our fire precautions rather than relying on that old bucket of sand that Calum has had for the past umpteen years.'

Morag hugged her friend as Penny joined them on the stairs.

'That's another way you're dragging Calum into this century,' Morag said with a smile.

'If only he'd charge his phone properly,' Cora replied with a look of exasperation.

The fire engine siren was getting closer.

'The list goes up,' said Penny. 'Arson and now another three attempted murders!'

Before they headed back to the cottage, Torquil phoned the station and was surprised when no one answered it. He phoned Penny directly and she explained about Cora's call, the message she had received and the petrol bomb attack.

'But you are all unharmed?' he asked urgently.

'A bit shaken by the enormity of what could have happened, boss, but we're okay. I think we were in professional mode and Cora was quick-thinking with the extinguisher.'

'Is there much damage?'

'No, it'll just need a good mopping up. Cailean was here with his crew and they did an inspection and assessed there was no further risk. The bomb was just a quarter bottle of whisky, so he doesn't think it was a serious attempt to start a fire. Especially with the lights being on upstairs and everything.'

'Just a warning, then,' Torquil said. 'And with that message from Mungo, it's pretty clear it was from him. Right then, the rain has stopped for now, at least. I'm going to tell the others, and so you can tell Cora that I'm sending Calum home to her. I'll get Ewan to accompany him on Nippy, as it's dark and I don't want him going across the moors alone on his scooter. There's been enough incidents for one day. Ralph will go back, too. We've monopolised his time enough today.'

'Are you coming back soon, boss?'

'Yes, we'll need to have a team briefing when I get back. Apologies to everyone that we might be late, but maybe see about getting some food in.'

'No problem.'

'And we'll need to do a press release, but tell Cora what I told Calum. No release until I clear it. If you could get in touch with Scottish TV, preferably Kirsty Macroon herself, and say I'll be in touch about recent developments on West Uist. Keep your cards close, though; she's a professional and will try and get you to reveal more than we want at the present.'

'And since Declan O'Neil is involved, this could be a huge story.'

'Precisely. So right now I'm going to go up to the cottage with Ian Gillesbie and the twins in their van so he can do his examination of the scene, and I'll interview Declan O'Neil. I left the Bullet there anyway.'

'You ride carefully, too, boss. Remember, you're getting married soon.'

While Ian set about measuring, sampling and photographing the scene at the cottage, assisted by the Drummonds, Torquil sat in the kitchen with Declan and Vincent. Briona Grant had made them tea and then went back to the estate office, having said to call her when the others were ready for refreshments.

'I'm not staying here tonight,' the actor said. 'I've phoned The Commercial Hotel and they had a room ready for me. I'll take the Mercedes.'

'Actually, that won't be possible yet. I'll want it going over forensically.'

'Why?'

'In case there are residues of whatever killed your associate. Alistair is being treated in Stornoway and we hope he makes it.'

Declan shivered. 'Can I get a taxi?'

Vincent waved a hand. 'I can drive you, sir.'

'That would be great, Vincent,' Torquil said. Then, addressing Declan: 'Now, can you tell me where your friends got that cocaine?'

Declan shifted in his seat. 'Steve had some in a money belt. He's got a — I mean, he had a pretty serious problem with it. Weed, whisky and coke. He did everything pretty intensely, though never heroin, thank God. He'd been in rehab several times. I and Alistair try to put the brakes on it with him.'

'But you all did coke while you were here?'

He nodded guiltily. 'Me just once, them more often.'

'Do you know his supplier?'

'I think he had more than one. It depended where we were. We moved about a lot.'

'In between your acting?'

'Acting is a strange job, Inspector McKinnon. It's intense for a long time until a series has finished. Then it's the old adage: you wait on tables, serve behind a bar.'

'Surely you are beyond that? You're a successful actor, you drive a Mercedes E-class and I presume you can always fall back on your singing.'

Declan gave a wan smile. 'Life isn't always what it seems, Inspector.'

'What was your relationship with Alistair Pitcairn and Steve Rollinson?'

'It's quite complicated. Alistair is my agent and Steve was my producer. But we were here as business associates.'

'You were representing a consortium?'

Declan looked momentarily surprised, then he nodded his head. 'Your uncle must have told you about our golf match. Yes, that's right.'

'You weren't here scouting for a TV show?'

'No, but I expect people were speculating that is why we were here.'

'This consortium, what is it called and what was the business venture?'

'The Ciderman Consortium. We want to expand into West Uist. It has great tourist potential.'

Vincent suppressed a sarcastic laugh.

Torquil smiled at them both. 'Does it, Mr O'Neil?'

The actor bristled slightly. 'Yes, we think it does. Which is why we were exploring the possibility of buying Dunshiffin Castle and converting it into a hotel and conference centre, and also buying the golf course and turning it into a real championship course.'

'Anything else?'

There was a tap on the door and Wallace put his head round it. 'Excuse me, boss. The SSCE would like a quick word.'

Torquil nodded and went through.

Ian signalled him over to the other side of the room. 'I thought you should see this,' he said, pointing to a briefcase from which he pulled out several files with a gloved hand. He fanned them like a cabaret magician showing giant cards to an audience. 'I think I've got all that I need for now. Did I hear you say you want the Mercedes checking out as well as the hatchery?'

Torquil did a double take when he saw the names on the files: Arran MacCondrum, Frazer McKenzie, Henson Dingwall, Lachlan McKinnon, Charlie McDonald, Elspeth MacLauchlan, Rab MacQuittie and several others.

'Aye, the car, the hatchery and Arran MacCondrum's house, but they can all wait until tomorrow, Ian. You've done enough for one day.' He took and opened his uncle's file and his jaw tightened. 'Leave this with me and you three have a hot drink before you head back to Kyleshiffin. Where are you staying tonight, Ian?'

'At the Masonic Hotel.'

Torquil nodded. 'If you don't mind coming to the station in the morning, we'll have a team briefing and I'd like your input. Then I can let you know about some things I'd like you to focus on when you go to the MacCondrum house. Meanwhile,

I'll take these.' He slipped them back into the briefcase and went back to the kitchen.

'Vincent, can you let Briona know that Mister Gillesbie and my two special constables have finished and could do with a cup of tea over there?'

As Ewan's cousin went off to alert the estate office manager, Torquil put the briefcase on the table and pulled out the files. 'And perhaps you can explain how the Ciderman Consortium obtained the information in these files and why you needed them?' He selected Arran MacCondrum's and that of his uncle. 'We'll start with these.'

Morag and Penny had phoned Henson at The Crow's Nest and organised a carry-out of a selection of food, including his take on fish and chips, scampi, and cartons of cullen skink. They had kept them warm in the bottom of the kitchen oven.

When Torquil eventually joined them, sometime after nine o'clock, he announced that they should eat first and talk after. As they were all hungry, they pitched in. Then, with teas and coffees at the ready, Torquil called the briefing together.

'It is really going to be a brainstorming session as much as anything,' he said, standing by the whiteboard with the marker pen. 'First off, though, did you get through to Scottish TV, Penny?'

'I did, boss. Kirsty Macroon said to give her a bell as soon as we have news and she'll try to get it on the news programme, but if it's really big enough they may interrupt a programme and do it as a bulletin.'

'*Sgonneil!* That's brilliant. But we'll need to play fair by the *West Uist Chronicle*, so I'll speak to Calum and Cora first.' He picked up his tea and took a sip. 'What about the Royal Mail, did they give us any joy?'

'They could all have been sent to somewhere off the island, then sent opportunistically from anywhere. They were not very encouraging.'

'What about the background checks?'

'I was working on it, but will have to carry on tomorrow. Declan O'Neil's had a warning in England for brawling. No charges, but he has a temper, apparently. There was a lot in the glossies about it. There was some word that his career was stalling, but it was only speculation. His soap role seems to have put him back up there.'

'Any drug or alcohol history?'

'A couple of trips to rehab. One when he was in the band Quicksilver and another after they broke up. Both to a private clinic in Glasgow, but he's not had a problem since.'

'Nothing on the others?'

'Steve Rollinson had three rehab trips to the same facility in Glasgow over a ten-year period. Nothing yet on Alastair Pitcairn.'

Torquil nodded and pointed to the whiteboard. 'Another question there, then. There were a lot of question marks already over Arran MacCondrum's supposed suicide, but as you all now know this is a murder investigation, which we had already begun and which Scottish TV have reported on.'

Morag cleared her throat. 'Boss, I should add that when I interviewed Elspeth MacLauchlan, she told me she and Arran had been engaged years ago when they were young. Ironic that they ended up on opposite sides of the salmon farming issue. They broke up after affairs.'

Torquil added the details Morag recounted to the whiteboard. Then he drew a line down the board and wrote the name 'Declan O'Neil' and circled it. Then underneath he wrote 'Steve Rollinson' and under that 'Alistair Pitcairn'. He drew a square round Steve's name and a circle round Alistair's. He added a cross beside Steve and the words 'in hospital' beside Alistair. Then beside them he wrote 'cocaine' and 'cyanide' with arrows to the two poisoned men.

'The cocaine found at the scene! We will wait for the analysis, of course, but it looks like they had potassium cyanide mixed with their cocaine. In my interview with Declan O'Neil, he told me that he had snorted some with them, but not on this deadly occasion. He wasn't there, having been to Kyleshiffin.'

The briefcase that he had brought back from the cottage was lying on the tennis table with all the clothes and effects they had taken from Arran MacCondrum's body. He opened it and took out the files.

'These were files Declan O'Neil told me the Ciderman Consortium had assembled on various West Uist personages, including both Arran MacCondrum, Frazer McKenzie, my uncle Lachlan and these others.'

The team all expressed surprise. Torquil explained that they were all people that Declan told him were to be contacted in their various business ventures to procure and obtain their ends. Those ends were to buy Dunshiffin Castle and much of the old McLeod estate, St Ninian's golf course and some local businesses.

'Did you dig anything up about the Ciderman Consortium, Penny?'

She shook her head. 'I searched Companies House Scotland and found no trace of it. It seems to be a bogus company.'

'Interesting. Declan O'Neil said that Alistair Pitcairn and Steve Rollinson had been approached by a high-powered Glasgow lawyer on behalf of the Ciderman Consortium. They appeared to be a blue chip deal with huge finances behind them. We'll need to do more digging.'

'Why your uncle?' Morag asked.

'The golf course.'

'And folk like Ross McNab and Henson Dingwall?' Penny asked.

'Local businesses they wanted to buy or put out of action,' Torquil replied. 'Like Henson Dingwall and The Crow's Nest. They wanted to recruit him as a chef for their hotel. Apparently the consortium had somebody try to sully the reputation of the place.'

Penny snapped her fingers. 'Cora told us about that. She was going to tell us about letters that folk had given her just before the fire attack.'

'She told us afterwards,' agreed Morag. 'She gave us the letters. One was given to her by Henson. She also managed to take a picture of the chap as he left The Crow's Nest. She and Calum had been eating there and this chap started a kerfuffle and was rude to Elspeth MacLachlan and about the food in the café. Ross McNab squared up to the fellow, who she described as being like a heavyweight wrestler. She sent me a picture of him and I've printed it out.' She handed it to Torquil and he attached it to the whiteboard with Blu Tack below the three names. 'And here are photos she sent of the letters that Henson and other folk had given to the *Chronicle*,' she added.

Torquil looked at them then handed them back to Morag to circulate around the team.

Penny went on, 'She also told us that they think they saw this chap from the *Chronicle* window. Frazer McKenzie drew up in his Jeep. They thought he was driving a bit erratically, as if he'd been drinking. They seemed to have some sort of conversation, but when they went down both had gone. Then they found two dead crows tied to the handlebars. It spooked her because one of her letters from Mungo —'

'— said a blackbird would peck off her nose!' said Torquil. 'I remember. I can't blame her for being scared.'

'But Calum was annoyed at the time because he thought we'd kept the news from him about Arran MacCondrum's death being considered suspicious.'

'We need to locate this man,' Torquil said. He drew another line down the board and wrote the name Frazer McKenzie. Once more he drew a square round it and a cross beside it. Underneath he added the word 'gamekeeper' and under that 'shotgun', and in brackets 20 gauge Beretta Silver Pigeon. 'So let's turn to Frazer's death. All the evidence suggests that he shot himself with his own shotgun. We will attach the photographs once Ian sends them through.'

'They are horrible,' said Ewan. 'Poor Calum lost his dinner after seeing him like that. And after what we'd been through at the Cruikshank Cottage —'

'You did as much as anyone could expect of you, Ewan,' Torquil replied sympathetically. 'Calum Steele, too.' He went to the briefcase again and drew out three letters. They all immediately recognised the precise, stencil-written letters. He passed them to Morag as well. 'I went over Frazer's cottage before I came back and I found these in his desk. They are, as you see, letters from Mungo accusing him of poisoning birds and threatening to expose him. Which it looks as if Calum may have done more effectively. According to Declan O'Neil, they wanted to persuade Frazer one way or another to leave the Cruikshank estate and work for them once they had bought Dunshiffin Castle and its lands.'

Douglas shook his head doubtfully. 'But were the letters enough to make him commit suicide?'

'Calum said it was all his fault,' Ewan volunteered. 'That was before he recovered himself. But I think he felt a bit guilty about that article.'

'Cora was feeling worried about that, too,' said Morag.

Torquil pointed to the poison-pen letters circle with the question mark beside it. 'I said that we'd be coming back to that, which we certainly need to. It looks like Mungo has had fingers in many pies. He's sent poison-pen letters to folk all over West Uist, including myself and the padre. And crucially he's sent them to Arran MacCondrum and Frazer McKenzie, both of whom are now dead. Arran MacCondrum was drowned and his death was made to look like suicide. Frazer McKenzie seems to have actually committed suicide by blowing his brains out.'

'And Mungo sent that warning to Calum and Cora and lobbed a petrol bomb into the hall of the *Chronicle* offices.'

'Thank the Lord you were all okay!' exclaimed Wallace.

'The thing is, it seemed more of a warning than a real arson attack,' Morag said. 'It was a pretty tiny petrol bomb with a quarter whisky bottle.'

'Maybe so, but if it had not been put out, it could have been catastrophic,' said Douglas.

Torquil nodded emphatically and added the word 'arson' underneath the name 'Mungo'. 'We cannot ignore he's the common factor here. And he's been going on and off for years.'

'I looked at that file of all the letters, boss,' said Penny. 'I just can't understand in this day and age why someone would send poison-pen letters by snail mail? Not when social media is full of all sorts of hate mail and poison.'

'We've all thought that. This seems to be a character with an obsession. Every now and then, he gets the craving to spread his malicious tripe, then he gets satiated and disappears again. Psychology and criminology texts imply that happens with serial rapists and murderers.'

'Maybe it's him showing how clever he is, doing it again and again,' suggested Morag. 'It's his way, and everyone of every age gets post. Not everyone even has a computer on West Uist.'

Torquil nodded. 'It's his brand.'

'Do you think, then, that Mungo is one of the two people involved in the MacCondrum murder?' Penny asked.

'In which case he may have escalated from just maliciousness to blackmail, murder and to pushing folk to suicide.'

Torquil picked up his mug and sipped his tea, then grimaced as it had gone cold. 'I'm making a habit of not drinking your tea, Ewan,' he said with a wry smile. 'Well, it's time to phone Superintendent Ross and then give Calum and Kirsty Macroon the press release.'

Later that night, Mungo read the *West Uist Chronicle*'s latest blog with glee. It had been thrown together rapidly, as expected. The little present had really upset Specky Short-arse and his little Nosy Nelly.

MUNGO THE ARSONIST FAILS MISERABLY. A predictable headline, but the little slob was rattled. He was at his most pompous this time and indignant as hell. He described the heroism of the police and of his dear Nosy Nelly.

The post that followed was irritating. DEATH OF ARRAN MACCONDRUM WAS MURDER. Well, so be it. It just meant that the plan had to be accelerated. But that had worked beautifully.

The post after it was most gratifying, however. CRUIKSHANK GAMEKEEPER DIES BY HIS OWN

HAND. Good, they had suggested that Mungo's letters may have tipped him over the edge. No mention, of course, of Specky Short-arse's malicious little piece. But the readers wouldn't forget it.

And then the coup de grace. TRAGEDY AT DECLAN O'NEIL'S HOUSE PARTY. And of course the squirt couldn't resist mentioning his heroic part in saving one of the guests. That's if he survived!

Mungo listened to the late news and was a little deflated to see that there was no mention of any of this.

Oh well, there was always tomorrow. All in all, it had been a most satisfactory day.

But there was no rest for the wicked.

CHAPTER TWENTY-FOUR

Over breakfast the next morning, Torquil filled Lachlan in on all that had happened the day before.

'I heard Crusoe bark when you came in last night, but I had been busy working on the church magazine all evening and had a toddy before I turned in. I am guessing you had a hard day.'

'Hadn't you seen Calum's piece on the computer?'

'Crusoe and I hadn't seen a soul all day, and I wanted an internet-free day. I'm guessing there was bad news.'

'Where do I start? Arran MacCondrum was drowned all right, but not in the sea. He was murdered.'

Lachlan stopped with his porridge spoon halfway to his mouth.

'Your golfing opponent, Declan O'Neil's two associates were poisoned with cyanide; one is dead and the other is in hospital in Stornoway.'

Lachlan put his spoon back in the bowl and sat back, looking astonished.

'While Ralph was treating Mister Pitcairn, Ewan and Calum discovered Frazer McKenzie had blown his brains out with a shotgun.'

'Mighty me! I can hardly believe it.'

As Torquil filled Lachlan in, he listened with increasing horror. When he was told about the petrol bomb attack on the *West Uist Chronicle*, he placed his hands together and looked upwards as if in momentary prayer.

'And you think that Mungo did it?' he asked after a few moments.

'It seems likely. Which makes one think that he is one of the two people involved in Arran MacCondrum's murder.'

'If he *is* a he!'

'We're using a generic he for now. But he's been at it on and off for years, hasn't he?'

'Aye. I have one of his letters from years ago.'

Torquil stared at him. 'Have you still got it?'

Lachlan thought for a moment, then dabbed his lips with his napkin and rose. 'I can put my hands on it straight away, actually.'

He went off to his study, Crusoe trotting at his heels. There was the sliding of a steel filing cabinet drawer and then the shuffling of papers.

'Here you are. I felt guilty when I received it twenty-six years ago.'

He handed it to Torquil, who examined the notepaper. It was lined and smelled faintly musty.

'That was the sort of paper folk used back then. Cheap notepaper that you could buy from any newsagent or post office,' Lachlan volunteered.

Torquil read it:

Dear Minister Mannie,

You are the worst example of hypocrisy there is. You rail about people in your sermons without knowing anything of what goes on in their life. In your pulpit you hold them up as examples of how uisge-beatha can ruin a man, his family, his life, but you do it in ignorance. You don't know what others did and you don't know what they might have tried. You are useless, all you clever lawyers, doctors and ministers. And you all go off to bed with your dram after a good day saving folk. Well, you don't deserve it. May you die in your bed and your soul burn in uisge-beatha hell.

Sincerely, Mungo.

Torquil whistled as he looked at his uncle. 'That's some venom spat at you, Lachlan. Why did you keep it? Did you show it to the police?'

'I kept it to teach myself humility. And no, I didn't show it to anyone, I felt too guilty. Besides, lots of folk received them and we just ignored them.'

'Did you receive others?'

'Aye, a few years later Mungo woke again and started sending them out. I wasn't so affected by them and just threw them away.'

Torquil nodded. 'I better get off. Can you watch Crusoe again?'

'No problem.'

'And can I take this for comparison with the recent ones? It looks like the same stencil.'

'Good luck. I'll forego golf this morning. I think I've got a lot of praying to do today.'

As arranged the evening before, Ian Gillesbie attended the station for the briefing. While he was there, he printed out all of the photographs he had taken at the different scenes, and they were all duly attached to the whiteboard under the appropriate cases.

As they ran out of space, the wall itself was used for the photographs that Torquil had taken of the inside of Arran MacCondrum's house. The smaller ones had been blown up to A4 size.

After a recap, Torquil showed the others the poison-pen letter that his uncle had given him. 'It is stencilled the same as the others, and the letter itself may be a bit longer than Mungo writes these days.'

Ian looked at it and at some of the other ones in the file. He shook his head. 'If he'd been using a typewriter, it might have been possible to trace it, but a stencil, well — you'll only know which stencil when you find it.'

'Will forensics be able to tell much from the paper?' Wallace asked.

'If he's left prints, but I suspect he's cleaned them. Probably used gloves.'

'So, a graphologist couldn't tell anything?' Torquil asked.

'Doubt it. A psychologist might.'

Torquil folded his arms. 'My uncle wondered if it was the same Mungo. I suppose with the time gaps since he was first troublesome, that is a distinct possibility. It might be son of Mungo. Daughter of Mungo. Grandchild of Mungo, even. But we don't have much to go on. So let's get going. We've got a whole mass of things to follow up which may or may not be related.' He pointed to the picture of the big man that Cora had taken. 'This man needs to be found. I'm going to call Calum and Cora and get them to put this up on their site. Also, print a load of these and let's get them up in all the shops and businesses. If he's still on the island, we need to bring him in for questioning.'

'Are you doing a press release to Scottish TV today?' Morag asked.

'Aye. It'll put the spotlight on the island and I don't really want journalists swarming across and getting under our feet, but it's important. I'm going to talk to the procurator first, though.'

Since Penny had worked with Ian Gillesbie before, she was given the task of driving him up to the Cruikshank estate to go over the cottage and the Mercedes. Having photographed, taken swabs, samples and virtually examined every crevice inside the car, Ian had spent time under the bonnet and in the boot.

'Nothing apart from cheroots,' he told her. 'Although I can still smell marijuana has been smoked inside. I have a nose for these things.'

Penny phoned Torquil, who was standing in the restroom with Morag staring at the whiteboard and trying to make sense of it all.

'Ian thought it would be sensible to check the rest of the guns while we were here. Is that okay, boss?'

'Sure, make sure they are all accounted for.'

Penny and Ian went over to the estate office, where Briona seemed to be barely able to go through the motions of working, apparently still in shock. She called Vincent McPhee over and then gave him the keys to the gunroom and the cabinet.

'How many people have keys like this?' Penny asked.

'Those are the estate office's, which I keep locked up, and there was Frazer's.'

Ian nodded. 'I think those matched the ones on his keyring. It was in his trouser pocket and I took it with his other effects.'

Briona and Vincent took them to the gun room and Vincent opened the cabinet. Only one shotgun was missing, the one that Frazer had used.

Again Penny relayed this to Torquil by phone.

'I'm looking at the pictures from the Bothy now,' came Torquil's voice. 'I'm not quite clear on something. Where is the shotgun now?'

'Ian says it's bagged and is in the station already. He unloaded it, so it is safe and ready to go back with him to go to forensics and ballistics.'

'Is Vincent there?' Torquil asked.

'Yes, beside me.'

'Ask him was Frazer a right- or left-handed shooter?'

Penny did. Then: 'He was left-handed.'

'Ask if the Beretta Silver Pigeon gun was fitted for him?'

A moment later, the reply: 'It was.'

Torquil expostulated on the other end of the phone. 'Ask Ian if he found a phone on the body or in the Jeep.'

Again the question was relayed. 'No, boss.'

'Say nothing, just get back here as soon as you can.'

Calum had been pleased to clear the air with Torquil, albeit by telephone. He agreed to post the picture that Cora had taken on her phone, saying this was a man the police urgently wanted to interview in connection with the arson attack on the *West Uist Chronicle* building.

The post that he put up was in the form of an Old West wanted poster, with the picture of the big man framed above a description of him as mean, ugly and built like a professional wrestler. He estimated his weight at about seventeen stones and his height as six feet four or five.

Underneath was the picture of the fire that Cora had taken before using the extinguisher to put it out.

'What if he comes here, Calum?' Cora asked anxiously as she looked at the post on the blog. 'He's almost a foot taller than you.'

Calum was strutting about the office with his telegrapher's eyeshade on. He stopped and turned on his heel to face her. Drawing himself up to his full height, he slapped a fist into his other palm. 'Don't worry, darling. The bigger they are, the harder they fall. I am an exponent in the Bob Bell art of self-defence.'

The editor's natural bravado had fully returned and he genuinely felt capable of dealing with any eventuality. The Bob Bell he referred to had been a course of judo instructions printed on bubble gum cards when he was a youngster. He had never actually got as far as having a lesson in judo, but he had once succeeded in replicating a throw when he had been attacked from behind.

The post was seen by many people across the island, including Jimmy Meikle, the big Glaswegian former enforcer of one of the main Glasgow criminal gangs. Old Archie Jingle had put him in touch for this job, which had proven lucrative and relatively simple. He had planned on heading back on the ferry once he had received his final payment. Seeing his face plastered across the internet had given him enough cause for concern to phone the contact.

'I told you never to use this number here. You are supposed to wait for my call.'

'That was before some halfwit plastered a picture of me on that Micky Mouse blog. Where did he get it?'

'That's what I want to know, too. Stick with the plan.'

'This is going to cost you extra.'

'Agreed.'

Once the whole team were back, Torquil explained his concerns. He had the bagged shotgun in front of him and opened it enough for them to see it without him actually handling it.

'Frazer McKenzie had this gun fitted for him as a left-handed shooter. That means the stock is cast on. The stock is offset slightly left so that a left shooter can get his eye over the rib to aim it without rolling his head. Cast off would be the position for the right shooter.'

He pointed to the photograph of the shotgun between Frazer's legs. 'See, the barrel is still held in his left hand and his right thumb is through the trigger guard. It's the wrong way round. A left-handed shooter would use his dominant hand to pull the trigger and he'd hold the barrels with his other.'

Ian slapped his head. 'I should have noticed that.'

'So you're saying he didn't do it,' Penny said. 'Someone else did.'

'Exactly. Frazer McKenzie was murdered, too. And that's why there was no phone found on him or in the Bothy or in his Jeep. Easier to just take it away than risk trying to wipe messages from it. The same with Arran MacCondrum's.'

Ewan pointed to the picture of the big man. 'I saw Calum's Wild West picture of him. He says he looks like a wrestler. He could be a tough one to deal with.'

'Well, we have just the man to deal with a wrestler, haven't we?' said Wallace.

'Aye, he could toss the fellow like a caber, or knock him out with his hammer,' agreed Douglas.

Torquil graced them with a thin smile. This was no time for levity, but he realised they were just trying to ease some of the tension in the team. 'I'll ask Calum to modify his post and say not to approach this man, just in case. The public should contact us if they see him.'

Penny frowned. 'So are we any the wiser about who did this, boss?'

Torquil tapped the name Mungo. 'This joker sent letters to both murdered men, and it seems both murders were staged to look like suicides.'

Ian gathered up his notes. 'If it's all right with you, Inspector McKinnon, I'll get off to the MacCondrum house and then go over to the hatchery. The sooner I get everything over to the labs, the better. I'll email over all the pictures I take, and I'll let you know directly if I find anything I think you need to know about.'

'We're grateful for all you've done, Ian,' Torquil replied. 'Wallace and Douglas will show you the house, drive you over to the hatchery and then get you on the ferry.'

As they left, Ewan snapped his fingers. 'I forgot to tell you, Torquil. SASA phoned. They have confirmed that the birds were all poisoned with carbofuran. It's an illegal pesticide that is lethal to birds. Interestingly, it is used by criminal gangs in some parts of the world to grow marijuana.'

'That's right,' said Penny with a shudder. 'And it's poisoned a lot of users who have smoked contaminated weed.'

'Right, Ewan, in that case I think you need to head back to the Cruikshank estate and have a search round to see if there is any of this carbofuran.'

'Will do. My cousin will help. He's a good lad.'

Torquil tsked. 'Right, so I'm back on the phone for a while. Superintendent Ross, the Procurator Fiscal, Calum and Kirsty Macroon need to be informed. We now have three murders on the island, a mysterious man to chase down and a poison-pen writer to unmask.' He tapped the whiteboard. 'What are we missing here?' He shrugged helplessly. 'And no arrests so far! It's not good.'

The *West Uist Chronicle* blog was opened innumerable times across the island with the stark revelations.

THREE MURDERS, POISON-PEN LETTERS AND THIS WANTED MAN. Calum did not hold back this time.

He put up pictures of Arran MacCondrum, Frazer McKenzie and Declan O'Neil and his two associates, which Cora had taken when they came off the ferry after the demonstration. He had circled Steve Rollinson in the picture and referred to him in the post.

He made it clear that Arran MacCondrum and Frazer McKenzie had both initially been thought to have committed suicide, but the police now confirmed that both were being treated as murders.

The wanted man was unidentified as yet, but had to be considered dangerous and should not be approached. Members of the public were advised to contact Detective Inspector McKinnon at Lady Wynd police station.

Mungo saw it, as well as the newsflash on the lunchtime Scottish TV news. Kirsty Macroon read out the details and names of the three dead men and then again did an edited interview with Torquil. One half of the screen showed the three murdered men.

'This sounds devastating news for West Uist. With three murders, people are bound to feel unsafe, is that not so, Inspector McKinnon?'

'We would like to reassure people that we are doing our best to keep everyone safe and that we have several fruitful lines of investigation going at the moment. We have a man that we would like to contact urgently, and I urge him to make contact with us straight away. We also have a lead on a poison-pen writer who we believe to be involved in two of the murders.'

The picture of the unidentified man replaced those of the three dead men.

In her half of the screen, Kirsty Macroon looked surprised. 'Poison-pen writer? Surely those only belong in crime novels?'

'This one signs him or herself off as Mungo and has been an intermittent nuisance over many years. We fear his activities have now crossed the line and three people have been murdered.'

'You said this Mungo was involved in two of the murders; is he connected with the third?'

'I cannot confirm this at the moment, but we have reason to believe so.'

Mungo was seething. As expected, he received a phone call almost as soon as the newsflash was over.

Checking that there was no one within earshot, Mungo answered. 'Yes.'

'Have you bloody seen the news and that idiot's blog?'

'Yes.'

'Is that it? You bloody well get my money and an extra twenty grand and get me off the island. I've done every dirty little job you asked. I'm not being done for arson and murders I didn't do.'

'I'll take you off the island myself, but you'll have to wait for the money. Unless you'd like a cheque!'

A torrent of abuse and threats sounded in Mungo's ear, but failed to elicit a reaction other than: 'Have you finished?'

Then instructions were given with precise details of where and when to meet. 'You'll see my boat.'

CHAPTER TWENTY-FIVE

Morag brewed tea and handed Torquil a mug as he stood looking at the whiteboard with all that covered it.

'Just staring at them isn't making it any clearer, Morag.'

'It's a tangled web, right enough.'

'But how do I untangle it? Apart from Mungo, where is the thread to grasp? I feel bad that —' Then he snapped his fingers. 'That's maybe it. I need to call Lachlan.'

Declan O'Neil managed to get a call through to the hospital in Stornoway and was told that Alistair Pitcairn was still in Intensive Care receiving life support, as he had not yet regained consciousness.

His hands were shaking when he came off the phone.

'The bastard set us up,' he said to himself through gritted teeth.

He called the Ciderman Consortium office number for the third time. Once again, it went straight to unobtainable. No receptionist. No answerphone. It was as if it had disappeared off the face of the earth.

Lachlan had been praying and contemplating for most of the morning in St Ninian's Church. When his phone went off, he smiled to see it was from Torquil.

'Uncle, sorry to interrupt if you are busy, but what did you mean when you said you kept the letter from Mungo to teach yourself humility and because you felt guilty?'

'The letter hit a chord with me. I had given a sermon on the Sunday about the dangers of drink and the way it could lead to alcoholism, with all that entails. I had written it because of a case in the parish. A sad one. A young man lost his job, his wife and kiddy, all because of whisky.'

'I've got the letter in front of me, Uncle. It says … "you do it in ignorance. You don't know what others did and you don't know what they might have tried."'

'I often do say things in ignorance, laddie. I try to stop being ignorant.'

'And then it says… "You are useless, all you clever lawyers, doctors and ministers." What do you think Mungo meant? Could he have been referring to something specific?'

'It's possible.'

'Like a divorce, which would involve a lawyer. Something medical that would involve a doctor. And something spiritual that would involve a minister. But the recrimination implies that it was something that none of them had helped with.'

'Again, possible. That's why I kept it to teach me humility.'

'But do you remember the specific case you were thinking of?'

Lachlan was quiet for a moment, then: 'I think I do. It was a young fellow; he was from a fishing family, like so many were when we had a bigger fleet than the few we have today. He gave it up and became a ghillie on the Cruikshank estate. But either he wasn't good at it or nature just took a hand: the salmon fishing dried up totally. It has never really recovered on the island. Anyway, he took to drinking really heavily. He had a young wife and a bairn, just a toddler. Then his wife got pregnant again and his behaviour got more and more out of control. He was rude to his employer's guests and to folk who came to stay to fish their salmon river. It got worse and he was sacked. There were also all sorts of sexual shenanigans, if I recall. He was not great at keeping his breeks on.'

'Did he attend St Ninian's?'

'Aye, we had an active congregation in those days, more than now, I'm sorry to say.'

'Can you be more specific about the shenanigans?'

'I never really followed it. Young folk, a group of them there were, I think. There were rumours about his bairn and the unborn child not being his. People in the parish were talking, you know. Especially when the family left the island and went off to Glasgow. There was a messy divorce and some accident or incident. I understand the mother and her baby died. To my shame, I preached a sermon about the dangers of drinking.'

'That letter from Mungo says you were ignorant.'

'Aye, I admit I was. That's why I've kept it, so that I never get high and mighty again.'

'But ignorant of what? And why say lawyers, doctors and ministers? I am wondering if that meant there was some medical condition you couldn't have known about?'

'Possibly, but I didn't explore that; it wouldn't have been ethical. Nor would old Doctor Ailbeart McLelland have divulged anything about his patients, what with his Hippocratic oath.'

'Ralph's uncle is dead and I know that Ralph also would not divulge a confidence, but could there still be medical notes?'

'I doubt it. They would have followed the family to Glasgow. It was over a quarter of a century ago now.'

'Do you know any of the group of folk you mentioned?'

'I think Elspeth MacLauchlan was one, Arran MacCondrum was another, may he rest in peace. And —'

'You are sure about that?' Torquil interrupted. 'Arran MacCondrum?'

'Aye, I think so. And also Frazer McKenzie. There was a rumour that —'

'Lachlan, have you not listened to the news today?'

'No, I told you I was going to be praying and contemplating.'

'Frazer McKenzie was also murdered. We've had a press release on Scottish TV as well as on the *West Uist Chronicle* blog. It was another murder staged to look like suicide.'

'Not another one!'

'Do you know the name of this ghillie?'

'His name was MacNider, Kenny MacNider, and his wife was called Kathleen.'

'Are any of the family still in the parish or even on the island?'

'Not now. His mother Isabel MacNider died five years ago. I took her funeral. She was a widow and a stalwart of the parish. She was on the flower-arranging rota. She had been Ailbeart McLelland's housekeeper and receptionist until she retired. If she retired, that is. There was no announcement, as I recall. She just stopped working there.'

Torquil thought for a moment. 'And Marie Urquhart's mother was the receptionist when Ralph took over — that's right, isn't it? I remember Ralph saying that when we went out to the salmon farm to see Arran's body.'

'Aye, sadly she died a year ago and I took her funeral, too.'

'And of course, now that Ralph's practising from the cottage hospital, he uses one or other of the hospital receptionists, so he doesn't have a personal receptionist.'

'I hope all that helps, laddie.'

'Hmm. It might do, Uncle, but I'm not sure how. I may be clutching at straws.'

Mungo had been careful to slip away unnoticed. The rage inside was reaching boiling point, but it was important to keep it under control. Important details needed to be carried out with clinical precision.

And this unexpected intrusion by the plods meant the whole operation had to be accelerated.

But first, Jimmy Meikle's worries had to be extinguished. Then it would begin. Soon, it would be time for Mungo to say a final farewell.

CHAPTER TWENTY-SIX

Gordon, Micheal and Nialghus were feeling let down by the persistent absence of Rab and Marie from their rota duties. Rab was the most experienced at the salmon farm and Marie was the senior technician at the hatchery, but it had been left to them and the others to cover for them.

'I'm not convinced about Rab's back strain,' called Gordon from one walkway to Nialghus on another, as the three of them slowly went round each of the pens using hand shovels to throw feed pellets to the salmon the old-fashioned way, rather than by the automatic feeding orchestrated by the now defunct computer system. 'And Marie's never had such a bad migraine attack before.'

'We could do with the computers and cameras being repaired or replaced as a priority,' Micheal shouted to them. 'And what's going to happen to the business? That's what I want to know.'

'I guess it'll come to a shareholder's meeting, same as you see on TV,' said Nialghus. 'And little tiddler shareholders like us will be gobbled up by the big fish.'

'Like Rab, you mean?' Gordon queried.

'And like Marie,' Micheal called.

'But they're our friends. They wouldn't do that to us, surely. Not to their friends.'

Nialghus continued to scatter fish food. 'Look at what happened to poor Arran. Murdered! And was that by a friend?'

For some reason, none of them was keen on feeding the salmon in pen two.

Cora was feeling frustrated.

'I can't arrange a meeting with Ross McNab,' she said plaintively to Calum, 'and I can't get him on his office number or his mobile.'

'He's maybe down at the bottom of the deep blue sea, searching for fishies — or for treasure,' Calum returned jokingly. 'Why not try your other feature target, Henson Dingwall?'

'The Crow's Nest isn't open today, but believe it or not, I can't raise him either. I'm sure he'll be on one of his foraging trips.'

'Maybe everyone has actually locked their doors and is hiding under their beds after the murder revelations.'

'That's not funny, Calum.'

The editor leaned back in his swivel chair and laced his fingers behind his head. 'I know, darling. I just wish I could get a lead on this Mungo. I'd give —'

His mobile phone beeped, indicating a text had come in. Half-heartedly, he reached over his desk for it and clicked to read it. He suddenly shot upright.

'It's an unknown caller — listen to this. *Dear Specky Short-arse, you think you're such a clever clogs, don't you? Well, I saw the man you're so keen to catch. If you want him, you'll need to be quick, because he's flown like a birdie. Search the sea and look for the best view. Sincerely, Mungo.*'

Cora looked aghast. 'He's toying with you, Calum.'

No sooner had she said that than her mobile beeped to indicate that a text had arrived. She gulped and then read: '*Dear Nosy Nelly, did you like your present? You might call it a house-warming present. Or should that be house-warning? Watch your pretty nose. Best to stick close to Specky Short-arse. Or should that be steer clear of him? It's a gamble either way. Sincerely, Mungo.*'

'The cheeky bastard!' Calum cursed. 'He's goading us, Cora. Well, he'll not succeed. Come on, we'll call his bluff. Or would you rather stay here?'

'Alone? After that petrol gift? I'm coming with you. But shouldn't we report this?'

'After we've seen this fellow for ourselves. But don't worry, I'm a careful fellow and I always take precautions.' He slid open a drawer and took out an aged catapult. 'I was the school champion with this when I was a youngster — the unofficial champion, that is. Come on, let's go and scoop a scoop.'

Morag took the anonymous phone call on the station phone. The voice was disguised with a voice changer device that converted it into a troll.

'I've seen your man up at the Hoolish Stones half an hour ago. He's sleeping rough.'

'Who is this?' she demanded.

The line went dead.

'Damn it! We can't ignore it,' she told Ewan, who had just returned from the Cruikshank estate and had built up a healthy hunger, which he was trying to assuage with a sausage roll from Gordon Allardyce's bakery.

'I'd like to catch this chap, if he's a wrestler like Calum said. I'll finish this and then head up on Nippy.'

'I think one of the twins should go with you.'

'You heard what they said, Sergeant. I can handle this skunner. Besides, they're still out with Ian Gillesbie.'

'And Penny is out interviewing some of the WUCE folk. I suppose so, but take care. If you need support, ring me or Torquil.'

Torquil was in his office when Lorna phoned him.

'We've had a call from Glasgow. They saw the bulletin about the bruiser you want to interview. He is well known to the Glasgow force. He has several names, but his real one is Jimmy Meikle. He's not got a lot of brains but has plenty of muscle. Accordingly, he's an enforcer for one of the big gangs, only he's been off the radar for a while. There was speculation that he's either flitted and joined another gang or that he was feeding the fish in the Clyde. They were surprised to see him up here.'

'Which gang was he with?'

'Not that I know any, but they say he was part of the Dalgettie Gang. They had been big in drugs and trafficking, but the past few years they had been distancing themselves from old ways and were trying to seem more legit. Into hotels, landlording and gambling arcades. It sounds as if they needed his sort of skills less and less, hence the force thought he'd either flitted or his services had been dispensed with permanently.'

She sighed. 'It sounds as if it's been a tough couple of days over there. I wish I was with you.'

Then followed their usual hushed endearments before she rang off.

All the while, Torquil had been doodling on his notepad. He had written the name his uncle had given him, MacNider, several times. Then for no particular reason he'd written it in a circle, like the anagram wheel he and the padre had done for years when solving the nightly crossword in *The Scotsman*.

Beside it, he wrote the anagrams he derived from it: *Incredam, Candemir, Mandrice, Meandric, Ciderman.*

'Ciderman!' he exclaimed, underlining it.

Picking up the pad, he ran through to the restroom, calling for Morag on the way.

'The Ciderman Consortium! That's the link, Morag.'

He explained as he picked up the pen and underneath where he had written 'consortium' with 'Ciderman' in brackets, he wrote the name 'MacNider'.

'And I think we've just found Mungo. The original Mungo, that is.' He pointed to the copies of the photographs from Arran MacCondrum's house. 'Look, it's been staring us in the face all the time.'

And she listened with a dropping jaw as he explained.

'But I need to confirm this urgently, before there is more murder. Because that's what Mungo has planned. I think I know who his next victim will be, and I need to make them safe. You stay here, Morag, and find out how Alistair Pitcairn is doing.'

The mists were rolling down from the Corlins, threatening to reduce visibility as Calum rode the Lambretta with Cora behind him on the pillion along the coastal route heading towards the star-shaped Wee Kingdom. The road climbed towards the cliffs atop, and the automatic beacon was already sending a beam through the mist out to sea.

'So you think this is what Mungo meant by searching the sea for the best view?' Cora called in his ear as they reached the beacon.

'I think so. But there's nobody here and nowhere really to hide. The clifftop is pretty bare here.'

Calum stopped the scooter and cut the engine.

'Was he just toying with us?' Cora asked, holding onto his anorak.

'Maybe, darling, but I'm not taking any chances.' He pulled out his catapult and bent down to pick up a few loose pebbles. Loading one and pulling back the strong elastic cord in readiness, he advanced towards the cliff edge. The old redundant lighthouse built on top of the outermost basalt stack came into view and, as they approached the actual cliff edge, they could see the rocky beach below.

And far down, spreadeagled and face down on the shingle, lay the bloodied body of a man.

The mist had swirled down from the moors and reached Kyleshiffin. Torquil made his way down the near-deserted street, following the man moving furtively along. He recognised him straight away by his build and the way he walked.

'So, let's see if you are heading where I think you are, my friend,' he whispered to himself.

He turned onto the Bonniegate and went past a number of the shops, all now closed for the evening, until he came to the *Ionad dualchais uist an iar*, the West Uist Heritage Centre. Like the other shops it was closed, and the blinds had all been pulled.

Going past it, he turned up the alley beyond. Torquil tiptoed up and gave him enough time to reach the back of the building. He heard a key turn in the lock and the slow opening and closing of a door.

Morag took the call from Calum and listened in alarm to his message. The signal was not great, and his voice kept breaking up.

'So it was Mungo that texted you, and when you got there you found the body at the bottom of the cliffs?'

'Aye, it's on the beach. The sea is going out. We're sure it's the wrestling chap.'

'Have you examined it?'

'That's what I'm trying to tell you. We're at the top of the cliffs and the mist is coming in. There's no way down and it's a long trip down to the beach. Can you get some of your team there?'

'It'll not be easy; I'm just here by myself. The Drummonds are not back yet and Ewan McPhee is up at the Hoolish Stones on a wild goose chase, I think. That was Mungo's doing, too, I think. But I'll get someone there as soon as I can. It's at the base of the beacon, you say?'

'Aye, he may have thrown himself off the cliff. Suicide, is likely.'

Morag bit her lip when Calum rang off. She wasn't sure how confident she would be in accepting any case as suicide now.

Elspeth had come back to consciousness first. She blinked her eyes open in the dim light of the single lamp in the office of the Gaelic Centre. She was sitting tied to a chair with her hands secured behind her, and she had what she presumed to be duct tape wrapped round her mouth. There was a bitter taste and a horrible stifling sensation in her throat, as if she was suffocating.

Looking to her left, she saw Marie Urquhart also stirring and looking about herself in panic. Like her, she was tied to a chair and similarly gagged.

When they made eye contact, it was obvious that they were both terrified.

But when she looked to her left she was utterly horrified to see her lover, Rab MacQuittie, being tied tightly to another chair. He was still unconscious and his head was slumped on his chest, his mouth also gagged.

'So, I have timed it all rather well, haven't I?' said Henson Dingwall as he tied a further knot, securing Rab's hands behind him. 'Welcome, all of you.'

'W-why?' came the muffled question from Marie. 'We … love…'

Henson gave a cruel laugh. 'We love each other? Don't be ridiculous — we screwed, that's all. I seduced you and you fell like a ripe plum. It couldn't have been simpler or more appropriate.'

Elspeth tried to speak, but her words were similarly muffled.

'And why you, Elspeth MacLauchlan? You cheap whore.' He turned and pointed to an old-fashioned writing case on the desk. 'Because of this. I am, if you hadn't realised it, Mungo. Or rather, I am the grandson of Mungo, whose real name was Isabel MacNider.'

Elspeth's eyes opened wide in astonishment and she mumbled something incoherently.

'That's right, my grannie was Kenny MacNider's mother and I am the toddler that her son Kenny and his wife Kathleen took away from West Uist after you shagged my father. Then either your fiancé Arran bloody MacCondrum or his good friend Frazer McKenzie got my mother in the family way. Between you all, you broke my parents. My father had started drinking when the salmon farm killed off the wild salmon so he seemed an incompetent ghillie. When he found out that his wife was pregnant by another man, he seriously started drinking himself towards the grave. Then his good friend Frazer McKenzie got him sacked, so that he could get the position of head gamekeeper on that miserable Cruikshank estate.'

Henson pulled on a pair of white gloves and with an old key unlocked the writing case and opened the front, which swung over to form a slope for writing paper to be placed upon.

'Behold Mungo's box of tricks! Poison-pen writing was my grannie's little hobby, her passion. It was easy for her as the local doctor's housekeeper to access the case notes of virtually everyone on the island. No one suspected that the nice, prim little woman who welcomed them to the doctor's surgery was tapping into all their dirty little secrets. All the affairs, the sins and the crimes against each other, she stored them all up and sent out her little missives.'

He picked up an aged stencil case and pulled out a small drawer to show the range of pens and the coloured notepaper that they had all received letters on.

'And the dirtiest of secrets was what you three did to my parents. It killed the love and trust between them and when the divorce my mother wanted didn't go through, she took her own life and that of what would have been my little sister.' His voice had been calm throughout, but he now leaned towards Elspeth and snarled. 'Because of you, you whore. She poisoned herself and my sister!'

Rab had come round and struggled against his bonds, gritting his teeth and trying to shout.

'Oh, relax, Rab MacQuittie. The chloroform I used on you may be making you all feel a bit ill, but it will be wearing off enough for you to understand what I'm saying, so you can appreciate why you are here.' He grinned at Rab. 'Except you, of course. You being here is a little bonus. I hadn't realised that you two were shagging each other. Even after quarter of a century, you're still at it. But being on opposite sides is a bit awkward for you, isn't it?' He looked at Marie and smiled. 'We know that, don't we, poppet? Shagging, I mean, and keeping it all a secret.'

He opened another of the little drawers and took out a diary. 'It's all in here, you know. My grannie was incensed that her son had been driven away from the island. She kept a log of everything. She knew all that happened. You, Elspeth MacLauchlan, breaking your engagement with MacCondrum and sleeping with my father. Then the men sleeping with my mother and impregnating her.' Again, his words started to rise in volume until he bared his teeth at Elspeth. 'Killing her and my little sister, in other words.

'Fortunately, grannie's brother, my great uncle had brains. He took me in and tutored me in the ways of the criminal fraternity until he decided we should be legit. He put me through catering college, had me train with top chefs in the best hotels until I became the young tyro chef of Glasgow. But that was when my old man, my father Kenny MacNider came back. A cuckoo home to roost. Home to die, really. He'd drunk his liver into a sponge. Cirrhosis and all the works. It turns you a bit mad, you know. Korsakoff's psychosis, the doctors called it, but I looked after him. I didn't care for him really, but I did take care of him.' He chuckled at his joke. 'He told me enough about my grannie and her hobby, and of how she had always supported him in her own special way. And of how as Mungo, she was famous in West Uist.'

He did a sort of pirouette and held out his arms. 'So, I vowed to get revenge on all of you. My Great Uncle Crofton MacNider, AKA Crofton Dalgettie in Glasgow snuffed it.' He breathed on his fingernails in a gesture of pride. 'With a little help from me. Poison, you see, is easy to obtain when you have contacts like we did. And I had a passion for it, all the different types. Pesticides, arsenic, thallium and cyanide. And, of course, chloroform — not exactly a poison, but it's not pleasant to take, is it? Well, all of them were easy for me to get, and Arran, Frazer and you three have sampled them this evening. It is so much cleaner than physical violence, like the sort I had to use on Jimmy Meikle a little while ago. I was waiting for him by the cliffs under the old beacon. He was looking for the boat and it was easy to sneak up and smash his head like an egg. I broke a few more bones to make it look as if he'd been overcome with remorse and jumped off the cliff.'

Henson rubbed his temples. 'Now, where was I? Oh yes, I am sure you are wondering about Declan and his cronies. They should all have snorted enough cyanide in their cocaine to be dead. They were totally expendable, you see. I had used an old friend of mine, a confidence trickster par excellence to set up this pseudo company, the Ciderman Consortium, to go round and buy or offer to buy Dunshiffin Castle, the local golf course, and the salmon farm. It was all very neatly done, getting them to take the cocaine I had laced with cyanide. That was where Jimmy Meikle the big stooge had been useful, you see. He'd laid down poison to feed the birds on the coast and on the moors, and he'd created a stir at the café just after he'd supplied them with the cocaine. That was part of the plan with the consortium, of course: to establish a high-class drug supply for the nobs who would come to the hotel. Or that's what they thought.'

He tittered. 'And they were making overtures to buy the salmon farm. Imagine that, the salmon farm that Arran MacCondrum, his father and his uncle had worked so hard on. The salmon that got rid of the healthy Atlantic salmon that the Cruikshank estate was renowned for in its salmon river and its wee lake. Well, he was pretty hopeless as a businessman, wasn't he? He had to sell his shares to his staff and we gradually inveigled ourselves in, gave him loans he couldn't pay back. And then Mungo, that's the new Mungo — me — arrived in Kyleshiffin all those months ago and got to know all the dirty little secrets. You've no idea how easy it is to pick up the gossip. Folk like to talk after a good meal. It didn't matter whether they were true or not; there was enough fodder for me to write my letters, send them off the island and have them sent back to their targets. And just like Grannie, my Mungo didn't make mistakes, didn't give the game away. The point was to flood the place with letters and in particular enough so that when Arran and Frazer were ready to leave this earth, there was apparently enough reason why they should have seemed depressed and ready to end it all.'

With his gloved hands, he picked up a wad of letters headed 'Ciderman Consortium' and looked at Elspeth.

'These are letters prepared earlier, which will show how you, Rab and Marie were involved in the plot to oust Arran MacCondrum and take over the salmon farm. The plods have somehow worked out that he didn't commit suicide, but was — executed — a much better word than murdered, don't you think? And so much more apt.'

He turned to Marie, who was trembling and staring at him in terror. 'You may wonder what Marie has to do with all this? Well, as you have gathered, she and I have been having it off for months. In my bistro, my flat, her flat, at the hatchery!' He giggled. 'Yes, at the hatchery. And that's where she was the time I arranged for Arran MacCondrum to come to the hatchery, only I had slipped her some ketamine, also known as cat Valium or purple in her gin, her favourite pre-sex tipple. We had the usual rough sex, of course, until she passed out on me. It's undetectable, but it put her right out of it, so that MacCondrum came in and saw this naked beauty in his technician's cabin. He was half cut himself, and it was a simple feat to chloroform him. For fun I blew some cocaine laced with cyanide up his nose, then I dunked his head in the nearest water tank and held him under. He drowned so easily.'

He waited, looking from one to the other, savouring their horror and fear. He gave that strange titter again.

'So when Marie came round, the deed was done. She was part of it, or so I told her. She was so confused she believed it all. I told her MacCondrum had said he was going to kill us both, so together we drowned him. She had wet hands and he was dead, so she had no choice but to help me get rid of his body. Then I spun the idea of taking him out to the salmon farm, which was my plan all along, to make it look as if he had topped himself in one of the pens. You may have noticed, Rab, that she wasn't herself that morning, apart from the shock. Well, that was ketamine working its way out of her system.'

Marie was shaking her head vigorously.

'Oh yes you did, Marie. You helped drown him. Or that's what I told you, and you were dumb enough to believe it.' He looked from one to the other again. 'And so here we are. At the finale of Mungo's little play. When they find your bodies — none of them bound, by the way — they will learn that Elspeth MacLaughlin was Mungo all the time. And I've got extra letters in here prepared in advance, due to go out to others.'

He tittered again, as if he was having difficulty maintaining a semblance of sanity. 'But here's where it gets interesting. There are love letters here, between you two ladies. And a letter to Rab, which I will write before I leave you all, arranging to meet here. And that will be seen to be the time that you chloroformed him and then forced him to take cyanide.'

All three started to struggle and shake their heads and scream, unsuccessfully.

'Yes, a lesbian romance. Bisexual, if you like — so many people are, don't you think?'

Another titter outburst, longer than the last. 'And here will also be the incriminating letters about having done Frazer McKenzie to death after he had twigged what you two were up to. I must say I was peeved that the plods had worked that out; it was a beautiful execution. I gave him a good coshing at that Bothy on the moor and then set him up to look as if he'd blown his head off. Brilliant, that — it got rid of the head injury I gave him when I knocked him out.'

He grinned at them. 'You all see that I didn't know which of them, MacCondrum or McKenzie, had made my mother pregnant and so both of them had to die.' He looked at his watch and sighed. 'Well, it has been fun, but I must go soon to prepare some dishes for tomorrow's menu. Everything has to look normal.'

He snapped his fingers. 'Oh, silly me, I didn't explain properly why Marie has to go, too. Well, sins of the father stuff. Or in her case, sins of the mother. Your mother got my grannie the sack at the doctor's surgery. But your mother is dead and can't be made to pay, so I'm afraid you'll have to.' He stroked her trembling cheek.

Returning to his writing case, he opened yet another small drawer and drew out a plastic bag full of white powders. Then he took a dropper with a large rubber bulb and inserted it into the bag. 'Just a good squish of cocaine and potassium cyanide up each nostril and it will all be over in minutes. You see, overcome with remorse after having stabbed Rab to death,' he said with a sorry smile at Rab, 'which will be done after you've had your cyanide, our two heroines make a suicide pact and there you have it. Then it is a matter of arranging the bodies, removing any bonds and curtain down. Play over, time for me as Mungo to become simple Henson Dingwall again. Elspeth is now Mungo.'

He looked from one to the other. 'Who's first, then? I think probably Rab. No point in struggling — you have to breathe and your mouth doesn't work, so it'll be quick. This is good grade coke and cyanide.'

He advanced on Rab and grabbed his hair to pull his head backwards.

It was then that Torquil banged the door open, leaped across the room and smashed Henson in the face with a straight right, propelling him backwards. A fountain of blood gushed from his broken nose and he smashed into the desk. The writing case slid off and landed on the floor, spilling out its drawers, letters and stencil set.

Moving quickly Torquil grabbed the bag of powder and the dropper and tossed them into the open drawer of the case.

'I've recorded your whole sordid confession on my phone, you scumbag,' Torquil said. Then, without taking his eyes off Henson Dingwall, he said to the three bound victims, 'Sorry, folk, but I needed him to incriminate himself before I pounced.'

'Ah, the plod,' said Henson, struggling to his feet and spitting blood. He reached under his top and unsheathed a knife. He sniggered. 'You know they say that the pen is mightier than the sword? Well, since you've spoiled my little play, I'm going back to the sword.' He lunged at Torquil, who dodged backwards.

'I'm making this up as I go,' Henson said as he slashed out again. 'They'll say you were killed in the line of duty.'

He slashed in the other direction and again Torquil dodged out of the way. But this time he darted forward and grabbed the wrist in both hands and bent it sharply, causing Henson to cry out in pain as bones cracked and the knife fell from his hand. Immediately, Torquil grabbed him by the shoulders and gave a swift headbutt in the face that sent him crashing against the wall.

Incongruously, Henson sniggered again. 'I had planned for some such eventuality,' he said, moving his lower jaw. 'Cyanide was the favoured suicide capsule in the Second World War. I had a very good dentist prepare one for me.'

Torquil's eyes opened wide in alarm. He grabbed him by his top and hauled him to his feet, then punched him hard in the stomach with his right fist. Henson groaned and a tooth sailed out of his mouth onto the floor.

'They only work if you swallow them, though!' Torquil said. And with another punch, this time an uppercut to the jaw, he sent him hurtling back against the wall, where he slid down unconsciously to the floor.

'Take that, Mungo, you miserable, murdering worm.'

Turning and rubbing his fists, he set about releasing the three victims. As they sat shivering, weeping and rubbing wrists, he called Morag.

'I need help at the Gaelic Centre, Morag. We've caught Mungo and a duped accessory and two very lucky people.'

It was then that Marie fainted.

EPILOGUE

Alistair Pitcairn was discharged from hospital two days later, and he and Declan O'Neil decided to move into the Commercial Hotel until all of the investigations were completed prior to the Procurator Fiscal's Fatal Accident inquiry. Both realised that they would have to answer further questions about the cocaine and the exact circumstances surrounding their involvement with the bogus Ciderman Consortium.

Marie Urquhart was charged as an accessory to the removal of the body of Arran MacCondrum and the concealment of a murder. She was remanded in custody over on Lewis.

She had confessed during her interview that she had an affair with Henson Dingwall and that she believed him when he told her that she had helped him to drown Arran MacCondrum. She had been so overcome with guilt, which she could not show, that she had gone to his house as soon as she could and laid flowers picked from the machair on his bed and had a cry into his pillow.

The body of Jimmy Meikle was recovered from the beach by the Drummond boys and a post-mortem examination confirmed that he had died from head injuries, most likely sustained in an attack from behind, on the beach, rather than from a fall from the cliffs.

Calum and Cora cooperated with Torquil's team in the way they handled the unfolding of the story, considering the sensitivity of the characters involved and the relationships that seemed to have been the root cause of Henson Dingwall's actions. A psychiatric assessment was pending on him as to whether he was a psychopath or suffering from a paranoid psychotic state. The name he assumed and worked under was a complete fabrication and he was charged under his own name of Henson MacNider.

After the successful hen-do dive to the *SS Lister*, which yielded several aged tins of fish and a bottle of sherry, Lorna and her friends had a simpler meal cooked by none other than the padre at the manse. The whole team were also invited, as were Calum and Ralph.

It was simple fare, which suited the girls rather than the planned meal at The Crow's Nest. All of them had been put off the idea of cyanide and seafood.

As they dined, Torquil explained how he had come to realise who the original Mungo was, and that Henson MacNider was her grandson.

'It was there in front of us in those old polaroid photographs of the group. Henson MacNider had the features of both Kenny MacNider and his wife Kathleen, simply masked by his curly black hair, beard and headband. The information that was hidden in that old letter from the original Mungo to Lachlan linked it all up, once I realised that the Ciderman in the Ciderman Consortium was an anagram of the family name MacNider. The diary that we have confirmed all that.'

Penny took up the story. 'And backtracking on Jimmy Meikle led us right back to the Dalgettie gang and the boss, Crofton MacNider AKA Crofton Dalgettie, who was Isabel MacNider's brother.'

Torquil nodded. 'And the Glasgow team will be looking back at Crofton MacNider's death to see if they can determine whether Henson, or Mungo as we think of him, murdered him as well. It is likely he also killed his father, Kenny MacNider, although it may have been a twisted way of easing his suffering.'

Lachlan shuddered. 'I was on his list as well, so it's a relief that he was stopped.'

Ralph sipped his Heather Ale. 'Well, since we have heard all about Lorna and her party's successful dive over the wreck, can we men finally agree on Torquil's stag-do?'

'Fine by me, whatever you boys decide,' said Calum.

The Drummond boys, Ewan and Ralph all looked at each other in amazement.

'Just so long as I get to make the first best man's speech at the wedding.'

Cora prodded him in the stomach with her elbow. 'Oh, Calum!'

A NOTE TO THE READER

Dear Reader,

Thank you for taking the time to read my novel. I hope that you enjoyed reading about the dark things that can happen on my idyllic little Scottish island on the edge of the world.

I have been a lifelong fan of crime fiction, but to my mind the use of the laboratory and the revelations that DNA testing can instantly give, somehow rob many modern crime novels of their sense of romance. That was why I set my story on the remote Hebridean island of West Uist, so that it would be far removed from the modern forensic crime thriller.

Also, because the island has the smallest police force in the country (now part of Police Scotland), it would not be another gritty, urban police procedural. Crimes would have to be solved in a very old-fashioned manner.

Having said that, in this novel there is a little more forensic work than in the others. This was necessary because of the forensic difficulties in determining drowning. I have also used personal experience from assisting at post-mortem examinations. At one time, I had flirted with becoming a pathologist.

I studied medicine at the University of Dundee and did some of my training in the highlands. I loved the sense of community in villages and determined that if I ever wrote a crime novel, it would feature a Scottish detective working in a remote place, aided by friends, family and the local newspaper. Years later, when Inspector Torquil McKinnon walked into my imagination I set about learning to play the bagpipes, although unlike Torquil, the winner of the Silver Quaich, I have never been anything other than dire. Nonetheless, playing around with my pipes helps me as I am working out my plots.

Since golf is also a hobby and I had played on the remotest Hebridean courses, those sheep-nibbled links complete with dive-bombing gulls had to appear in the stories. When I venture onto my local golf course I imagine the padre, a steady 8 handicapper, playing alongside me, advising me on how to hit the green, sink a putt — or solve the newest clue.

If you have enjoyed the novel enough to leave a review on **Amazon** and **Goodreads**, then I would be truly grateful. I love to hear from readers, so if you would like to contact me, please do so through my **Facebook** page or send me a message through **Twitter.** You can also see my latest news on the **West Uist Chronicle Blog** and on my **Website.**

Keith Moray

keithmorayauthor.com

Sapere Books is an exciting new publisher of brilliant fiction and popular history.

To find out more about our latest releases and our monthly bargain books visit our website:
saperebooks.com